Patrick Gale was born on the Isl infancy at Wandsworth Prison, which his father governed, then grew up in Winchester before going to Oxford University. He now lives on a farm near Land's End. One of this country's best-loved novelists, his most recent works are *A Perfectly Good Man*, the Richard and Judy bestseller *Notes from an Exhibition*, and the bestselling *A Place Called Winter.*

Praise for *The Aerodynamics of Pork*:

'It is packed with arch dialogue, affectionate caricatures and the feigned good humour more commonly found in memoirs written by chauffeurs of the famous' *Observer*

'A sad, funny and deeply searching novel. Plotting, characterisation and dialogue quicken the reader's pace, just as the delicacy of the unfolding love stories quickens the heart' *Publishers Weekly*

'A real craftsman, a master storyteller' *Independent on Sunday*

'Gale's concoction is irresistible: modern relationships with period charm. I couldn't have liked it more' Armistead Maupin

By Patrick Gale and available from Tinder Press

The Aerodynamics of Pork
Kansas in August
Ease
Facing the Tank
Little Bits of Baby
The Cat Sanctuary
Caesar's Wife
The Facts of Life
Dangerous Pleasures
Tree Surgery for Beginners
Rough Music
A Sweet Obscurity
Friendly Fire
Notes from an Exhibition
The Whole Day Through
Gentleman's Relish
A Perfectly Good Man
A Place Called Winter
Take Nothing With You

PATRICK GALE

THE AERODYNAMICS OF PORK

First published in Great Britain by Abacus in 1986

First published in this paperback edition in 2018 by Tinder Press
An imprint of HEADLINE PUBLISHING GROUP

1

Cataloguing in Publication Data is available from the British Library

ISBN 978 1 4722 5560 0

Typeset in Sabon 10.5/14.55 pt by Jouve (UK), Milton Keynes

Printed and bound in Great Britain by Clays Ltd, Elcograf S.p.A.

Headline's policy is to use papers that are natural, renewable and recyclable products and made from wood grown in well-managed forests and other controlled sources. The logging and manufacturing processes are expected to conform to the environmental regulations of the country of origin.

HEADLINE PUBLISHING GROUP
An Hachette UK Company
Carmelite House
50 Victoria Embankment
London EC4Y 0DZ

www.tinderpress.co.uk
www.headline.co.uk
www.hachette.co.uk

I dedicate this first-offering to the cherished memory of my brother Matthew, because he held the gifts of rage and love, but mostly because he could laugh like a drain.

(Notting Hill, February 1984)

There is something in us all, that does not come out in family life, or is suppressed by it, or rejected by it, or something. But I daresay it keeps the better and fresher for its own purposes.

Anna Donnc, *Elders and Betters* by Ivy Compton-Burnett

Criminals frequently follow a general pattern of actions when committing a crime. If it can be said that crimes have a personality then it is because individual criminals, by the methods which they follow, give their crimes noticeable characteristics. The criminal's method of working is known as his *modus operandi* or M.O. It is difficult to avoid acting in a way which is natural to an individual and upon this human factor the strength of the *modus operandi* system stands.

Police Training Manual: Section 63

FRIDAY one

When the leading lady is also the birthday girl, nobody and nothing gets in her way. This month's conjunctions, the most favourable for Lady Lion since she first strutted out in her birthday best, will make her invincible. So, tell those guys to watch out because for the next week the little firecracker in their lives is going to get everything she wants, and we mean *everything*!

On any other occasion Seth would have been mortified to have been seen reading the thing in public, but his last term was finished and, God willing, it was the last time he would take this train.

A thud of compressed air against the windows; the only sizeable tunnel of the journey. On the upward trip it required a ritual. When the darkness came, Seth had to say 'Abandon hope all ye who enter here', over and over in his head, counting on his fingers, until sunlight reappeared. The number of times he said it told him the number of days he had to wait for sex. It was always a fairly safe bet, more a reassurance than a matter for anxiety. Each time he said it about eight or nine times: each term it took a week for the hot-house atmosphere to send the wraiths of holiday sweethearts wilting into bland insignificance. Quoth the Raven, 'Nevermore.'

He reached up to touch the spot on his left temple.

Flushed a shade of angry prawn, it still wasn't ripe. He hoped Mother wouldn't think that he didn't wash. He prided himself on his ability to avoid the grease-bound ill temper of his teenage cousins.

The train was slowing down. Basingstoke. To one side, pre-fabricated buildings sporting familiar names, to the other, a housing estate. Expanses of turf, tidy concrete paths, golf course, shopping precinct, saplings in wire cages.

The platform was full. Seth lifted his things off the seat before him and placed them in the luggage rack, all things save his violin. Having ensured that this took up all the space to his left, he loosened his tie, undid his top button, placed a protective hand on the case, and closed his eyes in feigned sleep.

Doors opened and he could hear the carriage fill. Mumbled apologies and murmured thanks sounded around him. A titter of children stamped past in the aisle. Doors slammed and the carriage was once more in motion. He could feel someone's skirt against his knees.

'Excuse me?'

Her voice was firm and forties, faintly troubled. She had entered in a hurry and was now balancing between the legs by the door. He pictured her perfect creases and the vaunting caprice of her perm.

'Excuse me, young man?'

His fingertips reminded him that he was still nursing an unsuitable magazine on his lap. It was now impossible to lift the pretence. A drop fell from his armpit to run down his ribs and soak into a fold of cotton above his waist.

'Here. Take mine.' A man's voice from in front. 'I think he's been asleep for some time.'

There was a stir as he stood up, and she fluffed herself back into shape and lowered her rump.

'Why, thank you. So kind.'

That pinched 'O' of a crumb-anxious scone-eater.

Someone started to slide his violin from beneath his grasp. The saviour was making room to sit down. Seth produced his best deep-sleep mumble and slid his hand on to his lap, nestling his head further into the curtain. The man, whose voice had been youngish and pleasant, sat beside him, presumably with the violin across his pin-striped thighs. As seat springs stretched to his left, Seth checked the impulse to decline into his companion's lap, but allowed himself a slight stir to straighten an ankle twisted unnaturally in the hasty preparations for the tableau. The magazine slapped to the floor. The basilisk snorted her surprise. Forty minutes to Waterloo. Forty woollen suits in swaying, July proximity. The siren call of a youthful libido proved irresistible. Leaving the angels to their tears, Seth pursued a fantasy a while, then slid to earnest slumber.

Seth Felix Peake, fifteen years eleven months, was a regular misdemeanant only in the eyes of the Church and of those parents whose schools were founded later than 1850. He had not been expelled. In the academic opinion he was lost, but in the eyes of his mother, he had been discovered just in time.

FRIDAY two

It was clever; started by the wind, of course, but once set in motion it did seem to move by its own momentum. Maude Faithe, Mo to her friends, stared with genuine interest at the system of cogs, water, sails and weights labouring before her. A woman stood clutching a little girl's hand. Pointing, she cried, 'Do look, darling. Isn't it clever? Do you see how it works?'

Darling Maude looked again. She saw how it worked. The bright enamelled shades of the sculpture's parts no longer charmed her.

'Makes you feel a bit sick, really,' she thought, and moved on.

Plain clothes assignments made a nice change. The sense of cloaked power as you walked with the unsuspecting. Uniforms had their strong points. People thought you were kinky to like wearing a uniform, but it wasn't that; uniforms protected you. They meant you could walk along the street being yourself, but just being a WPC to anybody else. Made you sick the way people looked at your civvies, sizing you up. It had made her sick at school when they'd teased her for having only one skirt. In a uniform people stopped sizing you up and started accepting. There again, in a uniform they knew what you did and expected you to do it – the beauty of plain clothes was that you only had to do it when the spirit moved you. Cloaked power. It was a bit kinky when you thought about it, really.

Mo looked nonchalantly at the crowd around her. She was proud of her nonchalant look. How to watch unsuspected was the secret of cloaked power.

It was a pretty small area to watch, a green space near County Hall. She'd been sent to patrol a crowd like this the week before, in that converted railway shed. Always the same people. Always the tall, toffee-nosed women with headscarves tied to their shiny, black handbags, and sometimes their husbands, who were always in suits. Always the fairies, who tried to dress differently from everyone else, and so ended up looking the same. Mo could spot a fairy at twenty paces. And then there were the feminist types. People talked a lot of crap about how men aged better. Men only aged better because they didn't try to look so stupid. If a man grew his hair long and curly, and wore tight clothes, and showed his legs all the time, he wouldn't age so well either. Mo was glad some women had seen the light at last. It gave her something nice to look at.

Of course, Timson had made out that the organizers had asked for a fairly senior representative of the Met to come along and 'spread good relations', but she saw through his little lie. Making her snoop for small fry was the punishment he gave because she wouldn't lick his arse like the rest of them. Besides, wandering through a crowd in uniform would have been a wasted opportunity. She'd come in civvies.

All had gone well at first. It was even exciting at first. Women recruits were just starting to be given more responsibilities than looking after lost kids and acting as decoys in nightclubs, so she'd felt a bit of a pioneer. She'd been so proud when the papers came and took pictures one day. Until she'd read the articles, that was, and then she saw that all they were interested in was the sexiness of the new uniform. She started getting wolf-whistles in the street, which she never had in civvies, and when such attention began to be paid from her colleagues she complained.

Despite the warnings of the other women, she'd taken a collection of the offending newspaper cuttings together with reports of harassment to an appointment with a superior officer. There she'd demanded that since women were doing a 'man's job', they be allowed to wear the same clothes. The bastards in the office, all men, of course, had laughed and said that if she'd wanted to hide her legs so much she should have been a bus driver. Her blood boiling, she'd marched home, taken a pair of kitchen scissors and cut off all her hair-do. Reappearing for work the next day looking like some escaped nun she was spared the wolf-whistles, but she also ruined her chances of promotion for the next few years.

In the end it had come twice, each time as a reward for bravery. Constable Faithe rescued a man from a burning building and then ran back into the inferno and retrieved an unconscious child. Two years, and some exams later, Sergeant Faithe had captured a sex-attacker. She'd been on plain clothes duty in the danger area, on a Highgate estate, when a man had run up to her and, panicking, spoke of a dying woman in his nearby flat. She had recognized the approach and then a similarity to a recent photofit of the wanted man. On a quixotic impulse, she'd pretended to be fooled and returned to his flat. She knew that an attempted attack would provide the concrete evidence for his arrest. The attack came with an unexpected violence. Mo had overpowered him, but not before she'd received a severe knife wound in the thigh and a slash across one cheek. She'd remained in hospital for several weeks before emerging an Inspector, with a GLC award for services to women, and a face scarred for life.

Most had forgotten her quondam reputation as a troublemaker when she was sent out in charge of a team to keep control during a new equipment delivery at Greenham Common air-base. There were likely to be road-blocks by peace protesters, and it was the Force's job to see that the delivery found its way into the compound, and to quell any violence.

Mo had read all the articles, but had never believed that things would reach such a state that groups from the Met would be asked to help out the Thames Valley contingent. As she watched the cold drizzle on the van windows, she'd remembered a piece in the *Mail*. It had said how the campers slept out in the open, belongings protected by plastic sheets. No sanitation. No way of keeping food fresh. The writer had sought to shock, emphasizing the juxtaposition of the women's all too apparent intimacy and their squalid living conditions. They called each other 'love' and shared cigarettes.

'Must be made of iron,' she thought. Men in the back of the van laughed at a shared joke, others were reading papers or smoking. Just another day's work. Mo was glad she'd used a false name on her CND subscription form, glad she hadn't been too brave. Apparently there were lists.

No violence was likely so it was hard to see why so many police were needed. Surely an array of power apparent would be enough to clear the way?

'Please don't let them see me be gentle.'

The van stopped, doors flew open and soon they were making their way along a track deep in mud. There was a workaday feel about the movement. Mo gave out orders, answered questions mechanically, her mind intent on the *Mail* article and its photographs. They called each other 'love' and shared cigarettes. She rounded a corner and saw the gate. Across the gateway and on thirty feet of track before it sat women. They looked so incongruous there that at first she was struck only by their numbers. As she approached she saw that they were mostly aged between nineteen and thirty, muffled against the damp and cold, noses shining, cheeks flushed. The arrival of power apparent was barely registered on a single face. Mo heard a few policemen joking quietly, then one of them calling out,

'Hello, my loves!'

A woman started to sing something and the rest joined her, smiling amongst themselves, some rocking gently on the grass.

The first men had reached the group and were having bodily to haul protesters away on to the verge. Passive resistance. Mo had briefed her team on this. The supplies juggernauts were pulling up behind, waiting to get through. Mo arrived at the group, hating her regulation skirt. She had to be brisk, to hide her softness.

'Come on. Let's be moving you,' she said in the firmest tone she could muster and, bending down, she slipped her hands under the arms of the nearest woman and began to pull. She felt the body go quite limp. Her feet slipped in the mud. Women's voices called out.

'Hey! She's one of us!'

'Wotcha, sister!'

'Love the split-skirt, darling!'

She bowed her head, and hauled the woman back through the mud. It was ridiculous. Embarrassing. Whenever a protester was released, she lay still until her remover had walked a few paces, then hurried back to the group. Now Mo understood the need for numbers. Of course, arrests could easily be made – places like this were a mess of by-laws – but only as a last resort; arrests meant unwanted publicity. The material – not the enemy, official memos never spoke their mind – the material was too inflammatory. Tactful power was called for, but tactful power, Mo reflected, was difficult to summon in a skirt and three inches of liquefying mud. She marched back to the group and seized another pair of shoulders. A woman sang, 'You can't kill the spirit.'

Mo hurried towards the protesters. It was like some stupid Brownies game. Get two girls outside the circle before the whistle blows and the first one rushes back to Brown Owl. Another pair of shoulders, wool wrapped. More mud.

'On and on and on.'

A man's voice was raised. Mo glanced across. An arrest was being made. The accused would only sing in response to his questions. If it wasn't so bloody maddening, you'd have to laugh, thought Mo. Then she slipped and sat heavily in the mud. She swore. The protester stood and pulled her up with a smile. Mo thanked her, and blushed. The woman ran laughing back to her sisters. They laughed too and a new song was started.

'Lean on me, I am your sister.' The notes were distorted by giggles. 'Lean on me, I am your friend.'

Angry now, Mo staggered across in the confusion. Just one more try, then she'd arrest one. But as she bent, the girl she had meant to seize rolled over and huddled herself around Mo's ankles in a foetus posture. It was all Mo could do to keep upright. Her feet sank deeper in the mud as she tried to free them.

'Lean on me.'

She saw the face. The blonde hair cropped short, the pierced ear gently pointed, brown eyes staring straight ahead, mouth curled in a mischievous grin. The girl in the mud was beautiful. Mo froze, staring at her.

A man approached. Sergeant Higgins. Mo hated him. Cocky little bastard.

'Lean on me, I am your friend,' they sang.

'Spot of bother, Inspector?' He bent down and laid a hard hand on the girl's shoulders.

'Oi! What the hell d'you think you're doing, then?' he roared, and tugged her. The foetus closed tighter. Mo nearly lost her balance.

'Steady,' she said.

Higgins lost his temper. 'Go on! Get up, will you?'

The girl started to sing the first song again. 'You can't kill the spirit.' Her voice was high and sharp. 'She goes on and on and on.'

'Oh does she?' shouted Higgins and kicked her.

He didn't kick her particularly hard, but his boots were reinforced and the blow landed at the base of her spine.

The foetus unfolded at once, yelling a curse and rubbing her back. Instinctively, Mo dropped down and touched her shoulder.

'Christ! Are you OK, love?'

Higgins' voice intruded from above, shocked and mocking. 'You bleeding dyke, Faithe!'

Mo looked up. He was turning away. Her gorge rose. She sprang up and, without thinking, kicked him savagely on the back of the legs. He fell twisting awkwardly on to the mud.

The consequences of this rare loss of temper had been predictably severe. A report was made, and first Higgins and then she had been summoned to appear before their superiors. There had been the usual condescending mention of past record and achievements, then the grilling began.

'Inspector Faithe, did you attack your colleague because his violence enraged you? Were you protecting your good name, or had he, perhaps, touched on a raw nerve?'

Of course she had pleaded PMT and an abhorrence of Higgins' violent techniques. Defeated by such unwonted softness on her part, though they didn't believe her for a moment, they had suggested a transfer within the Met. Perhaps she could work for Superintendent Timson in the West End sector? A change of atmosphere. Maybe even a little investigative work? They could have been a bunch of ruddy doctors suggesting that a little light gardening was good for the nerves. It was punishment plain and simple.

As she gazed through the crowds, Mo wondered how many telly heroes ever had to see bleeding sculpture exhibitions on the South Bank. She glanced at her watch. Nearly three.

McEnery would be here soon to drive her back. McEnery the Perm. Everyone got a nickname after a year at the station. Mo had found her own on the toilet wall by a smutty cartoon.

I'm Faithe the Peg
Fiddle diddle diddle dee,
With my extra leg
Twiddle diddle fiddle dee.

A pickpocket. A real live pickpocket. Mo homed in. It was a girl. A punky type with spiky black hair and a leather miniskirt. She had slid into the back of a crowd that had gathered around a sculpture. A strong gust of wind had set it whirling like a tin firework. Its clattering bells had attracted valuable attention. Mo watched, marvelling at her technique. The kid's head craned with the rest of the crowd, pretending an interest in the sounds and colours, while her fingers slipped, an expert lizard, into her neighbour's handbag. She had on an oversized jacket with baggy sleeves, into which a wallet, then a bottle of perfume and then a cheque book were slid. Then, with the distracting grace of a master magician, she yawned loudly, covering her mouth with the offending hand, thus sending the ill-gotten contents of her sleeve well out of sight. She remained apparently rapt while her elegant victim strolled away to another exhibit, then placed her hand in her pocket, shaking it as if to search for loose change. Mo walked over and stood beside her. She wished her civvies ran to an Italian handbag complete with trailing headscarf. She would stuff a wallet with papers reading, 'I know all but, for a kiss, will keep silent.'

She saw McEnery strutting through the gate, in uniform, punctual to a fault. The wind died and the wheels grew less frenetic. As Big Ben chimed three, Inspector Faithe decided, for the first time, to wield the great cloaked power on behalf of the underdog. Letting go of her ID card in her pocket, she turned with a smile to the thief.

'Great, isn't it?' she said, and walked away.

FRIDAY three

'I suppose we should wake him,' said the kind young man.

'British Rail apologizes to passengers on the Intercity service from Bournemouth for any delay, and hopes that no inconvenience has been caused.'

Seth blinked awake.

'Too much bed and not enough sleep?' An unexpected shot at ribaldry from the gorgon. Seth smiled up blearily, his tongue waking dry. She turned and left the carriage, in search of chocolate.

'Here. Let me help you.' Pinstriped suit, well cut dark brown hair, blue eyes, square jaw, a hint of suntan. Seth watched him lift his suitcase off the rack and swing it down to the platform in one long movement of impeccable animal grace.

'Thank you,' the boy swallowed, and stepped down beside him.

'Your violin.' Strong white teeth.

'Oh. Thanks. Goodbye.'

'Bye.' He marched away, pink paper neatly furled under his arm. No comment.

There was Mother. Darling Mummy was running to meet him.

'Darling!'

'Hello.' They hugged and kissed – humming to avoid having to say 'I love you'. She laughed.

'Who was that devastating man who handed down all your stuff?'

'Oh. Just a man.' He recalled the *Cosmopolitan* lying on the carriage floor. Make way for the little firecracker.

As the Volvo swung out over Waterloo Bridge, she unfurled an eloquent hand in front of Seth's face, her eyes ahead, her tone abstracted.

'Down there. Ilena's new exhibition opened today. Dear Ilena. It's called *Waterstretch and Metalbeam* or something, but very good. Very good indeed.'

They had to stop for a bus. He glanced across and was met by her strong green return. 'But' was so like her – involuntary making of allowances for everything she encountered. Prizes to everyone for trying. He looked the other way to hide his spot and glimpsed the exhibition through the railings. A little knot garden of moving bars on the concrete. Dear Ilena worked on kinetic/sonic structures in a converted warehouse on the canal in Islington. Finding her at a poetry reading in Camden, Evelyn's set had embraced her with an almost unseemly appetite for the new. Seth suspected her of lusting after his mother.

'They've cut off your curls, but it's rather nice.' Did Mother know about lesbians? Did she need to? 'You filthy little man!' The car in front was lurking indecisively between two lanes as they approached the underpass. 'Out of my way!'

'Next stop Moshinski's?'

'Of course. But it's the last time. I'm getting a girth.' The first evening of the holidays was marked with a visit to a pet Hungarian cake shop.

'How's Father?'

'All right, I suppose. He's gone ahead to Cornwall.'

Tall and forty-six, Evelyn Peake's silver helmet of hair, emerald stare and superb carriage accentuated the fact that she was more pre than Raphaelite. Her only softness was a pair of full lips. A warrior-maid who had taken on wedlock as the cardinal trial of her strength. She brought out in most women those characteristics that men have earmarked as quintessentially feminine, those that all women of integrity eschew. Her father died in a hospice for the alcoholic elderly. Her mother had drifted off to a nursing-home on the south coast where she masticated vacantly among the potted palms while the eighties crashed on the pebble-dash outside. Evelyn had never missed parents who had so rarely been around. While Father had drunk his way from outpost to outpost of an illusory empire, Mother, made uneasy by her plain offspring's baleful eyes, had left her for longer and longer stays with her own parents in Hampstead while she visited Nice – for her health.

Faced with such shoddy examples of human endeavour, Evelyn emerged rigorously self-disciplined and altruistic; a tall, thin Protestant. She drank in a first-class musical education from her grandparents. The latter had met at the Paris Conservatoire, married and become a much-lauded cello-piano duo. Evelyn was not gifted – they saw that straight away – but she was blessed with determination and intelligence. With their encouragement and her perseverance, she not only gained a teaching diploma on the cello, but won a scholarship to visit Paris to study under Emmanuel Jakobsen who was then making breakthroughs in the sonic education of deaf children. She returned, qualified, to London to find that her mother had returned from Nice, having run out of money after a cancer operation, and out of admirers in her efforts to disguise its cruel effects. The ravaged creature was trying to form the home she had never had, with the tremulous shell that remained of her husband. To her grandparents' dismay, Evelyn moved with the freakish pair into a house in Kensington. They urged her repeatedly to look to herself and after a year were relieved to see her marry an intelligent, albeit mature, young man and start a new life. With their wedding present, she founded what was to become a highly successful music school for the deaf, working under her maiden name of Davenham. Within a year of her marriage, her father got violently out of hand and was sent to the institution where he died of cirrhosis of the liver.

'Be a devil. Have that chocolaty thing. I'll have the coffee one and then we can swop half-way through.'

Evelyn laughed. 'Oh, all right, Tempter.'

She was sure he was beautiful. Aware of the blindness of parents, she was constantly on the watch for the reactions of others, for proof. The waitress liked him, but that was her job. She often saw men look at him, though, which must clinch the question. The same sex was the truest, because the cruellest judge. She liked his high forehead, and those almost black eyes. Then she saw the spot.

'Are you sad to be leaving school for good?'

'Oh, not really. Another two years would only have been more of the same.' He remembered that she had paid most of the fees and threw her a smile, 'Can't wait for Trenellion again. What are our plans?'

'Well, Netia's being dropped off by Benji at about eight.' She lowered her voice. 'She thinks he's rather nice so I may have to make him stay for dinner.'

'Which one's he?'

'He reads English at Caius. You remember – he was in that Shakespeare with her last summer. The tall, blond one.'

'Oh yes. More tea?'

'No thanks. But we must go round everywhere locking windows and turning off valves in case I forget. And I must shut up school. We can do that on the way home, before Neesh gets back.'

It was a lie he had learnt: a benevolent question to be asked, whose answer was immaterial, whenever he could sense her discomfort. Once the questions had been those of any infant; now, stripped of any shred of credibility, their posing had entered the realms of comfortable ritual.

'Then what?' he prompted.

'Well, all my packing's done. You and Neesh will both have brought home mounds of filthy washing. I vote we take it all down and wash it at Saint Jacobs. Just pray that bloody twin-tub has been fixed. I wrote to Mrs Stock about it.'

'Mrs Pym.'

'Yes, to Mrs Pym. But she's so very absent-minded.'

'What about music?'

'Oh, that's all done. I picked up the copies from Swiss Cottage yesterday morning and Peter and Grigor took it down in the van today along with all the stands and t-bars and things.'

'Dear Grigor, with his awful "yokes". How's his eye?'

'Beastly. Well it was. He'd got one of those floating retinas – retinae? – and had to have it lasered back on. He only had it done a couple of weeks ago, but thank heavens he says his sight is safe for driving now. Oh, thank you.'

The waitress clicked a saucer on to the table. The bill lay

under a sugar lump. She smiled at Seth and walked away. He smiled back without his eyes. Evelyn detected the first shifts of sexual calculation.

'Now we must hurry.' She reached for her bag.

'No,' said Seth, 'let me, for once.' He seized the bill and walked to the till.

Determined that deaf children had enough frustrations without the added barricade of what she called 'the School Concept with a capital S', Evelyn had fought formality throughout what had been her grandparents' house. Every room was brought to life, not only with plants and small trees, but by a menagerie of birds. Out of term time the mynah birds, parrots, canaries and rose finches were farmed out with pupils' families 'to inculcate in each child', the prospectus said, 'a sense of responsibility and love; restoring to him, and her, that trust of others which disability may have undermined'. Even the dullness of the instrument cases lined up in the hall for collection had not remained unchallenged. Cello cases were sky blue, violin cases apple green, trumpet cases canary yellow, and so on. Each case bore a name tag inscribed in magisterial marker on one side, and in crayons, lovingly, on the other. Elspeth, Marianne, Eustace, Candida, Dan, Joe, Phoebe and Quintus. Seth had met Phoebe at the Christmas concert. She had carroty hair in bunches, and a winning grin that almost distracted one from the flesh-pink box dangling incongruously from her neck. Joe was said to be the more promising.

'You check the doors and windows down here and I'll do upstairs.'

Seth wandered into the main room. The light streamed

in across the garden. He took the burglar key and tightened the locks on each section of the large bay window – the only generous window in the house. Then his eye fell on a violin case lying on the window-seat. SFP on the lid. The dusty snakeskin of his childhood. He opened it, lifted out the small, and now unfamiliar instrument, tightened the bow and began to play.

Evelyn was marching back across the landing when she heard Brahms. She sat in a white painted rocking-chair. Her features took on the unguarded loveliness they had so often worn in an unwatched corner of the room where Seth practised. Her eyes filled with painless water. The reaction was Pavlovian but heartfelt; one offered tears to Brahms as a token of grateful humility.

The boy was prodigious beyond question. Over thirty years of music-making she had heard countless children perform. Many had attained a technical mastery far beyond their years, but there lay no mystery – the Japanese had demonstrated the childish openness to technique. Such technical precocity could execute a piece of Vivaldi without blemish, but faced with a Brahms sonata or a Beethoven quartet fell short of grace. Passion could no more be compassed by dexterity than a ten-year-old could be expected to understand the vagaries of lust, but when Evelyn first heard Seth play Brahms she had been as shocked as if her son had gravely proposed incest. He seemed uncannily to comprehend sufferings of maturity, torments transmuted into the bony code of a score. She wept in silence, as this boy who had never known any woman beyond his nearest kin, perceived and gave fresh voice to the longings of a man old enough to be his father.

FRIDAY four

Sixteen, Lydia Villas, was one of a row of snug cottages in Hackney. Most of Mo's neighbours had forgotten or had never known that she was a policewoman – the newspaper articles were far in the past, and she changed into civvies at work. Not a trace of her job to be seen. She'd memorized the handbooks at training school then thrown them away. She was useless at gardening – hadn't enough patience – but there was a snot-rag-sized lawn at the back, which she kept trim, and she planted a few bulbs and seeds when Mum reminded her. She didn't live alone because there was Andy. Some years before, the local pet shop had burnt down and this tabby tom had been one of the refugees. Now he was family. He'd lie on her bed until she was asleep then let himself out and reappear at breakfast for a saucer of milk, some bacon and a barrage of ribald teasing about his night on the tiles. She let him share her breakfast, but dinner was left-overs from the station canteen – cold sausages, bits of bacon rind, crusts of sliced bread soaked in milk. Bella, the canteen cook, said she reckoned Mo ate it all herself because she was too mean to buy her own. Silly cow. Mum offered to buy her a budgie once. That was before Andy. Mo hated budgies; ugly, boring birds.

The house was comfortable but a bit lifeless. Mo sensed this on the rare occasions when she had someone round, but somehow she could never find the energy to cheer it up.

A refuge. The only pictures were two photographs by her bedside: one of Mum and Dad, and one of Maggie. She'd bought the three-piece suite at a sale in Heal's and she'd bought a big colour telly with the money from when Dad died. It was a special German one, with remote control so she didn't have to wake Andy when he was asleep on her lap. Mumsy had been on an over-sixties holiday to Spain last year and had sent her a straw donkey with little baskets for pepper and salt pots. It stood on the mantelpiece with the calendar. No bookshelves – Mo couldn't see the point of buying books when you could get them from the library, but she had one book. Maggie'd given her a collection of prints by Gustav Klimt on their last birthday together. It lay in pride of place on the coffee table.

They'd met in the Gateways Club the very first time she'd been there. Not a bad advert for the place. She'd plucked up courage, spent a good hour deciding what to wear, had a couple of whiskies in a nearby pub, then turned up at the address she'd learnt off a toilet door. After five minutes, this girl had marched up to her and asked for a dance – simple as that. Mo was living with her parents, looking for a job after finishing school and Maggie was at art college, training to be a textile designer. For three amazing years they'd shared a flat over an Earls Court supermarket. Maggie had gone off to college each day and Mo had worked as a barmaid in a local pub. No one had batted an eyelid; lots of girls were sharing flats in the sixties.

It had happened soon after her twenty-second birthday, the birthday of the book. She'd come home from working at the Boltons and had been surprised to see that there were no lights on in the flat. As she opened the door a policewoman had touched her gently on the shoulder and said,

'Miss Faithe?'

She'd asked if she could come in and then, when they were sitting down in the lounge, she'd told her how Maggie had been killed on the flyover when her car had skidded in the rain and went under the wheels of a lorry. Maggie had had a little red sports car with a soft roof. Mo had listened in silence then broken down and wept on the policewoman's shoulder. It was all fresh still, right down to the smell of her hairspray and the little blonde curl she had teased out from her uniform hat to hang in front of each ear. Some girls became nurses because they'd had a big operation when they were kids – Mo became a policewoman.

She had moved back home to Mum and Dad's place in Tower Hamlets until she'd earned enough for a mortgage on a house. Material possessions had figured pretty small with her and Mag – nothing much to show for three years' marital bliss. Mo'd been glad of this as it helped her make a clean start. All she had (the flat had been furnished) was the book, and the photo that stood at her bedside – Maggie on Brighton beach, sunburnt, and smiling with a slight wince because the sun was in her eyes. There had been a lot of clothes that she'd had to sell to pay for Mag's backpayments on the rent.

She had to identify the body as the police couldn't find any next of kin immediately. The shock of seeing her laid out in the hospital chapel had been intense, but oddly soothing. Accidental death was so unreasonable that her brain demanded solid evidence that her lover was not going to appear again the next night with a slight bruise on her temple and a wicked story about the nurses on casualty duty.

The secrecy had been the worst part. No other women friends. They'd lived on their own little island of joy. None of Maggie's family had suspected that they were anything other than best mates. The funeral had been torture because she'd had to sit back and let the family – who'd taken no interest in the girl for three years – monopolize her.

Since Mag there'd been no one. Mo had joined the Force, worked hard and played little. She'd lusted, but lust was just lust – an indulgence, like the occasional ciggie or a glass of port. Maggie had loved her and that was enough. When she was blue there was always Andy to hug – he was a big cat and could take a good deal of squeezing before he complained. She was lucky to have had love at all. From what she could gather from the women at work and their tales of woe, she had tasted an uncommon passion.

'Hello, you filthy animal. Come here!' Mo slung the unprotesting Andy on to her shoulder and unlocked the front door. He rubbed her neck with his head and purred in her ear, making no attempt to jump down when they were inside. Mo talked to him as she hung up her helmet, kicked off her boots, and walked into the kitchen to make them some tea.

'What've you been up to today, then, And? Out with the girls, eh? Off with those girls? You filthy bastard! Look what you're getting for dinner then.' She scraped the contents of a small plastic pot into his bowl. 'Sausages, beans and a nice bit of kipper. Cor!'

Stirred at last, Andy landed heavily on the lino and set on his food, his tail sinking slowly – a happiness meter. Mo filled the kettle, slung a couple of bags in the pot, and laid out some kippers under the grill. She sat with a yawn on a chair, scratching her scalp that itched from the heat, and flicked on the radio. A cheery London station with lots of adverts and equally inane jingles.

'And we finish our six o'clock reports with the story of a man who has written a novel more disposable than most. Damien Bell has just published a book where each chapter has an alternative after it. You can read the happy version on pink paper or the sad one on blue. Mr Bell's publishers say that he had asked them to print the whole thing on perforated paper so that the unwanted chapters could be torn out where required . . .'

'Bloody stupid,' muttered Mo as she turned the kippers.

The telephone rang. She swore and switched off the grill. The kettle had come to the boil so she filled the pot before walking out to the hall.

'Hello . . . ? Oh, hello, er, sorry, I'm not that good at . . . oh, May. Hi, May. How are you? . . . Good . . . Tonight? Well . . . OK. What sort of time? . . . Right. And you'll drop in here on your way, will you? . . . Can you remember the address? . . . Right, May. See you in about an hour. Thanks for ringing. See you.'

Mo walked back to the kitchen and re-lit the grill. She poured herself a cup of strong, black tea and squirted some pre-packaged lemon juice into the mug. Andy had finished his tea and rubbed himself against her ankles as she sat down once more. She thought of the phone call.

'Ruddy Nora!'

FRIDAY five

On the way, Evelyn stopped at the petrol station to fill the tank for the next day's journey and found that wallet, cheque book and some scent had vanished. Familiar with the Peakes and their crises, the little man said they could pay another day. She checked back at Moshinski's but the waitress only stared at Seth again and said no she hadn't seen them, Madam. They drove home.

'Thank God the cheque card was old and the book almost empty. I've got a new card and there's a new book in an envelope on the hall table. I'll cancel the credit cards by phone. The scent was my best. I suppose I have to make a statement. Oh, blast and damn! I'll drop you off to do your packing.'

The fridge had not yet been cleared. The contents would be eaten for supper. Seth stole a pork pie and felt at once the satisfaction of a thorough homecoming. Then, cat at his heels, he ran upstairs ripping off his tie and unbuttoning his shirt as he went. The hateful uniform was hurled into a corner of his unnaturally tidy room and some faded jeans and a shapeless cotton jersey were donned in its place. Then, luxuriating in the sensation of walking on a carpet, and without stout, black shoes, he toured the house.

He and Venetia had been allowed to redecorate their own rooms recently, with a certain amount of supervision.

Evelyn was a great believer in self-expression. Elsewhere she had expressed herself at length. There were paintings and drawings everywhere, but she had an italianate distaste for clutter that was at odds with the irrepressible late Victorian spirit of the place. The modern classicism of her colours and furnishings was here gently subverted by a chaplet of plaster marijuana leaves, and there by a piece of florid stained glass. Seth left Father's study until last. Half-mocking, half with serious intent, Huw Peake had said that he thought it unfair that he should be denied self-expression simply because he was held to be colour-blind. Half-laughing, half-piqued, Evelyn had granted his boon, although she was meeting the decoration bill.

The walls were white, the windows hung with Venetian blinds. There was a desk with a telephone, lamp and typewriter, regimented bookcases, a waste-paper basket and two hard-backed chairs. There were no pictures and no carpet save a small rug under the desk. The only quirky touch in the spartan ensemble was a hamster cage gathering dust on the highest shelf. Placed there originally when the beast died seven or eight years ago and the children were still in shock, and left there for want of a suitably rational explanation to Doctor Peake as to why one was bothering to move it.

Seth remembered the death of Fifi (christened Fiordiligi) all too well. An aggressive hamster at the best of times, who delighted in hanging by her teeth from the youthful hand that dared to feed her, she had developed a tumour of the brain.

He slid the case on to the typewriter and heaved the whole to the floor. Then he opened the top drawer of the desk. The photographs. He set them out. Mother on one side, Father on the other and he and Netia in the middle: the nuclear family. He picked up his picture and his father's again and sought similarities. Father was good-looking in a wasted sort of way. He had the devastated glamour of the occasional tramp. At about thirteen years, Seth had resented the man intensely, but only insofar as he felt that this was expected behaviour. They had never quarrelled. Now he would just have him dead. Always so cold, so unremittingly rational, never treating children as children. He laughed at, not with. There was something immasculine about him. He had a 'masculine' intellect, to be sure, but there was a timidity, too, that shocked his son.

Recently they had been visiting some friends in Fulham and were driving home when they found themselves in a traffic jam, caused by the crowds leaving a football match. In the distance they could make out a sea of blue and white surging out of the gates and surrounding the cars up ahead. Then, as they drew nearer, breaking glass could be heard above the shouting. It transpired later that a match had been lost by the home team. Mother, sitting in the front passenger seat had turned to Father, crying, 'For God's sake, Huw! Don't just watch them – turn round!' But for a moment he had remained frozen at the wheel. Seth had stared at the beads of sweat rising and trickling down his temples. Then Netia had lost her nerve and screamed, jolting the man into action. On the way home, no one had mentioned his behaviour. Conversation had kept to the horror of the mob, the lack of policing and so forth, but later that evening, Seth had commented on it to his mother. She had become suddenly grave.

'Sometimes, darling, your father suffers from agoraphobia. You know what that is? It's because of the war, you see. He had some terrible experiences.'

Whenever this tender tone came into her voice when she spoke of Father, it puzzled him. He had sought to understand their relationship, but could form only a piecemeal, over-deductive analysis. She had felt guilty for wanting to leave Grandpa and Granny to pursue the interests of a career, and felt that forming a family of her own would do something to redeem herself in the accusing eye of her God. Marriage being a sacrament. Father got on with his theological history, she with her teaching and goodness; a horrible coupling beneath the civilized restraint of its dress. Taking for granted that she loved him because she was his wife, he showed no affection, only an acceptance of custom. His philosophy denied her religion, his misanthropy mocked her public spirit. She was too grateful to him for having been in the right place at the right time ever to admit to herself that she did not love him. She respected his work and she could quite understand their ideological differences.

'No one,' she would say, 'could have encountered the Nazis and not been scarred to their very soul.' She liked to suggest that he had suffered an appalling experience in some infernal theatre of war and been left with an unshakeable misanthropy, but Seth recognized this as the glamorizing of a shocked imagination.

Huw Peake's interest in theology was a wholly destructive one, concerned less with the exploration of belief than with the puncturing of the bubble mystery. He had none of Mother's rapture. With neither love nor worship, he had only scorn and terror. A man with no faith in his neighbour's innate goodness needs must suspect the stability of the public. A man whose life is dedicated to the establishment of hard realities needs must quail at the prospect of their destruction.

Seth, confirmed a year ago today, opened the drawer and returned the photograph of his father together with those of mother and son. Then his eye caught Venetia's and slid from it to Mrs Peake's, now uplifted in the dimness of the desk. He smiled at the tricks they had played on themselves. Venetia, Mother and Granny were strikingly alike, and yet Mother had grown up plain by being forever told how pretty her mother was, and had reversed the process on Netia by drumming it into her identical head that she took after Granny, who was once so lovely. None of the three was especially beautiful, but the fluctuation of self-esteem over the last two generations had wrought a startling effect. Mother stared at the top of the picture frame, fine but distant, as if to say, 'So? I'm not Vivien Leigh, but just feel the strength of character!' By contrast, Venetia had been taught to use her face to win. Though merely a younger version of her mother's, its eyes sparkled, its lips pouted slightly. He had once watched her sitting in a corner with a mirror, learning how to flare her nostrils. They were confidently flared in the photograph.

Venetia would be home soon. She had not missed Trenellion once since their childhood, had even been driven there peppered with the remains of a severe bout of chicken pox. Though she knew she would argue with Mother on the way, and often be beside herself with boredom, she had twice turned down offers of glamorous trips abroad just to sit in a Volvo and be driven for hours to a place she always swore she was seeing for the last time.

Delighted at the arrival of a live dolly in the household, nearly sixteen years ago, she had adopted Seth at once. Surrounded by the chattels of her miniature domesticity, she would chide him for failing to understand the invisible tea she fed him, and then press him to her hard little chest to quiet his bewildered tears. As she had grown older and found silence, he too had learnt the arts of peace and would sit quietly while she pored over a school book, drawing a picture or reading, in mime at least, a book of his own. His time was shared almost exactly between mother and sister and he never sensed any jealousy in the air until, around his seventh birthday, Netia suddenly regressed from her calm affection to infantile hugging and cooing. He was frightened by the violence of this new display, then disgusted when he saw that it only occurred when Mother was present. He sensed the aggression involved and recoiled from it, spending more and more time at his solitary music-making.

Seth placed his sister on top of his mother. From the drawer her smile was almost saucy. He was jealous to a degree of her poise. She never blushed, never sweated, never dropped anything and, if she had, one could be sure that it wouldn't break. Venetia had no accidents. Her life contained no spots or fillings, no crumples or rips. Since nothing ever seemed to go wrong, he often wondered whether she had enough experience to appreciate the extent of her good fortune. But how long did luck last? Her horoscope sign was Virgo; dreadful in old age, that at least was some consolation, but he wished that something could go wrong now. He wished with all his heart. Just a little something – a token gesture to curb her hubris for her own sweet sake.

He heard tyres and slammed the drawer shut. There was a strangled scream from a klaxon. He pulled on the shoes he had brought down with him, ran across the hall and opened the front door. Netia with the friend from Cambridge.

'Seth darling!' She laughed. 'What have they done to my poor baby's hair?'

Venetia acted a lot. She was rather good. Seth remembered her companion of the moment as her most recent co-star. A well-dressed snake. Netia leapt out over a door of his vintage car and ran to hug her brother. Her chest was not much softer than it had ever been. Then she laughed some more and kissed him on both cheeks so that she left lipstick marks. She smelt divine. Stepping back she looked him up and down appreciatively.

'Yes. He's grown some more.' She rubbed a hand on the shaved back of his head. 'Ooh, it feels so *sexy*!' she growled.

The companion of the moment stepped up behind her with her suitcases, the leather of his soles ground, satisfied, on the gravel. She spun round and laughed again. Venetia laughed a lot when she hadn't seen one for a few months.

'Benji, may I present Seth Peake, heir to the family name, protector of its honour and the only bro they've ever let me have? Seth, this is Benji Buckhurst.' She put on a childish lisp. 'My bethteth fwend.'

Blushing like a shaved mule, Seth held out his hand which Benji's cool white one grasped and wrung. Netia sprang up the stairs with a cry and a mew to pounce on a cat who was wreathing a welcome in the porch.

'Delighted to meet you at last, Seth,' said Benjamin. His eyes opened very wide on the 'delighted' and he squeezed Seth's hand a little too long. Feeling another, deeper, blush coming on, Seth turned to walk up the steps, tripped and just caught his balance on the railings. Netia hooted.

'Legs too big for you now, are they? What size are your feet?'

Seth reached her side.

'Nine,' he lied.

'Oh poor thing! Benji's are only eights.' Hating Benji, Seth walked past her towards the kitchen. At times like this one had to hide as much of one's lower body as possible under a large pine table.

'Where's Mummy?' Netia asked as they sat down. Benji remained standing to scrutinize the spines of the cookery books.

'Oh. She's at the police station. Someone nicked her purse, her cheque book and a bottle of scent when she was out this afternoon.'

Netia's almond eyes rolled inexpressively.

'No!' she laughed. 'How awful! Did she lose very much?'

'Thank God, no. And the card was old and the cheque book nearly finished. She should be back any minute. She's been making her statement for hours. God knows why, because she can't have much of a statement to make. I'm meant to be doing my packing.'

'Oh rubbish. You've got to talk to us. So all she knows is that they've gone?'

'Gawn but not forgotten,' Benji intoned in a lugubrious

voice. He and Netia collapsed in fits of laughter. Seth got up and made for the boiling kettle. As its whistle subsided, he heard that they still hadn't quite recovered. He turned and managed a half-smile as he asked, 'What . . . ?'

Netia pulled her face together.

'Oh. It's a line from this term's revue, *Sizewell Revisited*. It was terribly funny. You know Bella? Oh you *know*. Bella Macpherson. She did this brilliant bit about Brideshead meets the Nuclear Holocaust dressed as Charles Ryder in drag, and it ended with her saying, "Gawn but not forgotten".' She laughed again but soon gave up. 'It's months since I've seen you, darling,' she said, as Seth put the teapot on the table. He opened the fridge and took out a milk bottle.

'Jug,' she said flatly. He poured out a jugful and replaced the bottle.

'We were burgled only two weeks ago,' offered Benji.

'Oh dear,' said Seth, 'was an awful lot taken?'

'Yes. I should say. But Perkins caught them.'

'Is Perkins a detective?'

'No, the gamekeeper, actually.'

They watched as Venetia, faultlessly, poured the tea.

'Benji lives in a real live castle, darling.'

'Really?'

'Yes,' Benji affirmed.

'Whereabouts?'

'Near Buckhurst.'

'Does it have a haunting and glamorous name?'

'Just Castle Buckhurst,' said the heir.

'Oh, of course. Silly me.' Seth blushed so his sister made it worse for him.

'Seth's the only boy I know who blushes – I mean, *really* blushes.'

Benji mustered a kind smile. 'It's meant to be a sign of sensitivity and acute perception,' he said, as though speaking tactfully of an absent limb.

The front door opened.

'Mummy!' Netia laughed, and ran to hug her.

'Hello, young lady. You smell divine. Seth, you're puce. Have they been talking about something improper?'

'No. Castles, actually.' Her son mutely welcomed his ally.

'Hello, Benji. It is Benji, isn't it?' She shook hands. Seth watched for his wince at her unexpected strength. It came. God bless Mother.

'Isn't Benji's car wonderful?' he declared.

'Splendid,' she said.

'Benji and I had a marvellous drive from Cambridge. It was so sunny we had the roof down, so the wind was in our hair. And we sang songs at the top of our voices. I think some people thought we were drunk.' She laughed her haven't-seen-you-in-ages laugh. Benji rose.

'That reminds me. Buckhurst is a long way to go yet and I've no headlights.'

'Oh. Must you?' asked Evelyn, vaguely.

'Yes, I'm afraid I must,' he replied, and shaking hands graciously all round, he left with Venetia beside him to wave becomingly from the steps.

'Thanks for the lift, *mein Engel.*' The engine roared, the klaxon blared and the future Lord Buckhurst was gone.

'I didn't realize he was Buckhurst as in the Castle.'

Mother laughed kindly, 'Oh you poor thing.' She lowered her voice. 'He's a bit of a prat, isn't he?' She noticed the tea. 'Yes please.' Seth poured and dribbled some on to the table. He mopped it up with a hanky. 'Dirty boy,' she muttered, then, 'Oh, the *police*!'

'Was it murder?'

'*Dreadful!* I had to wait hours, then fill in a form, then another, then give names and addresses and say why I was leaving for Cornwall and when would I be back and so on. Then I had to sit and nod politely while they read the whole thing back to me. I thought I'd never get out.'

Netia walked in and put her hand on Evelyn's shoulder.

'Hello, Mummy,' she said.

'Hello, Poppet.' Evelyn patted the hand. 'Now sit down and tell me all your news while I cook something. Seth, have you packed yet? Well do so now, please, so we can load up the car tonight for an early start.'

They wanted to talk.

FRIDAY six

'Hi there. Great. I'm Gemma. Come on in.'

'Er, hello. I'm Louise,' said Mo, and did.

Bleeders had listed it as a 'consciousness-raising session'. She'd been glued to one of these on Channel Four a couple of weeks back. Seven intelligent women sitting in a circle talking about themselves. No men. No sizing each other up. Just talk and sympathy.

'Welcome to Thornhill Square, Louise. Still a bit of a mess, I'm afraid. We're doing it all ourselves and there's a lot to do.'

As the door closed behind her, the curiosity that had brought Mo thus far wailed that it wanted to go home.

'Come on down. We're all in the basement as it's the only bit straightened out.'

Following, Mo's eyes strayed up and around. At least three floors. All theirs. The girl was only about twenty-two. Glancing at the quantity of sheet-draped furniture, Mo bet she was a social worker. A large room leading up some steps into an overgrown garden. A large, shaggy dog asleep on the sofa in the corner and two women bolt upright on floor cushions.

'Now, everyone, this is Louise. And Louise, this is Emma and that's . . . er . . .'

'Fay.'

'Yes. Fay.'

'Hi.'

'Hi there.'

'Hi.'

Mo recognized Emma. She lived with her sister a few streets away from Lydia Villas. She ignored her conspiratorial smile.

'Well it looks as though that's all we're going to get. Louise, if you'd like to sit on the futon . . . yes, that mattress thingy there. Great. OK?'

'Hopelessly middle-class, ducky,' thought Mo, watching her practised descent into a cushion.

'Hey, we live round the corner from each other, don't we?' asked Emma, a nice enough looking sort with short red hair and pink denim dungarees.

'Well . . . I thought, perhaps. Lydia Villas?'

'Panton Street. Up to the top and second on the left.'

'Oh. Right.'

'Contacts, contacts. It's what it's all about,' Gemma said in a stupid voice. Behind her hung a big, framed print of that picture of the protester putting a flower in that guy's gun. There was a pause which she broke by clapping her hands together. 'Well, look, we can't really benefit from these sessions until we've all got to know each other better, so I suggest we just chat about anything under the sun, OK? 'cause I know most of these things get really formal, you know? with set topics and guest speakers and all that shit, well I think we should try to avoid that, so as I'm the mug who had this bright idea in the first place, I'll take the plunge and just start talking and then you all react and we'll just go where the conversation leads us. OK?' They murmured gratefully. Gemma set her lips, stared at the carpet and began.

'Well look, I'm in my early twenties, OK, and I've had, well, maybe three long-term relationships, and the obligatory sleeping-around-just-got-my-first-packet-of-pills bit of course, but the one thing I really want to do, and actually the one thing I think perhaps I *need* to do, is sleep with another woman.'

'You couldn't sleep a ruddy wink,' thought Mo, and then the door opened.

'Hi there.'

'Oh. This is Robin who'll be doing useful things like making us tea.'

'Hi.'

'Hi.'

'Hi.'

'Actually, I just brought you some apple juice. Is that OK? Run out of milk.'

'Great. Thanks.'

'Well. I'll get back to my bread-making.'

'Not just a pretty face,' said Gemma. 'Makes great date loaf.'

'Well, this is something I've been worried about, too,' said Emma. 'I mean, I think men are too possessive of women and women are too possessive of, well not of men exactly, but of the idea of men. I reckon a guy should be prepared to let a woman sleep with another woman because I think they could both learn something really valuable from the experience. I think men should, at least, be prepared for some alternatives to vaginal intercourse.'

Mo took a gulp of apple juice. Piss, she thought. Fay, extraordinarily out of place in a short skirt and lipstick, piped up.

'Well maybe I'm just old-fashioned, or conditioned or something, but . . . and it does make me feel guilty sometimes . . . but I really, well, I have tried other things but . . .' Mo watched her discomfort and tried to imagine her with her skirt over her head.

'Well I find I just *need* it. Nothing else will do.'

'How about you, Louise?' asked Gemma.

'Wouldn't say no,' thought Mo. 'It's great with a woman,' she said. She had drained her glass and set it on the floor. 'Frankly, I wouldn't know about men.'

Fay shifted uneasily. Gemma was fascinated. A three-dimensional lezzy. With a scar. On her futon.

'Would you call yourself a gay woman, then?' she asked.

'Guess so,' said Mo.

'Don't you think that's rather limiting to your sexuality? I think separatism is a very real danger.'

'Look, love. You're a woman, not a man, not a motorbike. I'm a dyke. You don't eat tripe, because a look and a sniff and you can see what you're not missing; same goes for men.'

Sycophantic laughter; not just a lezzy, but a character, too. Robin came in with a plate of flapjacks.

'Ever slept with a bloke, Robin?' asked Mo.

'Fraid not,' he said.

'Leave him out of it,' said Gemma and he retreated.

'Isn't it unfair of you to be jealous of him and to expect him to let you sleep around?' asked Mo. Talk and sympathy my arse.

'It's not the same thing.' Gemma threw up a tight laugh.

'Sex is sex, isn't it?' suggested Emma.

'But . . . is it *really* as good?' asked Fay, getting prurient.

'Look. You don't need the pill, you don't have his cum dribbling down your inside leg, and you don't wake up black and blue from his pudding-fisted search for the "start button".'

That had been her last contribution. Cow Gemma had seized on the reference to the pill to steer the rest of the discussion on to 'straight' issues. Would a 'male pill' make them feel less secure during sex? Did sterilization make one less of a woman or merely less of a wife? And so on. Mo tried to be shocked at such blatant cold-shouldering then reflected that she had asked for it.

When the time came to leave, she wrote down her false name and number, put it down to experience, and started unlocking her bike.

'I gave a false name, too,' said Emma, 'my name's May.'

Then, as Mo sat astride her BMW and fidgeted with her helmet straps she heard how May not only lived just around the corner from her, but had had her long-term suspicions confirmed that the woman May lived with was not her sister, but her lover of nine years' standing, and that she was unlikely to let her reluctant neighbour escape without handing over her genuine phone number. She'd complied. Tonight's call was the fulfilment of a threat.

FRIDAY seven

Evelyn and her daughter listened to Seth's footsteps as he ran upstairs, then Netia said, 'Pain about your purse.'

'My wallet?'

'I mean, your wallet. Where did you go today?'

'All over the place. But I know it happened at Ilena's exhibition by Waterloo Bridge. I had to pay to get in, and everything was there then. I'd have found out sooner, at the cake-shop, only Seth paid.'

'Observing the sweet ritual for the last time?' Venetia found it hard to be funny. She was home. There was a pause, then Evelyn rose swiftly, emptied her tea into the sink, and opened the fridge.

'What can one make with pâté, kippers, mashed potatoes, eggs, half a lemon and some cheese?' she asked, as she peered into various pots and bags.

'Leave the lemon for the garnish, then have a sort of fishy potato-cake thing, with pâté and toast to start, and bikkies and cheese to follow.'

'Wondergirl. I can't think straight this evening.' Evelyn switched on an old radio that perched on the fridge. Radio Three: 'And now, to carry on our apocalyptic theme, some Messiaen; two movements from *Le Quatuor pour la Fin du Temps.*'

'I haven't had a period for five and a half weeks,' murmured Netia.

The Messiaen began. Evelyn chopped a kipper in half.

'What was that?'

'I said my period's overdue.'

'Oh.'

'And before you ask me, yes I do take all possible precautions and the chances of my being in a certain condition are about a zillion to one. I feel foul.'

'Poor darling. Does this often happen?' The kippers, now lacerated, were gradually hidden by a soft fall of grated cheese.

'Never. I'm normally regular as a ruddy time-bomb.'

'There's not much I can say that helps really?'

'No.'

'There's no pain, just tension?'

'Yup.'

The quartet swelled. Some lightly dehydrated onion and red pepper joined the fish and cheese. Three boulders of mashed potato later, the whole lot rolled into an electric mixer and lay around the stationary blades. While Evelyn banged her way through a greasy pile of cast iron saucepans, Netia pondered the position of woman in society. Rather, she pondered her own as a woman who appears to be pregnant with no rational explanation.

At a dispassionate distance she could see that her circle at Cambridge was sexless – all talk and little of the hard-gutted reality. She knew closet debs who talked dirty at parties but always left when the first glass was kicked over. She knew 'Hooray Henries', who cultivated manly laughs, but had probably done it with juniors at school. These went around in droves, for security, then got drunk from time to time and laid some hapless and quickly forgotten tart from the biochemistry department. Then came the Token Perversion – desensitized, Debrett-cleansed creatures like dear Benji. The place was an obstacle course in which one had to gain a reputation while retaining a certain hazy integrity. She had discovered within a fortnight of her arrival in College, two years ago, that slander could prove an invaluable armour against ill-repute. In a society where proclaimed virginity was a mark of feminine weakness, it was as well to have her secret masked by the misinformed complexion of jealous surmisal. All it took was a lusty laugh in the right place, the occasional hint of debauchery, and a healthy inverse honour was fast established. She had a fine double-act running with Benji along these lines. United in their disdain, they threw a series of costumed parties that might best be described as 'naughty', and successfully cast the nature of their sex-lives and, indeed, the purity of their own relations, into uncertainty.

At the touch of a button, fish, egg, potato, onion, pepper and cheese were as one.

After her Finals in English, Venetia wanted to visit New York. She could easily apply for research, but it had to be abroad. If not research, then advertising – on the creative side, of course. She knew she would be a rat leaving a sinking ship, but the suicidal heroism behind this pejorative left her cold and smiling. Americans were so bland, their intellectuals so temptingly open to The Great Literary Bullshit. She looked up at Mother's strong back at the stove and hated all the seventies values it stood for: self-sufficiency, do-it-yourself, get-your-rights, pick-your-own, plant-a-tree, save-a-whale. What the hell! Life was too short for saving left-overs. She intended to get out, smoke, drink and enjoy herself while she was young, then swell to a fat and famous prime. She had yet to learn to smoke, however, and regretted the integral part that sex seemed to play in such aspirations.

Daddy had touched her once. There had been Seth's seventh birthday party, then Mummy had gone to visit Granny for a week, so he had said that he had to get her ready for bed. As she had lain there in the soapy water, unaccustomed to this male presence, he had touched her. Every night until his wife came back, he had knelt on the bathmat and touched her. It had been their little secret. Nothing had ever been said, but now she remembered every time, and it put her off. Not that she was hung up on it. She was the last person in the world to be called neurotic. She was simply keeping her options open. And her legs crossed.

'When's Daddy coming home?'

'He's not. He's gone ahead to Saint Jacobs.'

'That's rather sudden.'

'Not really. He wanted to be alone to work for a few days.' Venetia pierced a grape with a fingernail.

'Oh for Pete's sake, Mummy, don't lie. I'm old enough, aren't I?'

'What?' Evelyn turned around, smiling, genuinely bewildered.

'What did you row about this time?'

Evelyn was unflinching, supremely calm. 'Netia, we didn't "row" about anything. He just needed peace and quiet, that's all.'

'All right.' That twistless-knickers tone. 'I'm sorry. No row. *Pax vobiscum.*' Netia almost ran upstairs. Evelyn sighed and, turning back to the stove, prodded the six fishcakes that lay smouldering there on a griddle. Suitably liturgical for Messiaen, she thought.

There was a scratch at the French windows. As she turned and saw a cat waiting to be let out, she saw herself reflected, pinny at waist, flushed from the heat, fish-slice in hand: the perfect little woman – only she'd been too tall to play lacrosse with the other girls.

She had married Huw when she was twenty-four and he was thirty-eight. It was something of a cliché, she had always known, for an underprotected, rather plain girl to seek the protection of an older, brilliant mind. Her heart full of Daphne du Maurier and the Brontës, she had been blind to the blatant sexism of the match. After the initial shock at his atheism, she was attracted by the thought that his ego must play the part for him that God played for her in shoring up her night-thoughts. She could love an atheist if his godlessness had stature. Unfortunately, Huw's rigour of mind was far from Marlovian. His firmness of unbelief permeated his whole manner with an unappetizing negation. Where she would answer a pestering child with 'Wait and see', he had said 'I think not'.

She had had her first baby at twenty-six, her second at thirty. A difficult birth. The pain of Seth's arrival into the world had left a trace of suffering in all her dealings with him; her love was founded on the hurt of his creation. In his depth she found a pleasing counterpoint to Venetia's less complicated brightness. Seth could play brightness, just as Netia could play Medea, but she sensed that he was a ponderer, not a playboy, at heart. She walked to the door and called the children.

The discomfort of living with a man who laughed at her

every mention of the sublime was considerably soothed by the presence of children. A house, a husband, a son, a daughter provided the raw materials of her happy marriage; she had only to wait for the appropriate spirit to perform a transfiguring miracle. Needless to say, the tongue of fire never descended, but between them Venetia and Seth had provided a focus for devotion and concern. 'Those were the last two movements from *Le Quatuor pour la Fin du Temps* by Olivier Messiaen, performed by members of the Gudrun Ensemble under director, Gerry Hackett. And now, two songs: Fauré's *Après un Rêve* and Tchaikowski's *None But the Lonely Heart,* performed here by Helmut Schreier, with Daniel Grossman at the piano.'

'All packed and I've put it in the back of the car.' It was Seth. 'That smells good. Left-over rissoles – my favourite.' She smiled. Needless to turn round. She could hear him laying the table. 'Why's Father gone on ahead to Cornwall?'

'He had some new ideas for a book and wanted to be alone with them.'

'How exciting. Have you mustered a pudding, or not?'

'Just cheese, bikkies and fruit.'

'Right. Three little knives.' He felt the texture of her lie and loved her for giving him the opportunity to protect her wound. 'Here comes Neesh,' he went on brightly.

FRIDAY eight

As they walked together from the bus stop, Mo confessed, 'You know, I've never been to this place before.'

'Never been to the Carved Red Dragon? Where've you been all your life?'

'Is it good, then?'

'Ruddy marvellous. It's always packed, and really friendly and that.'

'You heard the band before?'

'No. But they're meant to be really good.'

'Didn't . . . er . . . Josie want to come?'

'She doesn't like pubs – says the smoke makes her feel sick. D'you smoke?'

'Off and on.'

'Bit like me. Can't smoke at home, of course.' May laughed, and stuck her hands deeper into her dungarees' pockets. She was so relaxed and talkative that she didn't seem to have noticed Mo's tension on the bus. Unremarked, Mo's shyness had evaporated. May wasn't butch, precisely, but she had a total lack of self-consciousness that was appealing after the simpering inhibition of the girls at work. Mo was relieved that she still hadn't asked what she did. Perhaps straightforward employment was too unalternative. As May swung open the door of the pub, Mo stiffened again. The room was full. Smoke stung her eyes, and the blare of the juke-box combined with the shouts and laughter from the all-woman crowd had her momentarily confused and on edge. May steered her over to the bar.

'We've just got time to drink before they play,' she yelled, looking at a nurse's watch that dangled from the breast pocket of her dungarees.

Mo relaxed at the bar. Familiar ground. She pulled out her wallet.

'What'll you have?' she asked.

'Oh. Thanks. Mine's a pint of heavy.'

'What?'

'Heavy – bitter.'

'Oh.' Mo started to laugh then had to cough. 'Two pints of bitter please, love.'

As the girl pulled the pints, May leaned her back against the bar and looked around the crowd.

'See anyone you know?' asked Mo.

'Yeah. One or two. Hello, Mand!' May waved in demonstration. 'How about you?' she asked over her shoulder, 'see any of your friends?'

'No. Like I said . . .'

'Oh yeah. Your first time. Thanks.' She took the pint. 'You've gotta meet Mand. She's a card, really. Runs the hostel over by King's Cross.'

'Oh. Right.' Mo turned around, taking a gulp of bitter. A willowy bird with lots of wispy hair and gold-rimmed specs was coming over.

'Hi Mand.'

'Hello, May love.' The women hugged.

'Mand, this is Mo. You know, the new-found neighbour I told you about?'

'Oh yeah. Pleased to meet you, Mo.'

'Hello,' said Mo.

'Here, Mand,' asked May. 'What's all this about Trish?'

'Oh God, the poor dear. You know she was having all that trouble with the drains behind the co-op?'

'Yeah?'

'Well the man from the housing department came round and told her that it was only going to get worse and that it was a condemned building anyway, so there wouldn't be any money for it. Well, she tried to put up a fight, you know, squatter's rights, and all that.'

'Yeah?'

'And then her little girl, you know, Becky, she caught some infection and the health visitor reported it and they've said either she moves out into one of those council-aid hotels in Bayswater, or the kid gets taken and put into care.'

'No!'

'Yeah. Awful, isn't it? Nothing she can do, of course. I said she could come in with me, but she doesn't want to give up the co-op. I mean, there's a real call for those posters and books and things now, and it's doing quite well, really, but the minute she moves off the premises, they'll be in there boarding the whole thing up or knocking it down or something.'

'Christ!'

Mand turned on Mo. 'What do you do, then, Mo?' she asked.

'I'm a . . . in social security.'

'Hey, quick!' May saved her, 'they're coming on. Let's get to the front.'

Mo had seen there was a stage of sorts at one end of the large, flock-papered room. A couple of women had jumped on to it and were tuning up guitars and adjusting amplifiers. May plunged forward through the crowd as it began to turn in their direction. Her companions pushed in her wake. Mo managed to stand with May in between her and her interrogator and they were soon pushed right to the edge of the stage by the people behind them.

'Jesus!' she exclaimed, 'they'd better be good.'

'They are,' offered a stranger with plaited blue hair, 'heard 'em at the Greenham benefit last week. Fucking brilliant.'

'Great,' said Mo vaguely, glad of her civvies.

The two women left the stage then, as the lights were turned off overhead and a pair of spotlights hit the back wall, a woman's voice called out over the speakers.

'And now let's have a big Friday night welcome for The Graces!' A cheer and a burst of enthusiastic applause. Mand whooped like a cowboy and three women bounded up into the pool of light – the two who had already been on and a third, who seized Mo's attention at once.

Small; just over five foot. Hair was cropped short and fluffy; it looked white. The letter-box red of her lipstick and her boiler suit made her hands and face seem almost as colourless. She ran forward to the mike, a sax slung round her neck, while the others took up their stations at the guitar and drums. She clutched the mike, smiling impishly across the audience, playing with its expectation, then simply muttered, 'Hi there,' breathlessly and launched into the first number. It was clear from the first that she was the crystal around which the group had formed. Dynamism, clarity of a hard, young voice, prevented one from looking away from her as she danced and sang. The song was an old hit given an arch new twist by its novel surroundings. Over the music of the introduction, she shouted the familiar words and raised an immediate laugh at the line she was taking.

'This song goes out to all those fellas who think their kisses are as sweet as candy; well Honey got them beat by a million miles . . .'

The gig lasted about thirty minutes and Mo's eyes were on the singer for every one of them. She was knowing, sometimes savage in her performance, yet her appearance was innocent. There was an air of mimicry about her gestures; a precocious child playing before a mirror in her mother's make-up and clothes. The pattern was the same throughout the session – the band took songs that had become familiar radio fodder, and robbed them of their heterosexual currency. Songs were still sung to girls, but with a difference. Mo's girl, who was standing almost in front of her, sang each number through, then improvised on her saxophone. Delivery so assured that the instrument was a crooning extension of her voice. She used it to toy with each melody as her performance had already played with each lyric. Mo was captivated. She hadn't seen a live band since her days with Maggie. The overt membership of the audiences made her feel too old. Now, whenever May leant over in between numbers to say, 'Good, isn't she?' Mo would merely grunt her assent and continue to stare. She didn't care if she was making a fool of herself, she knew she wouldn't be coming to the place again and was unlikely to meet the other women after tonight. She watched the diminutive singer, intent, with a childishness of her own, on storing up her every move and inflection and on winning, if only for a second, a glance in return. The girl seemed to be too blinded by the spotlights to make out any particular faces in the crowd, but Mo was at the very front, bathed in a wash of reflected light. She knew she could be seen.

The last song was a ballad. A gentle brush rhythm on side-drum. The girl played the melody on her sax first, low and reflective, then, backed by acoustic guitar, she sang. Sang to her new lover of how they had communicated through glances, through overheard conversations, even through unconscious sympathies – a shared love of warmth, of a certain flower or a piece of music – and as she sang her eyes strayed slowly across the faces before her and came to rest on Mo's. Mo's first instinct in her surprise was to look away, but she held herself and stared back. She expected the girl's gaze to travel on, but found that it had checked itself, returning her stare. Safe in the semi-darkness, Mo raised her face gratefully for the crux of the lyric.

'So how dare you tell me that our first loving day together was today?' Then the lights went out, the crowd pushed forwards and there was a roar of thanks.

'Amazing! Really amazing!' exclaimed May as the lights were switched on overhead.

'Yeah. Great,' said Mo.

'My round. Come on.'

May led the way back to the bar. The latter was crowded in the rush for fresh drinks as the room turned back into a pub. May brought them all pints, and they sat on the edge of the stage. Behind them, the two instrumentalists were packing up their things; the singer had carried her sax off-stage with her. May and her friend had a great deal to talk about and Mo was quite content to sit in silence, listening half to the buzz around her, half to their talk. Demonstrations, natural sponges, group meetings, problems of sisters-in-militancy. She tried hard to think when she had last been in a pub for anything other than work. Her days behind the bar in the Boltons. She'd been a chirpy creature then, with a smart line in answering back the teasing enquiries of her customers. They'd called her Mo Sauce.

To her right, Mand was being smitten by period pains.

'Oh God in Heaven! Here we go,' she moaned. 'It always gets me just here.'

She pointed to a part of her spine and rubbed it.

'Is it very bad?' asked May.

'Comes and goes. Ow!' She swore. 'Only thing to do is lie flat on me back and lift me legs.' She lay back on the stage and raised her knees. 'Be a love, May, and lean on me legs – it helps flatten me back out.'

'Sure.'

Mo looked away as May stood and leaned heavily on her friend's knees with a laugh. Bystanders looked on in amused understanding.

'Ooh, that's *great*!' moaned Mand, and Mo managed to place her accent at last. Somewhere near Liverpool. She took a swig of bitter and wondered whether she should be getting back to Andy.

'How'd you get that amazing scar?'

She twisted round. The singer had sat down beside her. She was wrapped in a black greatcoat to hide her distinctive red. Mo blurted,

'Knife. Bloke with a knife.'

'Shit!'

'It's a long story.'

'I'm a good listener.'

And so, when all she wanted to do was to say how wonderful this girl's performance had been, Detective Inspector Faithe haltingly recounted the story of her encounter with Harman the rapist. She didn't mention that she had met him in a professional capacity, however, but cast herself as a public-spirited, bluffly courageous victim. The girl sat rapt.

'Does it still hurt ever?' she asked, when Mo had finished.

'Only when it gets sunburnt – no pigment left.'

'Sorry. Maybe I shouldn't have asked you to tell me. It's just that I saw it on stage just now – well, saw you – and then it and . . . you know . . . I wanted to know.'

'You were brilliant,' Mo faltered. 'I didn't want it to stop.' The girl laughed.

'Really? I wish I could say the same – hate the sound of my own voice.'

'Why?'

She pulled a face. Mo analysed the accent. South of the River.

'I never used to sing. There was another girl, Judy, she's with Big Sister now – lured away by the money, you see. I used to stand near the back and play this.' She patted her sax case. 'But after Jude left, someone had to sing, and Bo and Denny are both a bit rough.' Mo laughed, she laughed, and they caught themselves staring at each other again. Mo looked down.

'Can I get you a drink?' she asked.

'It's OK, I bring my own,' she replied, pulling a half-bottle from the folds of her coat. She swung it to her lips then offered it to Mo.

'No thanks,' said Mo. There was another pause. The girl broke it.

'I'm Hope Linden,' she said. 'A copper found my dad in a fruit box in Linden Gardens so that's what the foundlings home called him. Stupid isn't it? What's yours?'

'Mo. Mo Faithe.'

'Faith and Hope; we'll go far.' They chuckled.

'D'you live near here?' dared Mo.

'No. Further west. Near Marylebone.' Mo raised her eyebrows. 'No,' Hope smiled, 'not *that* bit of Marylebone. I don't pay a penny for it. It's a squat on the top floor of this old office place. Used to be something to do with the Post Office. Now it's totally empty – just a few old filing cabinets. They know I'm there.'

'Don't they mind?'

'No way. I'm clean, and I keep it a bit drier than if it was left empty. It needs too much doing for them to put it on the market, and it's derelict council blocks all round. View's brilliant, but it's a bit cold at nights, so I need this.' She waved her rum bottle with a grin. 'Where d'you live, then?'

'Hackney,' said Mo, 'Lydia Villas.' Hope pulled out a felt-tip and wrote on her hand.

'What number?'

'Sixteen.'

'Sixteen, Lydia Villas. I want to be a taxi driver one day, so I've got to look everywhere up in the old *A to Z* and learn where places are. You have to get the Knowledge.' Her laugh was dry and breathy.

'Why d'you want to be a cabby?'

''Cause it pays better than this. I'm on the dole too, you know.' She nodded at the stage. 'That'll hardly buy Shreddies for a week.'

'You should go pro – properly, I mean, with a manager and everything.'

Hope laughed and played with the handle of her case.

'Managers don't grow on bloody trees.' She must have been about twenty-five, but sometimes she looked about thirteen.

'But honestly. It was really good.'

Hope stopped smiling. Her fingers lay still on the case and she looked back at her new friend.

'Can I come round and play, one day?'

'Yeah. Great,' Mo snorted, taken aback.

'OK, I will. Swop you for a hot bath.'

'Hey, Mo! Have you met Jill?'

Mo turned back to May. Her back had been fully turned and she was put out. There was a small woman in a black beret with a round face who said hi.

'I'll say this for you, Mo love, you're a pretty fast worker.'

Embarrassed at their laughter, Mo glanced over her shoulder. Hope had gone.

SATURDAY one

Years of practice had not perfected the art of the early start. As always this day had seen them rise at six, but only leave four hours later. After an organ recital on the radio, two string quartets, a lunchtime concert and a poetry reading to celebrate July, they arrived in Tivorbury to buy a late picnic. After promising to be back at the car in half an hour, Seth was released in search of violin strings.

Seth revelled in long car journeys. They provided the same excuse as train travel for indulging in fantasy. He marvelled at the audacity with which the bare-faced lie about the soporific effect of car travel was put about. Trains did make one sleepy – but then, they could be plain dull. Hurtling along in a steel box with only human fallibility between oneself and certain death was palpably too dangerous to be dull, and yet maidens, young men, even children were seen brazenly to sigh and close their eyes for a spell of auto-eroticism. Seth smiled at the unconscious pun.

He entered Bickerstead's Music Shop and at once was gravely intent. Music shops put him on his guard – the assistants were too often ill-informed Radio Two suspects. Bickerstead, whose back was turned when Seth walked in, was delighting a little too obviously in testing a new electronic organ, the kind that chugged along in an automatic bossanova rhythm while the player picks out a melody with one finger. Seth walked past him and smelt a waft of

Parma Violets. He glanced to the back of the shop, hoping to catch another assistant or perhaps to find the strings without their aid. Hopeless.

'And what can I do for you, Sir?'

The bossanova stopped. 'Sir' addressed to a fifteen-year-old felt as patronizing as 'my little man'. There had been a cousin of Father's, Harry, who had called Seth his little man and bounced him on his knee once, but he hadn't called again. Mother had drawn attention to his white silk socks in a darkly significant tone.

'I want to buy some violin strings, please.'

'Ah, yes.'

'I want a gut E and A and then two Ds and Cs, both in silver on gut, please.'

'Let me see.' The man opened a few boxes under the counter. Seth noticed flecks of dead skin in his thinning sandy hair as he bowed his head.

'If I might recommend these for the gut ones. Pendarotti.' He placed two yellowing packets on the counter.

'Pendarotti?'

'Yes. They're Hungarian. Unusual, but very good. You don't find many of them around now.' Seth pushed them gently back.

'They're a bit old I think and actually, this A here is rather frayed.'

'Is it?' Bickerstead, only his name was Pendle, peered in astonishment. 'Oh dear. Well they're very good value.'

'Look. I haven't got much time, actually. What are the very best in your stock for gut and for the silver?' Pendle told him sharply. 'I'll take those, thanks. What do I owe you?'

'Stuck-up little bastard, aren't we?' Pendle took the

money and passed a bag to the boy. 'Think we're the ruddy Duchess of the West don't we?'

'Thank you, Sir,' he said aloud. 'Goodbye.'

As the boy walked away, Pendle returned to his keyboard. Bossanova with a sax, violins and just a touch of celesta. Magic. The door bell clattered and he was reliving his night of glory as Carmen Miranda at Melville's drag ball. Was it really sixty-seven? Sick transit, Gloria Pendle.

Returning through the precinct, Seth glanced at a large ornamental clock. Ten minutes. He looked for a newsagent and found a large, impersonal one by a tub of geraniums. Thrilling to the luxury of an unknown town, he marched purposefully along the wall of magazines. The line of shamelessly economical browsers made it hard to see the titles, but the arrangement was invariable. Between Women's and Leisure he hesitated for a rapid glance around him, then seized the object of his quest, walked along to Foreign, and opened it.

'Is this your car, Madam?'

'Yes.'

'It'll have to move on, I'm afraid. Bomb regulations.'

'Oh dear. But you see, I'm a Friend.'

The warden smiled, wryly confident. 'I'm sorry, dear, but even His Grace isn't allowed to do anything more than get dropped off here, and *he's* got a Disabled badge.'

'Oh poor thing. What's wrong with him?'

Venetia got into the car, picking at a French stick.

'Broken hip. The old fellow slipped on a wet leaf in the avenue last winter. Nasty business. Terrible complications, he had.'

'Did he have to have . . . er?'

'Oh yes. A plastic replacement. It's marvellous what they can do.' She lowered her voice. 'I think *Her* Grace finds it comes in handy to have a badge for parking behind Sainsbury's. Oh well. Must be off. Now if you wouldn't mind . . .' She nodded at the Volvo. Evelyn dropped her smile.

'Oh yes. Of course.' She got in and shut the door. 'Damn!' she said.

'Still no Seth.'

'Well, we said half an hour, and there's still five minutes. But I think I can lose the wasp.'

She started the engine and drove slowly around the great Close lawn. She waved sweetly to the traffic warden and watched her walk down a side aisle towards the High Street. They continued their regal circle to where they had begun. Evelyn cut the engine.

'Bravo,' said Venetia.

'Damnably clever, aren't I?'

Evelyn switched on the radio. The news. A general election now seemed likely in the autumn of next year. A letter bomb had exploded in Whitehall wounding the hands of a senior minister's secretary, who was said to be stable in hospital. A Labour MP had been arrested by an *agent provocateur* in Earl's Court. Following arrests at the US Air Force base at Greenham Common, several women were appearing in court today on charges of vagrancy, obstructing a highway and breaking the peace. There was still no verdict.

'I hope they get a bloody big fine,' said Netia savagely.

'Why?'

'It would serve them right.'

'They're only trying to save the world for the likes of you.'

'Oh for God's sake, they're a bunch of communist lezzies.'

'Don't you think they're doing a good job?'

'What job? Knitting jerseys and singing flower songs? I think the CND were doing a perfectly good job until those stupid "wimmin" started joining in. They're extremists trying to draw attention to themselves. The whole thing's a carefully planned attempt to let some feminists make history. They've all got chips on their shoulders because the Suffragettes got all the pain and glory and now no one's interested – precisely because the Pankhurst gels did their job so well.'

The small clear voice of calm: 'I don't think you've understood at all. I found them very modest, rather lovely people.'

'How d'you mean, "found"?'

'As a matter of fact, I went there last month. The school was closed for half-term. I'd read so much in the papers that I was determined to go and tell them how great I thought they were being. So I made a couple of fruit cakes and bought a few bottles of whisky, and took them as a sort of keep-up-the-good-work parcel.'

Venetia stared for a moment in disbelief, then laughed.

'You are a joke, sometimes. Perfect *Guardian* Woman – right on, but never compromisingly so. It's a bit nineteenth century to go around taking pots of coltsfoot jelly to paupers, so she takes cake and booze to a load of dykes in Newbury.'

As he hurried back towards the cathedral close, Seth wondered who actually bought *Playgirl*. It had appeared in

British newsagents in the seventies, capping the rise in 'liberated' women's reading-matter. Or was he confusing liberation with licence? Did the liberated woman see male pornography as a means of subjugating men to her newly-acquired right to a sexual appetite, or would she view it as a weak indulgence? He looked down and saw that his damp fingers had made an imprint of soggy grey on the bag from the music shop. He folded the edges down a little, thought of Bickerstead, then felt a flush of shame-fed anger. The dreadful thing wasn't published for women at all! Crouching amongst the French scandal papers, he had become another figure in a successful marketing plan. In a few years' time he would walk out of the shop with it tucked into a copy of the *Radio Times*.

There was a pause. They both felt foolish all of a sudden, as they had on all the other rehearsals of this confrontation.

'Soon,' thought Venetia, 'she'll say it all boils down to the lovely differences of character, she'll turn up the radio and I'll be back on bail for a few months.'

'Still no Seth,' said Evelyn.

'He's probably having trouble in the shop. He's a bit timid with assistants.'

'You haven't seen him in a music shop; he's fine on home territory.'

'When you think about it, Seth doesn't believe in much.'

'He believes in art.'

'So do I.'

'Yes, but you only criticize and dissect it the way your father does.'

'Well, I act.'

'Yes. You're right. I hadn't thought of that.' Evelyn smiled. The pressure had gone. She turned up the radio.

'Didn't you first meet Daddy on an anti-nuclear march, though; one of the first ones?'

'That's right – Aldermaston. But I never did work out why he was there. I expect it was "fieldwork". It became one of his favourite jokes that he didn't need to go to church or to meetings of the rate payers' association, because I so enjoyed going to them for him. He'd say I had enough conscience for two that I viewed the extra burden as a spiritual luxury.'

'And don't you? Isn't it rather like feeding for two?'

'Here's little S.'

SATURDAY two

'Happy Birthday, Boss,' said McEnery as they turned into the Bayswater Road.

'Thanks for nothing,' said Mo, 'I feel ancient.'

'Ha,' went McEnery lightly, and glanced in the mirror.

Mo had felt McEnery's resentment from the day of her promotion. She could take it or leave it, but it obviously meant a lot to the girl. Strapping them together like this was Timson's idea of a sick joke. Mo had managed to win support for her plans for a trial of the all-women patrol cars against his considerable opposition. The little jerk had got his own back by recommending that she be sent out herself from time to time to monitor the progress of things, and by giving her The Perm for her number two. They stopped at the lights outside the Coburg Hotel and she reflected that there were better ways to spend a birthday.

'What did you make of that report?' asked McEnery.

'So-so,' teased Mo, 'usual reactionary crap.' She stared briefly at the plucked eyebrow and discreet lipstick.

'Delta five-two. Delta five-two. Call from an old lady in Ladbroke Square, number ninety-five, says she thinks her neighbour's been murdered. Probably gone to Bridport to visit her cousin Fanny. Check it out, would you? Over.'

'Roger, Harry.' Mo had snatched up the mouthpiece. 'Be there in two minutes. Over. Something to put the smile back on your lovely face, McEnery.'

'Saturday morning special,' clipped The Perm tersely, and accelerated towards Notting Hill Gate.

'Stay in the car by the radio. It's probably a false alarm as Harry says. They've caught Neighbourhood Watch fever round here. I'll call you if I need you.' Mo got out and climbed the steps to the front door. There were several bells so she rang the one marked *HOUSE*. The door was opened at once. The nervy old duck must have been waiting at the window.

'Oh, thank goodness you're here, Officer, I've been so worried!'

'What seems to be the trouble?'

'Well, my name's Avril Fairbrother. I'm the landlady here.'

A well-spoken old biddy; probably lived here all her life. Mo guessed the family house had been turned into bedsits to cover the rising rates. The landlady stepped out to join the officer on the porch and raised a timorous hand to the door across the railings to the right.

'It's Miss Stazinopolos. She's a fortune-teller, you know – but Greek, not a Romany – with the *Woman's Weekly* magazine. We're quite good friends and she often pops round, but she hasn't been out since Thursday. I thought perhaps she was ill, so I knocked on her door – I've knocked several times – but there's no reply. Her curtains are still drawn, you see? I tried telephoning her but she didn't come to answer it. I called in and saw her on Thursday afternoon and she didn't say anything about going away.'

'Does she live on her own?'

'Oh yes. Quite alone.'

'Big house for a . . . for a single lady.'

'Yes. I'm rather afraid Marina's let things slip a bit. Very otherworldly, you know.' She gave Mo a meaningful look.

'And you haven't heard or seen anything unusual?'

'Not a squeak. But then I usually have the wireless on, so I could have missed something.'

'I see.'

'Will you have to force an entry?'

'I've got a magic key, love.' Mo smiled and walked down the steps and up to the other door. Avril hovered by the railings and gave a sigh of admiration as the officer let herself in. Mo turned in the doorway and beckoned McEnery from the car.

An immensely stout woman, elderly, yet with jet black hair, was slumped in a chair where she had been tied up and gagged. There was no sign of a struggle, no blood, no mess. Not an amateur job. Mo hurried forward and crouched beside the prisoner. Still alive. Mo touched her chest and she opened her eyes with a start and began to moan. Mo freed her mouth. A torrent of Greek was released.

'Steady on. Steady on, old girl. It's all right. You're safe, now.'

Stazinopolos continued to chatter as Mo untied the ropes around her and the chair. Her practised eye missed nothing. Three milk bottles stood on the desk in front of the astrologer's mouth. Two were empty, one half full. A straw had been thoughtfully supplied with each.

'Get on the phone will you, and call Forensic and Medical. There should be some fingerprints, and she'll need some help – nothing but milk for two days.' McEnery, who had just come in, turned in her tracks and returned to the car. Stazinopolos subsided gently into English.

'Thank Jesu you come,' she panted. 'I thought nobody come. I try to call but no one hear me. He was so fast. I didn't see him come in.'

'Hang on. Hang on.' Mo whipped out her notebook and started to scribble. 'A man. Did you see his face?'

'No. Mask. He wore a black mask – wool.'

'Balaclava.'

'What?'

'Nothing. Go on. When did he come?'

'Thursday. Late Thursday night. I had had my bath and I was going to bed then I came down to find a book.'

'How late?'

'About twelve-thirty. I came down and was standing there by the bookcase. Suddenly I heard the door shut. I turn and see him.'

'How tall was he?'

'Oh. Very tall – maybe six two – and thin.'

'Then what?'

'He ran towards me. I try to scream but cannot – no sound. Then he force me down into chair. So fast. I cannot stop him.'

'Was he strong?'

'Yes. I did not think he would be – so thin, you see – but he strong. So he push me into chair and suddenly he winds rope round me. I start to cry out but he say, "Don't scream. Please don't scream. I no going to hurt you but I have to do this." '

'Was his voice young?'

'Hard to tell. He was well-spoken, I think, but so confused I can't remember. He gagged me then. Not tight but it muffle me. I was scared so I kept quiet.'

'What happened then?'

'He went over to my desk. I am an astrologer, you know.'

'I know. For the *Woman's Weekly*?'

'Yes. Well he goes over to my desk and starts picking over my papers. I keep all my predictions in separate files – for each month you see – or for separate people. Well, the file for this month and for August were lying in the top drawer. He search the desk-top then he open the drawer. He grabbed the file and turn to me. "Please tell me the truth so I won't have to hurt you," he say, "is this all that you've written about the next few weeks?"

'Now I was scared, you know, because he was so well-mannered and lunatics are often so, so I thought I must not lie. I just wanted him to get out so I shook my head like this and pointed with it, like this, over to the coffee table.'

'What was on the coffee table?'

'I had also written a special political horoscope for the *Observer* magazine, for next Sunday. I was going to take it in on Saturday but I was so scared that he might see it after I had said there was nothing so I let him have that too.'

'Did he go then?'

'No. First he burn them. He went to the fireplace and put all the papers he had taken in the grate and set fire to them with a match. Then he wait until they all burnt then he put the milk on the desk and slide my chair over to it. "You must drink this," he said, "it has protein and will keep you going until someone finds you. Don't be afraid." Then he go. He shut the door and stopped in the hall. I think he took off the bally-mask-hat thing before he leave by front door.'

'But you didn't see his face?'

'No. Oh my God!' She raised a fleshy hand to her forehead. 'I feel so giddy, I think I faint.'

'Hang on, lovie.' Mo braced herself for the strain, then, taking Stazinopolos under the arm, guided her over to the sofa where she allowed her to lie flat out, panting and softly moaning.

'Oh my God! Oh my God!'

Mo said that help would be here soon and thanked her for her statement. Was she hungry? No, Miss Stazinopolos was not. Mo looked up as McEnery walked in.

'They'll be over in four minutes,' said The Perm. 'Funny thing.'

'What is?'

'Jack got on the line to me and said there was another break-in in Chelsea last night.'

'Nothing funny about that. Friday night.'

'But it was another Greek astrologer, Papas Mercouri. He writes for the glossies. He came back early this morning and found that all his latest stuff was gone, along with his charts and maps. No fingerprints, no witnesses, not even a broken window. Very professional, Jack said, like a house-guest doing a bit of polite filching.'

'Oh Jesu!' The occupant of the sofa was roused to sudden action.

'You know him, or something?' asked Mo.

'Oh Jesu!' she repeated loudly, and rose unsteadily to her feet. 'No. I must just . . . please excuse me, ladies.' She swept out of the room and across the hall to disappear behind a door. A wooden seat banged down sharply, followed by a muffled Greek exclamation. McEnery smiled at the carpet and coughed.

SATURDAY three

Saint Jacobs was a diminutive fishing village that clung, Atlantic-beaten, to the rock face of North Cornwall. Placed at an inconvenient distance from the nearest beach or sizeable town, it had had the good fortune to attract only the more serious artist. Three miles west of this haven lay Trenellion. This was a mining community near the sea, designed and erected entirely by an inspired landowner in the eighteenth century; a mine, a church, some labourers' cottages and a school. In time, the landowner was proven less happy in his speculation than in his beneficence, the tin seam was soon spent, its master died of drink, and after three generations, his dream stood abandoned to the wind: a testament to vanity and a dwelling for grateful sheep. Trenellion remained in a state of increasing dilapidation until the years immediately following the First World War, when a trio of idealists undertook its renovation. The original landowner's latest descendant, who would grow up to be extremely rich, had befriended in his youth one boy who would grow up to be an architect of note, and another who would grow up to be Evelyn Peake's grandfather. United on leaving Cambridge by their modern beliefs, the three came to adopt the ghost town as a focus and then a cipher of their ideals. The cottages were repaired and considerably modernized, the school became a rehearsal room and small art gallery, and the church was made ready as an auditorium, its government-claimed lead roof replaced with a glass one. The mine had long since collapsed into an encroaching sea.

Restored Trenellion began as an informal retreat for the three friends, their wives, lovers and artistic acquaintance; a *Petit Trianon* where maturing Bohemia could find a little privacy from the interest of a swelling public. On the return of the new landowner from Spain however, his shock at the rapidly souring ideals there induced him to place his privileges to the support of popular suffering as well as the élite sublime. A pacifist festival of music and art was inaugurated. A group of talented amateurs and idealist professionals would provide two weeks of nightly concerts in the church. There would be lectures and exhibitions in the school rooms, and all profits would go to a worthy cause, agreed upon each year by a festival committee.

With each July, word spread, and by the time young Evelyn Davenham went to stay in their new house at Saint Jacobs for the first time, her grandparents, the Strakers, were joint directors of a very popular cultural event. In their retirement, the sole survivors of the original Trenellion set, they came to play an honorary role in the proceedings, handing over the helm to Peter Grenfell, an aspiring conductor who had come under Straker's tutelage. Evelyn had participated in every festival since she was fourteen. On her grandparents' death, she took on their role of social magnet and became Grenfell's 'right-hand man'. She organized mailing lists, fund-raising, and oiled the wheels of a now large undertaking.

A duty of the Festival Administrator was to hold a drinks party on the eve of the first day's rehearsals to welcome back the old faces and to introduce the new. The thought of this had given some cause for concern in the Volvo, but with the first triumphant cry of 'I can see the sea!', there were still at least forty minutes to go before anyone could be expected to arrive.

La Corveaurie, as Grandpa Straker had archly dubbed his house, was a vast barn, cleverly converted by the celebrated architect friend. The original shell had been divided into an open-plan lower half, with a gallery of bedrooms above, and an extension had been built to house a garage, a music-room-cum-library, and a bathroom. The whole was now a priceless, if lived-in, museum of thirties chic.

As they drove into the garage, an awesome fat woman in blue overalls appeared in the rear-view mirror. Evelyn heaved a sigh of relief. The guardian of *La Corveaurie,* Caerleon, Pendarrick and Dulgannon Reach. Evelyn had a memory block about her name and would smile too much in her effort to get it right.

'Hello. Hello again, my dears,' wheezed Mrs Pym.

'Hello.' Evelyn smiled and hugged her. She handed over a basket of little somethings bought in a swearing rush in Hampstead that morning.

'Oh! For me? You shouldn't, Mrs P.'

'Well, it's to thank you for being such an angel. Just little nonsenses.'

'Oh no, I'm sure they're not. Yes. Lovely. Well, haven't you grown, Master Seth!'

'We'll all have to call him "esquire" after next week,' said Venetia.

'Look at him blush. And my little Neesh. Lovelier than ever, my dear.' Netia pecked the doughy cheek and hoped that she would never sprout facial hair. 'I've left everything ready for the party, Mrs P. The receipt for the food and wine's on the dresser. Oh, and the water's heated up nicely for your baths. I won't come in now as I've got to get Roger's tea, but I'll see you in the morning to clear things up. All right?'

'Bless you. Is Huw working out in the garden?'

'Oh no.' Mrs Pym paused with a frown on her doughy brow. 'I thought he'd have told you. He left yesterday afternoon.'

'Left?' echoed Venetia crossly.

'Yes. Left for abroad, I think. There's a note on the table.' Nosing the unnatural, Mrs Pym hurried on, 'Now I must be off. See you tomorrow.'

No one said anything more so she waddled away down the lane.

Jaw set, Evelyn strode into the house, children trailing deflated in her wake. She snatched up the note and read aloud in her school voice.

'"Dear all. Afraid have had to rush to Vienna to pick Leon's drying brains – something vital in his new book that I have to check up on. Will join you soon. Hope Neesh and Seth had good terms. Love, Huw Peake." I see.' Evelyn crumpled the note in a palm. 'Could you two unload? Sweetly? I'm going to make a call.'

She walked into the music room where she could be private, and shut the door. She flicked rapidly through her address book to B for Berkowski, then dialled an extended number. Her knuckles were bloodless on the receiver. A distant voice said,

'*Bitte?*'

'Leon? It's Evelyn. Evelyn Peake. Huw's wife.' There was a pause. The voice continued, so old she could barely recognize it.

'Evelyn, my dear. How are you?'

'Fine.'

'And how is Huw?'

'Isn't he with you?'

'No. Should he be?'

'He left me a note saying he was coming to see you.'

'How delightful! When does he arrive?'

'I'm not sure. He left Cornwall yesterday but . . . Leon, sorry. This may be a big mistake. Can I ring you back later?'

'But of course. And how are all the children?'

'Big. I must go, Leon. Bye. I'll call you tomorrow, maybe.'

'Goodbye, my dear.'

She thrust the receiver back on to the hook. Almost at once it rang. She snatched it up.

'Penfasser 53642,' she said.

'Hello, Penfasser 53642,' Huw's voice was typically wry, 'this is . . .'

'Where the hell are you?' she interrupted him, turning to face the window.

'I'm in . . .'

'You're not in Vienna, because I've just spoken to Leon.'

'How very embarrassing for you. I'm in London. At home.'

'Why?'

'I have to pack and, as you've doubtless discovered, I still have to ring Leon to make arrangements. How is he?'

'Fine. It's bloody typical, you know. Couldn't this have waited?'

'I need to see him.'

'You could have rung him.'

'Too expensive.'

'And the children need to see . . .'

'Balls.'

'I beg your pardon?'

'They'll survive. Tell Venetia I hug her.'

'What do I tell people at the party tonight?'

'Tell the truth and shame the devil.'

'But at least you could have . . .' she all but stamped.

'I'm going. I'll ring you. Bye.'

'Huw, for God's sake . . .' He had rung off.

Evelyn fumbled for a cigarette in the box on the mantelpiece, failed to find a light and put it back. She stalked to the window and pulled it open, letting in a breath of sea air and a gannet's shout. She scowled, rubbed her forehead, breathed deeply once or twice, then rejoined the children. They were sitting, idle, on the sofa. She hated them to look so vacant.

'Where are the cases?' she asked.

'I'll get them now,' mumbled Seth, not moving.

'Yes please. We haven't got long.' She walked across to the kitchen, brightening her tone. 'Well, frankly, God bless Mrs Slim. Look – chairs pushed back, little bowls of nuts everywhere. Even quiche and pizza.'

'How's Daddy?' Venetia piped up.

'He sends you a hug,' said her mother, pouring herself a glass of wine. She glanced at her watch. 'Oh God, I must have a bath! I go first as I drove.'

'And bags I go second,' said Venetia, 'as I didn't get one last night.'

'I'll get the stuff in,' said Seth.

Evelyn sped upstairs. Soon her warm contralto rose above the noise of running water. As Seth walked to and fro from the garage, Venetia lay on the sofa and ate nuts.

'Listen,' she said, 'she's always so happy to get back here. I suppose it reminds her of Great Granny and Grandpa – makes her feel young.' Seth came in with the third suitcase, then flopped into a chair.

'Well, doesn't it you?' he asked. 'Saint Jacobs is in a time warp: The Land That Time Forgot. Hey, steady on! There won't be any left if you carry on like that.'

Netia noticed that she had almost emptied the little bowl of cashew nuts and felt odd. She wished she hadn't come. She could have stayed at home, getting on with her revision and keeping Daddy company when he got back. He had betrayed her by not staying. Sacrilege to say so, but she had never felt happy in Cornwall; she had never been musical enough. She dreaded the party. At least after tonight she would be left in peace to revise, but for the next few hours the place would be full of cheery faces talking music. As Seth laboured upstairs with luggage, she held the rim of the bowl to her cherry lips and filled her mouth with the last of the nuts. Seth called through the bathroom door,

'I've brought up your things. I'll put them on your bed.'

The singing stopped.

'Angel. Do you want to choose me something to wear?'

'OK. Mung bean, or administrative?'

'Oh, mung bean, I think. I'll be being bossy enough without dressing the part.'

Seth opened her case on her bed and, lifting a few things out, draped them across the counterpane.

'The cobwebby-pink designer tent?' he called.

'Fine. And there's a grey suede belt and shoes to match.' The bathroom door opened and Evelyn emerged from the sandalwood steam swathed in a Peter Jones towel. 'Your bath's running, Miss Piggy,' she announced over the banisters.

'Oh. Thanks.' Venetia stood and stretched. She swore dully as a trouser button pinged to the floor. She stopped to pick it up, a puzzled look on her face and started slowly upstairs. She yawned. Car journeys were so very soporific. Seth smiled at her and she hated him.

'Your things are on your bed,' he said confidingly. It felt good to be back. 'I'm just running down to say hello to the sea.' He hurried down the stairs two at a time.

'Don't be late, darling. Just a quarter of an hour.'

Opening the front door he remembered he had left the car unlocked. He walked across to the dresser where keys lived and heard Venetia's voice, edgy and low.

'No it still hasn't started. *Oh!*' The gasp of impatience was accompanied by the sound of a kicked bed-leg. Then Mother's soothing tone,

'Poor darling. I'm sure if you fret it makes it even longer. Just be patient.'

And then his sister: 'Sometimes I *hate* being female.'

Walking out along the harbour wall, listening to the slap of murky water on the stone he pondered the Female Mystery. From various snippets of conversation and magazines, he knew in strictly clinical terms the problems to be overcome in being a woman. Confronted with the emotional reactions though, with Venetia's impetuousness, with Mother's days of ill-disguised crabbiness, with

Matron in a haze of Diorella and Gordon's, he was left an outsider. Two herring gulls wheeled, yelling, over his head.

Perhaps their emotions were the seat of the problem – if indeed, it was a problem. It could be said that he had turned to his own sex because they were the only sex available, but that would not explain the profound sense of bathos at the new-born Venus' gender, nor the way so many of his contemporaries at school had managed to follow their genetic noses, so to speak. He had looked blankly at some of the less grotesque pornography the latter had amassed. Legs spread, breasts heaved; the crude poses were as aggressively territorial as the 'woman only' conversations at home.

Aged all of seven years, he had once stumbled upon Mother leaning across the kitchen table to examine something Mrs Pym was showing her in an unbuttoned blouse. He had started back unseen and spent four days in torment, convinced, until he took care to watch them intently at the altar rail, that they were both brides of Satan.

'That's Huw Peake's boy. Halloo there! Seth!'

He spun round and saw Bronwen. Elder statesperson of the artists at Saint Jacobs, Bronwen was a village 'figure'. Long and narrow as a rake, of an indeterminate age the other side of fifty, she always wore one of three paint-daubed smocks and a pair of fur-lined ankle boots. She dyed her hair with an infusion of something she gathered along the cliff paths, and over the years it had assumed a fiery ginger. Bicycling everywhere, she had the lungs of an Alpine shepherd and the hands of a lorry mechanic. She had been Seth's special holiday friend since his childhood. They had discovered each other on a cliff-top walk, and with juvenile obstinacy he had dragged her into the festival. She sat in the back rank of the contraltos and barked the tenor line.

'Hello, Bronwen.'

She seized his hand, slapping him on the shoulder as she did so.

'Glorious evening,' she snapped, 'you can feel the surges in your bones.' They began to walk back along the wall. 'Something special will happen.'

'Yes,' said Seth, happy to have her arm around his shoulders, 'it's good to be back.'

'You just arrived?'

'Yes.'

'I gather we have to go to some bloody drinks do at your mother's. How is she?'

'Fine.'

'Father?'

'He's gone abroad to do some research.'

'Good for him.'

In her room, Venetia pulled on the frock she had chosen, then found to her surprise that she couldn't do up the zip. She started to sweat. This was ridiculous. It had fitted her three nights ago. She tugged at a fastener, holding her breath. Why, she had barely eaten anything all day apart from those nuts! The zip slid up. She relaxed and heard a seam tear open.

'Shit.'

She looked over her shoulder in the mirror, at the stretch of skin laid bare where the stitches had given. Angrily, she pulled down the zip, tore off the frock and threw it on the bed. She looked into her case, rummaging through her clothes. There was a stripy 'ra-ra' skirt with an elasticated waist. She pulled this on, with a pink silk t-shirt, trod her way into some shoes, and opened the door. Feeling loud and fat, she went downstairs to talk music.

Bronwen picked up her bicycle and swung herself astride. It was a man's model, circa 1918. She claimed that the centre bar was useful for hanging things on during long journeys. Seth marvelled at her muscle power as she rode beside him up the hill. He had to walk briskly to keep up. A gust of wind billowed out her smock. Her legs were quite bare above her woollen knee-socks, so he looked ahead. Three Volvos, a dormobile, and a bright yellow French car – the kind that took apart for picnics – stood on the verge outside *La Corveaurie.* Bronwen threw her bike aside and marched up to the front door.

'I must go and have a bath,' Seth said.

'What do you want to go and have a bath for?' She smiled and ruffled his hair like a benign uncle. 'Funny little thing.'

They opened the door. The air was already full of chat and cheap wine. Seth ran upstairs.

Three more dormobiles had come from Trenellion while he was bathing. As he emerged on to the landing, he saw a host of known faces. The Pollocks had just arrived – one of the more substantial Festival families. He was a retired prep-school headmaster whose all-female progeny – a nurse, a typist, a music-teacher, and a newly-appointed deaconess – were a cherished topic of speculation among Festival wives.

Not that Old Maidenhood was not known to be a defunct concept. By the drinks table, Mother was deep in conversation with the director and the latest scion of the landowner's tree. Around the sofa, where Venetia was amusing herself with a new arrival in cricket whites, the Bevanses had struck up a madrigal. A clan that spawned to perform.

'Seth. My dear, sweet, *only* boy!'

It was Jemima Beale. Evelyn's best friend at school, she had gladly accepted the offer of godmotherhood to the second child. Unlike her friend, Jemima had shown more than the talent of an accomplished amateur, and had become a household name with her viola playing. Scorning to treat the alto instrument as an alternative violin, she had set about educating the musical public, and had won not only acclaim, but regular dedications of new concerti. She embraced her godson warmly.

'My *God*,' she ground her vowels, 'you *are* getting tall! You'll match Great-grandfather yet. I say, thank you so much for those lovely hankies you sent me for the birthday. Really sweet of you. Daniel forgot me, as always. When you marry, dear, be sure to make a note of your spouse's birthday, it makes for good relations. Were the O-Levels vile? When do you hear?'

As ever Jemima wasn't bothering to wait for replies. She was held to be good value at parties, because of her habit of homing in on shy men and letting them smile in sweet silence while she made conversation for two. Her glamour was easy on the eye, good for the morale. Seth was happy to be accosted.

'Now look, I can't monopolize you all evening, that wouldn't be fair on those dear Pollock creatures. Slap my wrist. No, but honestly, darling, a poor Professional's being mauled in that corner by dear Bronwen and I must go and save him before there's an ugly scene . . .'

Seth laughed at her retreating back. Venetia wailed at him from the sofa, 'Seth, hurry up and grab a drink so you can come and be introduced.'

Seth did as he was bid. The newcomer was much older than he had seemed at first glance. Seth surmised that the cricketing garb was the record of a youth that had stopped some fifteen years ago. Venetia had on her reunion manner.

'Seth, darling, this is Harry Barnes. He's over from New York to do some research for a new book, well, to give lectures officially, and he wants to meet a real live prodigy. He went to Eton – or is it Slough Grammar? – so you'll have heaps in common.'

Her brother blushed obligingly. Barnes remained seated as he held out his hand, forcing Seth to stoop.

'So you are he. How very exciting. Take a pew,' Barnes said. Seth sat on the sofa arm nearest his sister, and took a large gulp of wine.

'Neesh has probably been talking a lot of rot,' he said, 'it stands to reason you can only be good at something by neglecting something else.'

'Oh bilge. Don't believe a word he says. He's always been teacher's pet,' said Venetia, her thoughts elsewhere.

'Ah, but there's a difference between rank diplomacy and actual merit,' retorted Barnes, 'I believe I was a teacher's pet precisely because of my failure to shine. I was the only one who never put the teacher on the spot with awkward questions. He was eternally grateful and overlooked my marks as a reward.'

Seth thought Venetia's laugh excessive.

'You're a novelist, then?' he asked the man with thinning hair.

'Bull's eye, dear boy. Have you read any of them?'

'Well, actually . . .'

'Too busy fiddling to, I suppose.'

'It may interest you to know,' Venetia interposed, 'that a friend of mine has applied to write a thesis on you in his last year at Caius. You're not *wholly* neglected by English youth. He'll probably write to your agent any day now to ask you for an interview.'

'Well that's flattering, so long as he doesn't want to read any of my letters and diaries – they have to wait until after my demise, I'm afraid.'

'Or at least until you've secured your Nobel prize.'

Barnes roared with laughter and Venetia joined him, delighted to have found someone both witty and unmusical. Aware that his role as conversational property was now played out, Seth turned away to spare himself their charity.

At the last chorus of Fa La La's he took another gulp of wine and gazed about the room. Everyone was intent. No one was at a loose end. He dropped his eyes to stare at his drained glass. He had never managed to drink wine without leaving an unappetizing scum on the rim. He wondered anew whether this crippling disability was something one grew out of, like nocturnal emissions. A firm hand tapped him on the shoulder and a young man said,

'It's not that bad. Let's go outside and admire the view.'

Seth looked up. There was a hiss behind him. He turned

and saw a blond stranger smiling in the open garden window. Seth returned the smile automatically and stood up.

'Come on. It's getting terribly hot in here, and there's a marvellous sunset. My name's Roly. Roly MacGuire.'

'I'm Seth Peake.'

'I know that. Bronwen told me.'

Anyone with whom Bronwen had spoken of such things could be trusted. Seth followed the good-looking man out into the dusk, while behind him Venetia squealed with delight and the Bevanses went Hey Dinga Dinga Ding.

Evelyn had recognized the temptation to lay a garden in the plot of land outside the main windows and had resisted it. Her grandparents had left the space untouched. Not only was the soil impossibly salty and the area buffeted by winds, but she also felt that beds of imported plants would look quite out of place. It was the sort of thing people did in Polperro. She had only done what was necessary to let the plot 'speak'. There were only the flowers that nature had sown there. A lawn of sorts had been grown beside the windows, and carefully placed were pieces of sculpture in local stone and driftwood. The whole was stark but strong – exactly the effect that the mistress sought. Stepping outside, the young man exclaimed:

'Now that's good. Very good.'

Seth repressed the impulse to stare, and looked out to where the remarkable sunset was taking place.

'Yes. Isn't it,' he said, 'that's one of the things I hate most about London – that one never sees the sun go down. Well, you do from bits of the heath, but never properly.' The young man chuckled. Seth saw that he was laughing at him.

'Actually, I was talking about the garden.'

'Ah.' Seth reddened in the softening light.

'The sculptures are good. Whose are they?'

'My mother bought them locally. I think those two tall thin ones are by Virginia Rawsthorne, that's a Barbara Hepworth, that's a Bronwen experiment Bron gave us last year, and that's a Steiner she brought over from London. Not sure about the others.' They began to walk towards one of the grey gloss benches on the perimeter, facing across the fields to the sea.

'Bronwen's quite incredible. She had me cornered just now.'

'Are you a Professional, then?'

'A what?'

'A Professional. One of the pros in the orchestra. Bronwen tends to pounce on them, as they're new.'

'Oh. I see. No, I'm just a sort of artisan hanger-on. I'm renovating the church angels to pay for my keep.'

'Who's keeping you?'

'My cousins at Trenellion.'

'Really? Whereabouts do they live there?'

'Sorry. I mean at Trenellion Hall.' Seth faltered. 'What's the matter?' Roly pursued.

'That's the second time I've made that mistake in forty-eight hours.'

'I'm not really one of them. I'm the black sheep, thank God. We don't see eye to eye so I'm sent to lodge in their lighthouse.' They reached the bench and sat down. Roly looked at the view. 'You're quite right,' he said, 'the sunset's good, too.'

Behind them someone shut the sliding glass panel with a

click and the chatter of the party was replaced with the sounds of a distant harbour. The gulls had turned in. Roly looked at Seth and smiled with a gentle puff of breath through his nose. It was a wonderful nose, but Seth could think of nothing to say. He asked questions instead.

'Do you play any instrument besides the chisel?'

'Well. I used to play the trumpet.'

'Why only used?'

'I found the repertoire too limited, and I was better at art.'

'Like me. They wouldn't let me do German, because I sang in thc choir and classes clashed.'

'*Du bist ein Tenor?*'

'*Aber natürlich, Herr MacGuire.*'

'There. You still learnt some.'

'Only from *Kantaten une Lieder.* What makes you the black sheep?'

'They find it rather awkward because every girl they push at me becomes a good friend. On the whole, I prefer men.'

Surprised, Seth's cheeks burned. Involuntarily he made a startled sound. Roland had quite clearly expected no reaction and looked concerned.

'Sorry. Does that shock you?'

'No. I don't think it does really, it's just that no one's ever blurted it like that to me before.'

'You just took it for granted?'

'Yes. Either that – I knew instinctively – or they beat around the bush for so long that I guessed what they were driving at and put them out of their misery.'

'How?'

'Kissed them. Usually.'

'Seth, you're absolutely puce! Would you like some water or something?'

'Don't talk about it. People always talk about it and that only makes it worse.'

Roland laughed. 'You really haven't had a conversation like this before, have you?'

'No.'

Someone had just been using the bathroom lavatory and opened the window to clear the smell. There was a gentle sound of gushing water and a retreating whistle. *La ci darem la mano.* Seth glanced over his shoulder. Half the guests had left, to sort out who was going to sleep where and to save Mother from thinking she had to provide food on a grander scale. He turned back and stared at the vanishing rim of the sun. The shadows cast by the sculptures lay long across the grass. He couldn't look at Roly. He wished no one had left. Roly sighed and ran a hand through his hair. The movement caught Seth's attention and their eyes met. They smiled. Seth flexed his muscles to stand but Roly broke the silence and he relaxed again.

'This is an extraordinary house. You're very lucky.'

'Yes. I suppose it is. I couldn't bear not to have it to come away to every summer. Imagine having to work all year in some office off Oxford Street then blow your year's savings on a fortnight in Mykonos! I think if I woke up tomorrow and found myself in Pinner or Tring or one of those places where they have to live, I'd slash my wrists.'

Then there was a pause. A ghastly pause that made the boy's heart freeze in its dock. It was like the silence when Mother had chanced on an obscene doodle once. Roly took a breath and began to speak so unexpectedly that Seth actually jumped.

'That's just the sort of thing I've grown to expect from a privileged Hampstead kid like you. You lounge here on your exclusive designer bench, in your little man suit, with your glass of supermarket plonk, because isn't it fun once in a while, and you languidly dismiss half the population!'

'No, I don't. Not normally. I was only being funny.'

'Oh, whoopee. I suppose in your other life you're a fully paid-up member of the Socialist Workers' Party.'

'No. You know I'm not. But I do what I can.' Seth grew frantic. Arguments weren't meant to happen this quickly. They'd barely been introduced.

'"I do what I can" – like some Victorian matron bewailing the inefficacy of her charity. What precisely do you do?'

'I'm a member of the CND and I went on one of their marches last year. And . . . and I'm a member of the Anti-Nazi League.'

Roly clapped. Slowly. Seth wanted to run across the fields wailing. The whole situation was so thoroughly unpleasant and pointless. Politics got so personal. He felt as if Roly had punched him in the stomach when he'd expected him to shake hands. His blood rose. Pinko prat.

'Well you're not so sound yourself.'

'What do you mean by that?'

'Well . . . living off your rich relations who let you stay in lighthouses and . . .' Seth rapidly ran dry of venom. He stared at his hands, glad that it was almost dark now.

'You know that's got nothing to do with it at all. As I was . . .'

'Well, what's . . .'

'Will you let me finish?'

Seth loathed him. A prefect.

'No. I won't,' he said. 'It's got nothing to do with you anyway. I can say and think what I like without having to toe your pinko line,' he muttered.

Roly was standing now. He placed his glass on the bench beside Seth.

'I won't apologize,' he announced, 'because I mean everything that I've said.'

'No. No. I . . .' Seth looked up in the gloom.

'I think . . . we seem to have progressed rather fast and you're unnerved. I think you'll realize why I said what I said, should you give it a little thought.' He was inexorable. 'Now I think I'd better shut up and go away, I can tell I've hurt your sense of hospitality. Thank your mother for me, will you – I think I'd rather go home this way. Night-night.' He walked over to the wall and jumped into the field. Then he turned and called out, 'You must come and play me your violin some time. I'd like that,' before walking into the night.

Seth found his tongue but lost his heart, so said nothing. He sat dazed in semi-darkness, the light from the house pouring on to his back.

He was not politically unaware but he found that the gulf between ethic and practice posed too great a quandary to be worth contemplating. He thought of Socialism as he thought of organized Christianity – a moral caliper to support a halting conscience and on occasion to cause it a salutary twinge. He had long ago decided that he could not be an active Socialist, whatever 'an active Socialist' might be, without an unlovely measure of hypocrisy. He believed in equality as he believed in God, but he could no more deny that he enjoyed his privileges and would enjoy them all over again given the chance, than he could deny that he gleaned intense pleasure from things that any strict Christian would eschew. He would say that he felt trapped and conditioned, if only he bore his captors and programmers more of a grudge.

He sought loop-holes in Roly's harangue, miserable as he did so at the extraordinary turn taken after so promising an introduction. He grew indignant as he thought of the suggestion that young MacGuire, though obviously more privileged, had made his position the sounder of the two simply by saying the right things. By taking the aggressive initiative, the parasite and producer of useless (and doubtless ideologically suspect) sculptures, brushed over his own tracks, then stood pointing cruelly at Seth's. Bronwen's hearty laugh broke into his thoughts.

'So. This is where you're hiding. I thought perhaps you'd got bored together and gone off for a walk. It was rather appalling. Shouldn't be saying that, of course, or you'll go telling that mother of yours!' She laughed her laugh and dropped on to the bench beside him. 'I really came out to say good-night.'

A lie; she was trying to escape.

'God! What time is it?' Seth looked around and saw that the room was empty except for Mother and Venetia who were clearing up.

'Oh yes. They've all gone. It's safe to go back in now. Ha! I'd stay longer only she might try to cook something and she looks a mite too tired to produce anything edible.' Bronwen stood, her hair aflame in the light from indoors.

'Bronwen, where's the lighthouse? I've been here all this time and never seen it. Can we walk to it one day, or is it beyond bounds?'

'Oh Lord, no. We can walk to it. Crumbly path, mind. Takes about three-quarters of an hour along the cliff-tops from the church. Much quicker by road. Why?'

'Oh. Nothing important. Just wondered.'

'Read any Virginia Woolf?'

'No.'

Bronwen chuckled like a tiddly guardsman and ruffled his hair.

'You will,' she said. 'You will. Funny little thing.'

She strode across the fields. Seth heard her growling out some of the Bach they were to rehearse the next day. *Quoniam tu solus*; a bass aria.

SATURDAY four

When Mo arrived back home on Saturday night she paused with her key in the door to call out for Andy. He usually waited under a parked car nearby. He didn't appear. She called once more.

'Here, Andy?' Still nothing. 'Please yourself, you dirty bugger,' she muttered and let herself in. He ran out of the kitchen to greet her in the hall. 'How the . . . ?'

She was about to switch on the hall light when she noticed a glow under the bathroom door at the top of the stairs. There was a torch on the hall table, the heavy-duty kind encased in rubber. Taking this to protect herself, she silently climbed the stairs. She waited at the top, just outside the bathroom door and listened. There was a splash and a tap was turned on into what sounded like a very full bath.

'OK. Who's in there?' she asked gruffly. There was a gasp of youthful surprise then a giggling reply.

'Oh Christ, you made me jump! It's me, Hope. I've come for my hot bath.'

'How did you get in?'

'I slipped a Swiss Army knife under your kitchen window. Hope you don't mind.'

'No. 'Sfine.'

As the improbability of the situation washed over her, Mo found herself dithering on the landing, still clutching a large rubber torch and searching for her second move.

'I'll be down in a second,' said Hope.

'Oh. Right. I'll . . . er . . . be downstairs, then.'

She started downstairs then remembered that she was still in her bike boots, turned and hurried into her room. For the first time in years she worried about her appearance. She wished it were midwinter so she could pull on a baggy sweater and not feel fat. She pulled off her blouse and changed it for a battered white shirt she used for doing jobs around the house. The boots she pushed under the bed and exchanged for a pair of plimsolls before these too were rejected in favour of bare socks. There was nothing to dab behind her ears, because it tended to give her a rash, but as she wandered downstairs, running her fingers through her short hair, she wished she had an 'extra something'. She glanced into the lounge. It was far too tidy. She switched on the telly for some background noise and pushed a few cushions around. Her eye came to rest on the Klimt book, alone on the coffee table. She opened it and laid it on the sofa then, unable to find a page without some naked bird in a load of gold leaf, she flung it shut and took it into the kitchen where she left it on a worksurface. She opened the envelope that had come that morning. A blue kitten on a toadstool.

'Happy Birthday, lovie. Love and kisses, Mumsy. See you Tuesday tea-time. XXX.'

Andy mewed. She looked down at him as he paced at her feet and came to her senses with a self-mocking snort.

'You want your grub, don't you? And the barmy old tart's thinking about her hair,' she said under her breath. She recalled her drive home. 'Bought you a treat, didn't I?

Stopped off at your friends and mine in the Pakki shop.' She walked out to the hall and found the bag where she had left it. 'Look at that!' she said, lifting a package from inside for Andy's inspection, 'Turina Reddy-Meel Deluxe – your favourite as it's the old tart's birthday. Cor!'

She cut a corner off the packet and emptied the pinkish contents into his bowl. He ran to it with a rumble and she gave his broad back a rub.

'What's he called?' Hope was leaning in the doorway smiling.

'Andy.'

'Great. He's a real character.'

'Give you a lovely welcome, did he?'

'Telling me. Never make a guard dog. I borrowed this, is that all right?' She was wearing Mo's old towelling dressing-gown.

'Fine.'

'I've always wanted one of these – I hate getting dressed straight after a bath. I like walking around feeling all clean.' There was a pause as Mo stood up and rubbed an ache from her back. 'D'you want some rum?'

'Rum?'

'Yeah. My dole cheque's come so I just splashed out.' Smiling she brought a bottle from behind her back.

'Oh . . . er . . . great,' Mo said, quite out of her depth. 'Come through.'

'Cor. Amazing telly,' said Hope. 'No. Don't put the light on – I like the glow from the screen.'

'Bad for your eyes, isn't it?'

'Please? Go on?'

'OK.' Mo laughed and sat on the sofa.

Glad she had left off her shoes, she seized the opportunity and swung her feet up beside her. There was a cowboy film on. She expected Hope to sit in one of the chairs but she just pulled a cushion out of one and lay on the floor on her side, propped up with one elbow on it. Her hair was spikier than the night before, from the lingering water. She ran a hand through it and sighed happily.

'Mmm. Clean again. 'Sgreat.' She unscrewed the cap of the bottle and took a swig. She shuddered as the spirit went down then passed the bottle across to her hostess.

'Thanks,' said Mo with conviction, and followed suit. Twice.

'Are you pissed off because I broke into your house?'

'No. Well, I wasn't expecting you, so I guess it was a bit of a surprise, but I'm not pissed off. Why should I be? Nice surprise.'

'What made you think I wouldn't come?'

'Well . . . I didn't see why you should want to, really.'

'I wouldn't have bothered to say if I didn't want to.' She grinned. Mo noticed in the light from the telly that her ears were slightly pointed. 'You rich, then?'

'Not very, no.'

'Well you're not on the bloody dole. What d'you do?' Her tone was curious, but unaggressively so.

'I work for the Council. Housing offices,' Mo lied. She took some more rum. She didn't have a weak head, but she was unused to drinking spirits neat like this. She could feel herself loosening up and enjoyed the feel. They watched the screen in silence for some minutes then she asked her caller,

'Where d'your family come from?'

'Brixton. Dad and Mum started a greengrocer's. Dad's

brother owns a little nursery and Dad sells the stuff he grows. Mum's dead, though. Died about six years ago. Some kind of cancer.'

'How often do you see him?'

'Never. I ran away when I was fourteen.'

'Didn't he tell the police?'

'Yeah, maybe, but I'd cut off my hair and stripped it like this, hadn't I, and then I gave the DHSS a false name when I started claiming. 'Seasy. Thanks.' She drank deeper this time and the Indians swept down into the valley on their stolen horses.

'Why'd you run away, then?'

'He got married again. How about you?'

'Adopted. No brothers or sisters and my step-dad's dead. Mumsy lives in Tower Hamlets. He was a boxing coach.' She paused. 'Worked as a brikky, too.'

'I thought boxing and all that was all fake.'

'Wrestling is, mostly. Boxing's for real, though.'

'Oh. Here.'

'Thanks.' Mo drank again.

Andy walked stiffly in and jumped up into his armchair.

'Here, Andy,' Hope whispered to him as she crawled across to stroke his fur.

The dressing-gown rode up her legs as she moved. They shone white in the gloom. She wet her finger with some rum and held it under the cat's nose. He licked it and the rasping of his tongue made her laugh softly. For a while she talked quietly to him, rubbing his head with her fingers. The scene cut to a white woman tied up in a wigwam. She worked the gag free from her mouth and let out a piercing scream. 'Davy! Davy! Over here! For goodness' sake come quickly!'

Hope twisted to look at the screen, then turned grinning to Mo. Mo, who had been watching intently as she petted Andy, met her smile. Then her smile dropped and she stared. Hope did the same; a girl in Mum's Sunday best. Mo broke the tension, letting the air hiss between her teeth by way of a laugh.

'That's not fair,' she chuckled, 'I'm the only one allowed to stare.'

'Who says? Here.' Hope crawled over to the sofa and held out the bottle. Mo reached for it but the burglar pulled it away at the last moment and, shutting her eyes, held out her face instead.

Mo leant forward and kissed her swiftly on the lips, then pulled her up into a fuller embrace. Hope's eyes flickered open briefly then closed as she pulled her hostess towards her in turn. The dressing-gown was slightly damp to the touch. Hope's hair smelt of shampoo and her limbs were still warm from the hot water. The orchestra thrilled to the gallop of the cavalry and Mo slid down beside the girl on the carpet. Their kisses grew slowly softer and the younger woman suddenly broke away with a light push.

'Wait,' she said. 'Sit up a moment.' Mo sat up. Hope reached for the rum bottle, wet the tips of her right-hand fingers, then held her hand towards her lover's face.

'Now,' she whispered, 'I baptize you, Mo, for me, for me, for me, and . . . for me.' Each time she spoke she brushed Mo's forehead, nose and then mouth with the liquor. 'There,' she smiled. Mo laughed and they kissed once. Mo broke away.

'My turn. Here,' she said. 'I baptize you for me, for me,

for me, and for me,' here she dabbed some rum on to the delicate point of Hope's chin, 'and a little bit for Andy!' Hope laughed aloud and startled the cat from his chair, at which she laughed the louder. Mo hugged her to her.

'Is this for real,' she asked, 'or is it like wrestling?'

'You great wally!' Hope kissed her, then lay back with her head resting on the front of the sofa. 'I was really pissed off this morning,' she said.

'Why?'

'Well, I was walking along, right, and someone called out my name, you know, real friendly like, so I turned and all I could see was this piglet.'

'Piglet?'

'Lady Copper, wally.'

'Oh.'

'So, it turns out to be one of my best mates from school, right? Well, I didn't know what to say. I was too shocked, you know, so I just said, "Oh hello, Trace, how's things," and walked on. She used to be a right little rebel, too. Straight up.' Mo glanced to see if she was being put through some kind of test, but she saw that Hope was staring straight ahead, so she said,

'She might have . . . well.' She stopped then tried harder, 'Well, she might have been sort of subverting from the inside of things.'

'How d'you mean?'

'Giving people tip-offs about raids – things like that.'

'Don't be stupid. You pay *them* if you want that – you don't have to fucking go and join them too.'

There was an awkward pause filled only by the cries of slaughtered Ojibwa and the thunder of hooves.

'Come on,' said Hope at last, 'let's go upstairs. Them ponies are putting me off.'

Andy returned to his chair as they left and fell into a deep sleep. He woke an hour later, roused by the crooning strains of *Stranger on the Shore* coming from the bedroom, let himself out through the flap in the garden door, and went to pay a few calls.

SUNDAY one

Evelyn slept with her window open because she liked a warm bed in a cool room, and always drew back the curtains before retiring, so as to be woken by the sun. This morning the latter streamed into her sleep and stirred her with the birds. She dressed quickly, then slipped out of the front door and strode down the lane.

The sky was cloudless. The air stung her lungs it was so clean. She picked a pinch of periwinkles which she stuffed through a hole in her baggy cardigan, and soon she was humming *Die Forelle*. The village chapel stood only doors away from the pub. She had missed fisherman's communion, which happened at an unearthly hour and which she reserved for the last dawn of the holidays, but the doors still stood slightly ajar. She went inside and knelt in the back pew. The sun, still cool, spilled in from the high east windows and left patches of blue and green on the whitewash opposite. There was a faint smell of extinguished candles and an even fainter one of *vino sacro*. She thanked her god for bringing them there safely, prayed for her and Huw, that whatever their problem was it might go away, for Venetia, that she might find fulfilment, for Seth, that he might be spared from pride, and for Mummy, that she might be allowed to slip away peacefully in her sleep, but not just yet, please. There was a phlegm-charged cough behind her. She rose, took a last glance at the bare little altar, smiled good morning to the cheerless old bat who had drifted in to arrange the flowers, and left to buy some bread. Recently Huw had started to suffer from sick headaches. He had left his pills behind, in the bathroom. Evelyn stopped at the post office on the way home to mail them to him.

Seth had slept like a log. He jolted awake, found he was not in a dormitory, and relaxed. The knocking that had roused him was repeated and Mother walked in.

'Morning,' he said.

'It's a heavenly one,' she replied, pulling back the curtains and perching on the end of his bed. She smiled across at his sleep-creased face. 'I've been down to the harbour, so we've got fresh-baked bread for brekky. It's still hot.'

'Mmm. Here I come.'

'I'll go and wake Neesh.'

He started to dress as soon as the door was safely closed. Evelyn knocked softly on her daughter's door.

'Darling,' she called, 'it's almost eight o'clock. I thought you might want to get up and have breakfast with us so you can get a good start on your reading.'

There was a rustle of hurriedly snatched bedding and a dim murmur. Evelyn opened the door and peered round. It was stuffy inside so she walked across and opened the window. This brought a groan of protest. She gazed at the sweetly cross expression.

'Don't you want to get up?' she asked. 'It's a heavenly day.'

Seth walked in, tugging a jersey over his wet temples.

'Let her have a lie-in, poor thing,' he said. 'She always gets up early in college, don't you, Neesh?'

There was another, darker, murmur. The others laughed and left her in peace. They gorged themselves on hot bread and jam, swilled strong coffee from the bowls bought at the local pottery, greeted Mrs Pym's wheezing form, and were soon bowling along to Trenellion.

The windows were open wide so that the wind blew in their hair and the voice on the radio could hardly be heard. It spoke politely of fresh troubles in the Middle East, where things in the Gulf were coming to a potentially violent head, of a bloody reprisal in Ulster, of plans for new peace talks with the Russians, and the untimely death of a much-loved comedian. In the kitchen, Mrs Pym changed to Radio One because it was easier to work to and anyway Miss Netia preferred it.

'Oh look, it's a baby rabbit!' cried Seth.

'Did you get a chance to talk to Harry Barnes last night?'

'Yes. Well, a bit. He's more Netia's domain.'

'You know he's giving the talks this year. It should be rather fun – on reclaiming the nineteenth-century novel for the eighties.'

'That's good. She can pick his brains. Trollope's one of her special topics.'

'I think so. Who was that you were talking to for ages at the end?' She remembered the arrogant young man who hadn't thanked her for a piece of quiche. 'I was going to come out and find you, only Bron the Man said you were having an intense discussion and shouldn't be disturbed.'

Seth saw the tower of Trenellion Church rising out of the corn. A much-loved poet had likened it to a rabbit pricking up its ears.

'Oh that was Roland MacGuire. He's one of their cousins. He's here to restore the angels.'

'Ah, so that's the one. Hasn't he just finished at art college in Edinburgh?'

'Maybe. I don't know.'

'Nice?'

'Very,' Seth lied.

'You must point him out to me.'

When they had come in, Venetia had found it hard not to cry from the sheer tension of the situation. Even after they had left the room she had lain silent, not daring to lift off the bedclothes again in case she lost control. Listening to the chatter downstairs, to the radio, to the hurried greetings and goodbyes, she lay and trembled. Mrs Thing was downstairs now and would be busy hoovering and tidying things away from the night before. Gingerly Netia pulled back the sheets. Gingerly, she lifted the long *The Clash* t-shirt she wore as a nightie. She let out a convulsive little gasp and bit her lower lip. Her belly was indeed rounder by a good two inches. She jumped up, locked the door and examined her abdominal profile in the long mirror. The inexplicable bulge wobbled slightly as she adjusted her stance. She ran a hand over it. There was no pain. It felt quite firm, firmer than the relaxed muscle of a buttock. She cradled it in both hands and pressed, gently at first then with a hard, inquisitive thrust. This time it did hurt and she whimpered and sat back on the bed. Memories of sluttish sixties films came to mind, as she pulled on a dressing-gown, let herself out, and slipped unseen to the bathroom. There she turned on the hot tap to run a bath, locked the door, pulled the curtains, and knelt over the lavatory bowl. Sticking her forefinger into her mouth, she rubbed the back of her throat and brought on a bout of retching. Nothing would come up but a dribble of acid that burnt the back of her tongue. She had eaten nothing since those cashews the night before. She considered food poisoning then sensed that that would have entailed an upset stomach at the very least. She brushed her teeth to take away the taste. The bath water was unbearably hot but it seemed the right thing to do, somehow, so she forced herself to lie down in it. Wincing, she hummed a hymn and tried not to cry.

The nave and side-aisles were empty save for a mobile gantry of scaffolding which stood under one of the old angels. The original guardians of the rafters had been quite defaced by the combined forces of dry rot and beetle. Roly had had what was left of them removed to one side. Their decay checked, they huddled there, a mournful crew, and awaited a last coat of varnish before being wheeled to the museum. The committee had decided that it would be futile to attempt a precise re-creation of the originals. Rather, a troop of winged creatures with a modern feel could be aimed to encapsulate the Festival spirit. Roland's work was finished along one side and there were only two angels remaining to be carved on the other.

A crowd of players stood gazing up in admiration. Seth looked too, and was annoyed to feel a swell of vicarious pride in his new acquaintance's work. He walked along the nave taking each one in. The wood was very pale, so as to match the stone above, and yet contrast with the dark-stained beams below. The light was divided into shafts by the beams as it fell from the glass roof – to theatrical effect. Each angel carried a different instrument, each had slightly different plumage and each bore a different motif along the borders of its robes. The faces were uniformly sexless, as were the bodies, and grave.

'It must be awful to create something so original and yet be unable to sign it as your own,' Evelyn declared.

'Oh but you see, my darling, he *has* signed it,' answered Jemima. 'He's signed every one of them by giving it his own hair! Hasn't he, Seth?'

'Has he, Seth?' enquired his mother.

'Well, he didn't talk much about them last night,' said her son, 'but yes, I suppose he has, really.' And he blushed.

Peter Grenfell swept down the nave, his Swedish-born wife hurrying at his side, her arms full of music. He was carrying her oboe case.

'Good morning, everybody. Did we sleep well? Good. Now let's get going, please – we've an awful lot to do by lunch-time.'

The crowd was galvanized into action. The air was filled with loud questions about who was to sit at which desk, how did such-and-such think this passage should be bowed, and whether Peter wanted all the *da capos* left in. Beneath this, and the flurry of hastily compassed gossip, rose the tide of tuning strings and wind, and a buzz of activity at the harpsichord as Grigor illustrated an anecdote about a performance at last year's Salzburg Festival. Seth sat at second desk of the first violins and tuned quietly and quickly.

'Seth. It's good to see you again.'

'Hello.' He and Peter shook hands.

'I didn't see you last night.'

'I spent a lot of it outside.'

'Oh. Well the thing is that I was a little concerned that we've never given you any kind of solo spot down here. I'd give you a recital space only you'll appreciate that we have to give priority to gold-plated pros like Henry and Jemima – as a courtesy.'

'Of course.'

'Anyway, I had a chat with Evelyn last night and she reminded me that you'd led the fiddles in the B Minor at school last Easter.'

'Yes I did,' Seth laughed, 'just about.'

'She said it was very impressive, and I know how hard she is to impress. I thought you could sit one desk forward and play all the solos. Megan's just this minute got over dropping a baby and says she's only had time to look at the Berlioz, so she'd love you to lead for her. All right?'

Seth was so excited he could only smile and nod vigorously with a slight 'Ya' of consent. He stood and took up his new place. Jemima said a loud 'Hooray' and he caught a furtive shot of bliss from the cello front desk.

It was only when Peter dismissed them for a coffee-break half-way through the *Credo*, that Seth discovered that he was so tense his back was drenched in sweat. Embarrassed, he hurried out into the graveyard instead of following his fellows into the vestry for coffee and biscuits.

The church was now the part of the estate nearest the sea. An expert from the Royal Society had been called in before any restoration took place and had said that the ground was extremely solid and that no further falls would take place so long as no one was foolish enough to try any more mining. Seth climbed up and sat upon the graveyard wall, facing the church so that the wind from off the waves might dry off the unsavoury patch on his back. As he cooled down, he relaxed. He could hear the sound of the crowd in the vestry, and the singing of the choir in the old school. They were just reaching the *Credo*, so they too would be stopping soon. Somebody blew a bugle call on a trumpet. He slipped on to the grass at the summons, and started back for the next half of the rehearsal.

'Hello, Peake.' Roly MacGuire's voice. Seth turned, and saw him jumping over another part of the wall. They smiled.

'I didn't know you were here.'

'I saw you didn't,' said Roly, 'it's my secret – well, our secret now. I didn't want to be mobbed by women asking me to do their little girls' heads so I've found a secluded corner behind that bit of wall. It's perfect – the wind blows the chips into the sea so there's no mess.'

'I've seen them. They're good.' Seth pitched the understatement with care.

'Oh. Thank you,' the sculptor clumsily replied. 'Look, I've got to talk to you alone. I mustn't make you late. I'll see you out here in the lunch-break.'

''Bye,' said Seth but Roly was already walking back to his lair.

The *Crucifixus* had no sooner started than Seth recalled the stupid conversation of the night before and damned himself for having appeared so untroubled outside just now. He had agreed to meet with a childish alacrity.

Roly was too proud to apologize and, in any case, he had said at the time that apologies would be unethical – or some sanctimonious words to that effect. Try as he would, Seth could not fix his mind back on to the Bach. He looked on with disgust as he dared to play the masterpiece on automatic pilot even as he indulged in preposterous scenarios. Against the agonies and joys of the Passion, he crushed MacGuire with the declaration that his 'politics' were a hypocritical patter of bandied abstractions, and was made the object of the vanquished one's vengeful cliff-top lust, the Atlantic boiling beneath them, herring gulls mewing above.

'Fine. There are obviously a lot of problems to be ironed out later, but, as we all know, the principal problem is still rehearsing in the school. Kind Mrs Willis and her helpers have laid on a picnic lunch in the garden of number one. Would you all be careful of how you dispose of the mess, and please be back by two sharp.'

Seth hurried away before Mother could stop talking and notice that he'd gone. He dismissed the idea of grabbing ham sandwiches as uncool. He climbed the wall and jumped down on to the path on the other side. There was the workplace, the work-in-progress covered by a tarpaulin to protect it from gulls, but no worker. A two-fingered whistle, and Seth saw him standing on the cliff-edge some hundred yards further on. He waved. Seth shouted 'Hi' and ran to meet him. He curbed his ardour by a nod and a quiet 'hello'. The atmosphere was crippled. Roly was so palpably thinking only of what he intended to say when the time was right. They walked side by side, away from the church. There were a few desultory exchanges about the sea, the birds, the angels, and then the seascape was left to speak on its own behalf as they continued in silence. After about five minutes Roly stopped and sat on the grass near the brink. Seth followed suit. A ridge of lemon-spattered gorse bushes hid them from the eye of the church.

'You don't get vertigo, or anything?'

'No. Never.'

'Good.' Roly paused, then, 'Look. I know I said I wouldn't apologize about what I said, but I do. I'm very sorry. It was an ugly thing to do. Of course I meant what I said, but it was stupid to blurt it out like that. I must have been a bit pissed, I felt I knew you better than I do.'

Seth lacked words so he made a few noises midway between nurtured injury and returned apology.

'OK, I admit it was rank hypocrisy,' Roly continued, 'I'm no less privileged than you. I just needed a scapegoat and happened to be quicker off the aggressive mark than you. I'm very sorry.' Seth laughed. Roly looked hurt. 'What's the joke?' he demanded.

'Nothing. Well . . . it's just that I spent all night, and most of the morning, planning how to demolish your attack next time we met, and you've gone and done it for me, damn you! You've taken all the fun for yourself! You must be more self-centred than I'd thought.'

'Me? Really? Do you really think I'm self-centred?'

'Oh, you must be, or I wouldn't like you.' Seth played shoot-bang-fire-pop with some grass. 'I find overtly altruistic people unnerving. I can't fathom them out so I end up suspecting their motives. Mother's altruistic but she's the first to admit that she only does it because virtue makes her feel good. It always reflects back on to the self. I think it's healthier to bring the egotism to the surface and use it constructively. Saints get cancer.'

Roland laughed aloud, the sunlight in his hair.

'You really are an extraordinary person,' he said in an off-hand manner.

'You're not so dull yourself,' Seth countered. Roly put a hand on his shoulder and stared in mock amazement.

'Really?' he exclaimed. 'Oh, but that's wonderful!' They giggled, staring boldly into each other's eyes. As the mirth died on his lips, Seth placed his hand on Roly's thigh. Roly covered it with his own. Seth hoped he wouldn't have to stand up in a hurry.

'When do they want you back?' Roly's voice was grave.

'Oh, shit!' Seth swore as he glanced at Roly's watch, 'I'm going to be late, and I'm meant to be leading. Mother'll kill me.' He jumped up. Roly started to stand but Seth stopped him. 'No,' he mocked, 'I want to run away and leave you staring soulfully out to sea.'

He chuckled as the sculptor swung his profile out towards the horizon, then he raced back to the church, dodging the rabbit holes as he went and singing *All we like sheep* to himself. Roly sighed and lay back on the salty grass, his eyes on the intense blue above. A lark, disturbed by the boy's running, mounted into his field of vision. Its fierce song pierced his ears. He had an idea for a sculpture.

As the first two movements were run through with the chorus, Seth no longer found the thought of Roly a distraction. He no longer sweated with the effort. He was exhilarated by everything about him. Even Grigor's 'yokes' were funny. During the *Gloria*, however, he rose further into the music. He remembered watching Mother at work during his last half-term. All the pupils stood in a small white huddle in the middle of the sun-splashed gym. She had put the *Gloria* on the stereo system at full blast. Then she had skipped around the room smiling at the children and singing. '*Gloria! Gloria in excelsis deo!* Come on, Stephanie, let's dance together! *Gloria! Gloria!* That's it! Happy, happy, happy!' Without being told, they had all seized hands and danced in a circle around her, moaning tunelessly but joyfully, their sandals' buckles jingling as they went. *Gloria in excelsis!*

Seth glimpsed Roly sitting at the back of the gallery. A shaft of stained light lying across his face and hair. Angel hair. Seth threw him a smile and promptly missed an entry. When he next glanced that way, Roly was laughing.

At the end of the afternoon Evelyn came over with Jemima.

'Well done, Poppet,' she said, 'you must be whacked.'

'I'm bullying Evelyn into coming with my godson to have a drink and a bite to eat,' said Jemima, 'maybe he can persuade her.'

'Oh, do let's!' Seth enthused. 'An evening at J's would be funny.'

'So I'm a gas as well as talented,' laughed J.

'Well what about Netia, all alone, poor lamb?' asked Mother.

'I'd love to see her too.'

'No, honestly, Ma. She'll be fine,' Seth said, 'she loves being alone; she can read in peace, and there's no one to make her eat fattening food when she'd rather have a bit of lettuce.'

'Tempter, I succumb,' said Mother. 'Yes please, J.'

'Jolly dee,' said J. 'Incidentally, Seth, your mother was asking me who the gorgeous person was you were sharing a private joke with up in the gallery. I told her she must have been seeing things – there's never anyone gorgeous sitting up there. God knows, I've looked often enough.'

'Well who was it, then?' asked Mother.

'The angel-maker.'

'Oh,' she said, a wry smile reaching into her face, 'I see.'

SUNDAY two

As she slept with Hope in her arms, Mo dreamed of her former lover. She was in a panic, standing in the hall at the flat in Earls Court trying to open the door into the street. She had Maggie's driving gloves with her and it was vital that she called Maggie back to get them because a blizzard was blowing. Maggie had just left and Mo was standing there tugging at the door and calling her name. The door bell rang and the door opened. That policewoman was standing there again. Her mouth didn't move but there was a soothing voice, 'Yes, of course I'll give them to her. If you'll just sign here.'

Mo had signed and the young officer had walked briskly back to the car, Mag's little car, and climbed in. Someone else had driven her off, then the door had slammed back. Mo woke with a start. The front door slammed. It was morning. Eight o'clock and no Hope.

As her head began to throb into consciousness, Mo took the telephone in an unsteady hand and dialled.

'Jack? . . . Hi . . . Yes . . . I'll be a bit late, love . . . No. No problem; just a crisis with the plumbing, I'm waiting for him now . . . Yeah. OK. See you. 'Bye.' She dressed, splashed her face with cold water and threw a couple of Alka-Seltzer into a glass. For the first time in a decade she left the bed unmade. As she picked the papers off the mat and walked through to put the kettle on, Andy slipped in through the cat-flap.

'Hello, And. Yeah, I know, don't say it. Here.' She poured him a saucer of milk then shut her eyes tight as she stood up again, to wait for the giddiness to pass. She took a breath then drank the Alka-Seltzer. The grains left at the bottom of the glass sent a shudder through her frame. She took a swig from a carton of orange juice to kill the taste and noticed the message.

The Klimt book was lying open by the breadbin. Her wallet lay open on top of it, pressing down the front cover to stop it folding shut again. On the page where Mag's rounded writing wished Mo a happy birthday was scrawled, 'Why didn't you tell me you was a bluddy piglet? Thanks for the bluey. See you round, maybe.'

Mo snatched up the wallet. Her ID card stared from its plastic window. A fiver had gone. She dropped the wallet, swearing, and ripped out the defaced page of the book. It caught half-way and she had to shake the whole thing. The page tore completely and, as the book fell to the floor, a few pages of glossy prints slipped out. Mo swore again and trod on the wreckage, grinding it with her heel. Andy mewed and ran back into the garden. Mo bit her lip, dropped to her knees and, picking up the scattered and distorted pages, held them to her chest. A lump gathered in her throat as she rocked to and fro by the saucepan cupboard.

'Shit, shit, shit and shit,' she murmured and briskly used the back of her hand to catch a rebellious tear on the top of her cheek.

The kettle came to the boil, its lid bouncing lamely. Mo stood, sliding what was left of the book to one side, and started to make some tea. She felt sick. Andy came in again and jumped on to the chair to her left, with a mew.

'All right, go on and laugh at me you cold bastard. See if I care!' She held out her hand and let him butt at it with his forehead. The telephone rang. It was The Perm.

'Boss?'

'McEnery, good morning.'

'Hello. Has your plumber come yet?'

'What? Oh, yeah. He's just getting on with it.' Mo looked down at her cat and winked at him.

'It's just that some things have come up and Jack, I mean Sergeant Melly, wondered whether you could come and take a look.'

'What things?'

'It's in connection with the burglaries yesterday. There's been another one that looks as if it's the same person; same m.o. – seems to be a pattern.'

'Tell him I'll be right in.'

'Great.'

'Oh . . . and McEnery?'

'Yes, Boss?'

'Be a love and make us a cuppa?'

Mo gave Andy his breakfast, locked the back door and the cat-flap, took down her helmet and went out into the street. Andy followed her then trotted off to greet the milk-woman. Mo set off on her bike, wondering if it were possible to subvert from the inside.

'Here's your tea, Serge.' Sometimes The Perm could be all sugar and spice.

'Thanks, McEnery. After my job, or something?' McEnery laughed, and realigned her hat on the mound of tortured hair. 'Now. What's the news?'

'Burglary in a mews house off the Brompton Road; belonging to a Miss Katya Garcia. She's an astrologer, like Papas and Stazinopolos, but with a difference.'

'How come? Does she believe in it?'

'She's more scientific. She writes for "serious" occult magazines, gives lectures – things like that. She says she had a number of phone calls yesterday morning – silent ones, from a box. Whoever it was didn't put any money in. She got a bit nervous because she assumed it was someone trying to see if she was out. She had a lunch appointment she couldn't cancel, though. Just as she was getting into her car she heard the phone ring again, and decided that with so many calls it must simply have been a wrong number.'

'Silly moo.'

'She's next door giving her statement.'

'Fancy. Go on.'

'Well, of course she was wrong. She got back from lunch at about three-thirty and didn't notice anything amiss until she went back to her study to do some work. Someone had carefully rifled her desk and taken all her latest articles and papers. She's very upset about some lecture she'd been due to give to some society.'

'Fingerprints?'

'Nothing. Not even a hair. A meticulous worker.'

'Why didn't she report it sooner?'

'She did – straight away. But Chelsea didn't think to tell us until Forensic said there was a similarity to the other two. She seems very keen to help – anxious about her papers, I suppose – so I asked her if she wouldn't mind coming to make a second statement, to see how far they tallied.'

'She's in there, is she?'

'Yes, with Jack . . . I mean . . .'

'You mean with Sergeant Melly.' A woman's voice was raised, on cue, from the next room. 'I'll go in,' Mo said, 'and have a little chat.'

Miss Garcia was facing Jack over a desk, her back to the door. He had evidently given up taking notes, and was nodding sympathetically as she rambled. Her voice was wholly English, Mo noted at once. Perhaps she had been reared in Knightsbridge and had a Norland nanny, or something. She was smartly dressed, though without great show, and a pair of tortoiseshell specs dangled from her neck with her pearls. They bounced on her shallow bosom as she talked. She didn't seem to hear the door. Jack's eyes flicked to Mo's in rapid despair then dropped back to his patient.

'And you see it really is most important that I have those papers back. This couldn't have happened at a worse time, you know, just when everybody ought to be told.'

'Told what, Miss Garcia?' asked Mo. Garcia swung round in mild surprise.

'Who are you?' she asked.

'Detective Inspector Faithe, at your service, Madam.'

'How do you do?'

'Hello. Told what?'

'Why, my dear woman, that the world is about to change.'

'Change? How?'

'It's hard to explain in layman's terms, but by a gross generalization I can state categorically that the society we know and love can never be the same after this coming

Friday. It's quite extraordinary – the most concentrated prediction I've seen since the start of the last war – supported on all sides, you know. I was due to address the Royal Society of Egyptologists on the matter at a luncheon on Wednesday, and of course, now that that madman has rushed off with all my papers, it's quite impossible.'

'Well, can't you remember it all?'

'My memory's not what it was, but I doubt if I could ever have remembered quite so much data – even in my teens. Naturally, I could give the Society the bare bones of the thing, but they're a suspicious lot – understandably, since there are so many tricksters about nowadays – and I'd need facts and figures for support.'

'Miss Garcia, can you think of anyone, a professional rival perhaps, who might have wanted to steal your ideas?'

'No. I'd told no one and, well, at the risk of sounding conceited, I don't think that anyone who wasn't a real specialist could possibly have known what track I was following.'

'What sort of change is on the cards for Friday, exactly? Is the Third World War going to start?'

'Inspector, you must realize that the stars are not an open book, any more than the Tarot is. They rarely make categorical statements. They are a cryptic language, there to guide, to make suggestions, to provide advice.'

'Only the blind look for direct answers,' said Jack, with an air of having had this lesson already. Miss Garcia wheeled on her pupil.

'Exactly so. The point is . . .' The door opened. McEnery.

'Yeah?'

'Boss, there's been another one.'

'Where?'

'Kensington, in the Campden Hill area.'

'Who?'

'Seamus O'Leary.'

'*Daily Express*?'

'That's right.'

'Let's go.'

'Oh, thank God you're here. Come in, please.' O'Leary's jewelled hand wandered up to his yellowing hair to reassure it that the callers were friends. He giggled nervously. 'It's just like the telly, isn't it? You never think it's going to happen to you. I suppose everyone says that to you, don't they?' He giggled once more.

'If you'd just like to tell us exactly what happened,' said Mo, already taking notes in shorthand. She saw a trail of blood up the stair-carpet. O'Leary followed her gaze in an instant.

'Oh, that's his,' he said.

'McEnery, get Forensic, would you?'

'Right.'

'You haven't tried to mop this up, have you?'

'No. I didn't think I was meant to.'

'Quite right. Old Audrey Fox strikes again.'

'Do you read her too? I've read the lot. Sorry.'

'Go on.'

'Well,' he patted his hair again and took a breath, 'let's see.' His eyes played rapidly across the patterns of the wallpaper as he composed his thoughts. 'It must have started at about one o'clock, I suppose. I was upstairs in bed. Yes, now that I think of it it must have been about one because I remember setting my alarm radio before I went to sleep, and it was twelve, then.'

Mo was irritated that he couldn't pronounce his rs.

'I was woken by a noise,' he continued. 'You know that feeling when you wake with a start and you just know that something's just gone crash?'

She nodded her assent.

'Well, I sat up and switched on the light and listened, very still. There was another bang. It was someone walking into a chair, 'cause I heard it fall over and someone saying . . . well, a man swearing. I kept calm. The only phone is in the study – where the noise was coming from – so I couldn't call the police or anything.' O'Leary remembered who he was talking to and smirked. 'So I crept down, quiet as a mouse, and peered over from the stairs. Look, you can see from here – when the study door's open you can look in from the landing. Well, I saw him.' He paused for effect. 'His back was turned so he couldn't see me or anything.'

'What was he doing?'

'He was standing by my desk and going through all my things. I know it was stupid but, well, quite frankly, when I saw him there, bold as brass, that was it. I saw red, as they say. I came down quick, and went straight into the kitchen and took the carving knife off the wall. I'm not an aggressive person, you know, never hurt a fly, but just this once I was mad, I mean *really*. So I came and stood in the doorway like this, so he couldn't escape, and I said, "And what are you doing?" Right? "And what are you doing?" Well, he sprang round like a frightened cat at that. He had this balaclava on back-to-front with holes in for his eyes, so I couldn't see what he looked like. He had gloves on, too. I'd say he was about forty from his build, but it's so hard to tell these days, don't you find? Well, he paused for a moment, then he grabbed a handful of papers and started trying to open the window. You can jump from there down on to the garage roof and down to the road. I wasn't going to let him get out that way, so I ran for him. He saw me coming and waited till I got close – about here – and then he ran past me and out into the hall. I ran after him and saw he was trying to get the front door open now. As I came up behind him he started up the stairs and I just had time to lash out at him. I got him on the back of the leg, just above the heel, I think. Certainly bled a lot. He shouted anyway, and carried on up and into the bathroom. He was sort of panting. I think he was almost as scared as I was, by now!' A giggle slipped out with this. 'Well, then he locked the bathroom door behind him. I ran into my room next door and flung the window up just in time to see him driving off. He must have come in that way. The house is on a very steep hill, as you probably saw, and those back windows are on street level like the front ones. I'd had rather a hot bath and didn't want to spoil the wallpaper, so I'd left the window open to let the steam escape while I went to bed. Stupid of me, I know.'

'What kind of car was it?' asked Mo as she walked upstairs to inspect the escape route, wondering in passing what kind of people wanted spotlights in their bathrooms.

'Oh. Hard to tell. It's a very badly lit lane, such a back street you see, but it was definitely a small car. I could see that much. Maybe a Mini or a little Fiat.'

Mo walked around the scene of the narrative, taking notes under the occupant's eye. A fairy, of course. She'd known that as soon as she'd walked in. She asked him questions as she walked about, to make him feel useful. Funny the way he didn't look anything like his photograph in the papers – not surprising, though. McEnery's reaction had made her morning. The girl wasn't as cool as she liked to make out. The way he looked at the two of them, pretending not to be, reminded her of the old bag in the corner shop in Hackney. Everyone a potential thief. He had the same air of good preservation with an even greater lack of anything worth the time or expense.

'Well, Mr O'Leary, thank you for calling us. I'll leave McEnery here with you to explain things to the Forensic blokes when they come, while I go back and get to hunting down your victim.' She laughed under her breath. O'Leary opened the door for her. 'Thanks,' she said.

'Well, thank *you*, Inspector. Are you sure you won't have some tea?'

'No thanks, but I'm sure McEnery here will. Just one small thing,' she paused by the door of the patrol car, 'those papers he ran off with, they weren't plans for the end of the world on Friday, were they?'

'How did you . . .' he spluttered as she climbed in.

'Just a hunch.' She smiled.

O'Leary laughed a dismissal and closed the door. As he swept past McEnery into the kitchen he complained, 'It's those bloody do-it-yourself magazines – even the dykes are at it now . . .'

MONDAY one

Seth woke to the sound of raised voices from Venetia's room.

'Well why on earth didn't you tell me?'

'You didn't ask.'

'I could scarcely have suspected . . .'

'Oh *please*, Mother.'

'When did it start?'

'Look, I'm *not* . . .'

'Yes, but when?'

'The night before last, I suppose.'

'You've got to see a doctor. Now.'

'But they won't under—'

'No buts. Now.' There was a second's pause, then 'Seth?' Footsteps, and a knock on his door. 'Seth, you must get up now. It's ten past eight.'

'Coming,' he said, and jumped out of bed, snatching up some newly-washed clothes. Mother continued talking but Seth caught nothing save the announcement that she would go and make some breakfast. Irritated, he opened the door and called out, 'Hang on. I can't hear you from up here.'

Mother was moving fast this morning. She was evidently extremely worried about something. She glanced up as Seth came downstairs.

'You've got to get to Trenellion without me.'

'Why?'

'Netia's sick, and I've got to stay here until the doctor's been to have a look at her.'

'What's the matter with her?'

'Oh, nothing much. Just a tummy bug, or something . . .'

'Then why . . . ?'

'But I've got to stay in case it turns out to be her appendix.'

'Poor old Neesh.' He turned to run upstairs and see her but was checked.

'No, darling. Better not. It might be infectious. Look, you stay and eat your breakfast and I'll ring up the Hall and ask if someone can drive over and give you a lift in. I'll make apologies and so on now if I can. If no one can make it, the bus leaves at about eight-thirty, doesn't it?'

'Yup.' He sat down and shook out some cereal. Mother started to dial the Hall number. 'Any post?' he asked.

'No.'

She was lying. He could always tell. He started to eat while she spoke to Jane, the landowner's wife.

Upstairs, Venetia had expanded by another two inches. While Seth ate and her mother talked, she walked a little shakily to the bathroom where, leaning over the lavatory, she vomited copiously. Too much cooking sherry the night before. She brushed her teeth, wiped her lips and smiled wryly at her reflection.

'And the top o' the mornin' to you too, Miss O'Dowd,' she purred.

Mother rang off.

'You'd better wolf that toast down, darling,' she said. 'Jane said she'd try to send someone, but that perhaps you'd better go and wait for a bus at the crossroads, and take that if a car doesn't pick you up first.'

'OK. Will do,' he said, taking his plate and bowl into the kitchen. A form appeared in the front door.

'Hello, Mrs Er . . .' Evelyn was all smiles, 'sheer chaos this morning, I'm afraid. Poor Venetia isn't well.'

'Oh, the poor lamb. Nothing serious, I hope.'

'Oh, no. Just an upset tummy.'

'Such rotten luck. On the first day of her holiday, too.'

'Yes. But the doctor's coming now, so I wonder . . .'

'I'll go and hoover up there now,' answered Mrs Pym, already on the stairs.

'Oh Hell! Doctor!' Mother exclaimed, and searched for his number. In the kitchen, Seth was holding together the quarters of a torn letter he had found in the waste-paper basket.

Darling Evie,

This is fucking insulting, perhaps, but we have always told each other the truth. You asked me about H's headaches. I lied when I said nothing was wrong. It's too much to write now – better we discuss – but I watched him *chez toi* on Thurs evening and was scared shitless. Josh and I return Provence Tuesday next week.

CALL ME.

Love, Jodie.

Jodie was a clinical psychiatrist. Seth threw the pieces back into the bin and hurried for the front door, grabbing his violin as he went.

'Run, or you'll miss it.'

''Bye.'

As her son sped off, Evelyn sighed, stood and lit a cigarette. She smoked rarely. When she did, the drags were deep.

Upstairs Mrs P had finished hoovering and patted the bed to show that it was now tidied up and ready. Venetia clambered back in, making no attempt to hide her extra bulk. Then she raised expectant eyes.

'Did you?'

'Would I fail you, my lovely?' asked the other and, leering, she reached down, pulled up her skirts and nylon overalls to reveal a packet of cashew nuts tucked into the top of her stockings. Family size. She gave it a little pat.

Seth had often wished for chilly glamorous foster-parents. It was not that his family smothered him with their problems, on the contrary, they went out of their way to keep up cheerful appearances, but the blood relationship implicated him nonetheless in the emotional untidiness. A broken home implies a total, albeit jagged, break. Watching the approach of the bus, Seth decided that his home was a squashed one.

Just as he was climbing on board, there was a bellow from a klaxon behind him. He turned and saw a white MG rounding the corner, Roly at the wheel. He apologized to the driver and jumped down on to the verge.

'I had dinner at the Hall and stayed for breakfast. Your mother telephoning was a good chance to escape with a good grace.'

Seth climbed in, violin under one arm.

'What a lovely old car.'

'D'you like it? Wish it were mine. They let me use it to

keep me from wasting money on one of my own. I think it's about nineteen thirty-five.'

'Wonderful smell of old leather.'

'Kinky brat.'

They rounded a corner then had to brake to allow some cows to cross the road. The bus drew up behind them.

'I wish we were going further than the church,' sighed Seth.

'A bad day, is it?'

'Well, it would be nice to go further in the car, but yes, it's a very bad day. It's one of those mornings when I've got one family too many.'

'Well, I wouldn't know how that feels.'

'Why?'

'I haven't got one. My mother died in childbirth and my father when I was four. I was an only child and so were both parents. I was brought up by a nanny and a committee of Edinburgh bank managers and lawyers. There'd been something of a rift between my father and any relations he had. I think he was that sort of a man.'

'Straight out of Deirdre Comstock – can't have been very cheerful, but right now it sounds wonderful.'

'It wasn't nearly as melodramatic as it sounds. I'm an Aquarian so I like to feel special. I was too young to have known what I was missing by having no family; all I got was the occasional fantasy that I'd created myself – just materialized into a comfortable house with a nanny, and toys and a garden ready and waiting for me. Come on, darling!'

The last cow was dawdling in front of the long white bonnet. She turned slowly and stared at Roly before rocking gently on her way.

'She says she's not your darling.' Seth began to sweat. He felt they were trying too hard, like Neesh on an off day.

'Haven't you got a sister?' Roly asked.

'Yes. Venetia. She's in bed with suspected appendicitis.'

'Oh.'

'She's reading English at Cambridge. I suspect you'd say that she was ideologically unsound. My mother does, so you certainly would.'

'Is your mother a Socialist?'

'She tries to be, but it's rather hard. I think she's just a libertarian. She reads the *Guardian* and goes to meetings and marches, but it's all a bit Victorian.'

'How d'you mean?'

'Well, she does her bit, but she eats all her cake – if you see what I mean.' Roly laughed again. 'Am I so amusing?'

'Not really, but you'll do. Blast!' He had to stop again as a large flock of sheep crossed the road. 'The whole bloody animal population seems to be on the move today. Will this make you late?'

'No. I wouldn't normally leave home for another ten minutes.'

The bus driver cut his engine and leaned out of his window to chat up the rosy-faced shepherdess in jeans.

'Were you never lonely as a child?'

'Not at all,' said Roly, 'I was very self-sufficient. It's a big lie that only children are the lonely ones. I'd never any friends so I didn't miss their company. I made friends at school, of course. They sent me to Fettes which was a bit grim, but I had fellows in suffering. I used to meet Nanny by inventing trips to the dentist.'

'Do you still see her?'

'She died in January. Bad heart. She stayed on with me right through. I bullied the trustees into paying her keep as well as mine. I'd bring friends from art college back for dinner and she'd be great value. I think people thought I was a bit odd, but it was no odder than living with an elderly relation. She was my surrogate granny.'

'My granny's mad.'

'Is anyone normal in your family?'

'Venetia and my father, only he gets sick headaches and frightens people, which leaves just her.' Seth had a sudden image of Fiordiligi, mad, hanging by her teeth from his father's finger. 'Of course,' he continued, 'you were spared the parental trauma bit.'

'A note of envy?'

'Spot on.'

'And I suppose you used to fantasize that one day your true parents would come along to claim you from the family in which you'd been placed at birth to teach you humility?' Seth nodded guiltily. 'You *are* cliché-ridden.'

'Sorry.'

'I've never worried about the coming-out bit.'

'Why not?'

'It lays too much accent on who you make and not who you are. I just bumble on and if people arrogantly assume that I'm like them, it makes the revenge the sweeter when they find that I'm not.'

The last sheep were rounded up from the hedgerow by the girl, who waved her thanks as Roly started the engine once more.

'When did you finish art college?'

'I didn't. I left. I'd a bit of a revelation when Nanny died and saw that it was all a waste of time. I already knew what I wanted to do and people were already showing some interest, so I skipped the last two terms and sold the house.'

'What about the trustees?'

'Powerless. I'd reached my twenty-first last year. The summer's a misleading time to go studio-hunting, as the light's too good. I'll stay on here and find somewhere in London in September.'

'We could put you up while you looked,' Seth volunteered automatically. 'Where do you want to live?'

'Not Hampstead.'

'I might have guessed. Perhaps somewhere off the Portobello Road?'

'Warmer.' Roly smiled briefly. They drove on in relaxed silence. There was a steady wind from off the sea. Beneath a surly sky, the spry bell-tower of Trenellion Church came into view.

'Didn't someone famous say that that tower looked like a rabbit peeping over the corn?' asked Roly.

'Ronald Barclay.'

'The churchy Laureate. They read something of his on the *Today* programme this morning. Did you hear about the poisoner on the news?'

'No?'

'Rushed brekker?'

'Very.'

'Well they've arrested this man – the archetypal quiet civil servant. He worked in some unexciting post in an unexciting corner of the Water Board, or whichever branch of the Civil Service deals with water. It seems he was caught trying to feed cyanide into the whole Inner London water system.'

'God! Why?'

'Religious crank. He saw himself as the instrument of God, a sort of latter-day Tamburlaine.'

'Who?'

'Never mind. Middle Eastern tyrant.'

'How did they catch him?'

'Pure chance. Some security guard saw that a man's uniform had gone from its place, even though he was meant to be off sick. His suspicions were aroused and he found the Scourge of the Lord fiddling around up at the reservoir. Apparently they searched his flat and found bottles of poison and all these incredible maps and diagrams. He'd got access to all the right data. Knew exactly what he was doing.'

'But that's horrible!' Seth shuddered and thought of Jodie's letter. 'I've always been scared of maniacs. Vampires and werewolves are too fantastic, but axemen and poisoners really happen.'

Roly slowed the MG and turned to Seth with a sickly expression on his face.

'Then I suppose the time has come to break the news . . .' he intoned.

'Oh, stop it!' Seth laughed. 'But how could anyone find the privacy to do a thing like that?'

'No one bothers with minor civil servants. Bureaucracy spreads the information so thin that, unless they club together, they don't often get hold of anything that could endanger the State.'

'Just the whole of the Inner London water-drinking

population. You'd have thought his family would notice something.'

'We don't all have families.'

'No, I suppose not. Oh, sorry.'

'Are you going to have one – a family of your own?'

'I used to think I would, but no.'

'Too many mornings like today?'

'Partly.'

'Well, look out. You might start being unspeakable in secret, with no one to watch over you.'

'I shall have a good, upstanding man to watch over me. You don't have to be straight to set up home.'

'I can just see you settled on Primrose Hill with the Good Upstanding Man, a Great Dane, a tabby, and canaries in the conservatory.'

'Who knows. We might even adopt a little refugee.'

'That use of the word "little" speaks volumes. It so patently had nothing to do with size. I'll bet your mother talks about "little men" to avoid the rank snobbery of "tradesmen".'

'Sorry. Sorry. We'll try to be a better family, we promise.'

'You stay just the way you are,' Roly said, as he pulled up outside the church. 'I'm going to the lighthouse for some more breakfast.'

Seth saw Jemima smiling vaguely from the path.

'Shall I see you at lunchtime?' Roly paused and looked away for a moment. Seth wished he hadn't asked.

'OK.' He looked up and drove off. Seth wanted to eat a second breakfast with him. He turned to Jemima.

'Wotcha, cock,' she said, and hooted.

*

Doctor Fielding was a strong man, wholly unacademic, who played rugger. Evelyn trusted him. As he blew his nose he watched her hands fidgeting with the piping on a sofa cushion. He finished and put away the handkerchief.

'Well?' she asked.

'Evelyn, Neesh isn't sick. More importantly, she isn't going to have a child. She's not overeating and I can't prescribe any useful pills.'

'How can you possibly tell she isn't pregnant? You haven't had time to do a test.'

'There wasn't any need.'

'No need? The dear creature's swelling up like one of those sheep in Hardy.'

'Please let . . .'

'If you're trying to spare my feelings, there's no need. I'm your archetypal modern mum.'

'That may be exactly the problem.'

'What?'

'Modern mum. How many boyfriends has Netia had, as far as you know?'

'Well, she's very cagey of talking about them, but there've been at least five in the past four years.'

'Five? You're quite sure?'

'Five, six, forty! I don't care about her boyfriends, I care about her. What the hell . . .' Evelyn checked herself then went on quietly, 'what the hell is wrong with her if she's not in the Club?'

'Clinically at least, Venetia is still a virgin. But, she's in a rare state of hysteria in which pent-up sexual neurosis is made manifest in all the classic pregnancy symptoms. The poor girl is even giving herself morning sickness.' Evelyn was speechless. Fielding went on. 'I'm no shrink, but the problem seems to be that she feels the world – or at least her mother – expects her to be more grown-up and more highly-sexed than she is. Her mind throws a desperate sop to her oppressors in the form of a galloping pregnancy.'

'What can I do?'

'Just give her lots of the old TLC, and only talk about it if she wants to. Maybe she just isn't ready for sex. Perhaps she could do with a little old-fashioned maternal affection. Remind her what it's like to be a little girl. She isn't trying to irritate you; in a funny sort of way, not wanting to grow up is really a sign of affection. It's bound to come as something of a shock to discover that she's not the little vamp she made you think, but for the present you mustn't let her know that you've found her out. She made me promise that I wouldn't tell you – muttered something about "offending your Christian Modernity".'

'I understand, Robbie – take the cues from her. Frankly, how long do you think it will last, I mean . . . ?' Evelyn was growing breathless. Fielding reached out and held her hand. Professionally firm.

'Steady. Steady.'

'Sorry,' she tried to laugh, and sniffed, 'what I'm trying to ask in my feeble layperson's way is, how long is she going to remain in this state? Will she carry on swelling and go into a fake labour or something ghastly or does she just stop at this stage?'

'Well, I'm no specialist, but I do know that labour's almost unheard of. Given lots of peace and quiet, the swelling should subside on its own after a matter of days or even hours. Try to remind yourself that it's a physical hysteria.

Her body's gone into the same state of overdrive as her mind would after some appalling shock. I'd give her some tranquillizers, but I know how you . . .'

'No thanks. No tranquillizers.' Evelyn shook her head as she spoke. She stood, 'It's been so kind of you to rush over like this before your surgery begins. Can I get you some coffee or something? Some tea?'

Fielding walked to the door.

'No thanks. I've got to get back. Don't hesitate to call me if there are any developments that frighten you.' She opened the door for him.

'Horribly muggy,' she informed him.

'Isn't it. No, you go inside and put some shoes on.'

She looked down and saw to her embarrassment that she was in her bare stockings. She laughed and shut the door. She could hear Mrs Thingy hoovering the bathroom. She hurried upstairs after the sound. She had to raise her voice to be heard.

'Er . . . ?'

The girth turned and the hoover was silenced.

'Hello, my dear. Doctor gone, has he?'

'Yes. Now everything's going to be all right, thank God. Apparently, it's all some form of hysteria, that's all. Of course, there is the problem of people misunderstanding. The poor lamb will have to stay indoors for a few days. I can trust you not to . . . er . . . ?'

'Oh, Mrs Peake,' Mrs Pym looked hurt but faithful, 'of course I wouldn't.'

'You're wonderful. Now I must rush.' Her face burning, Evelyn turned and went along the landing. She paused briefly at Venetia's door then pushed it ajar. 'Darling?'

'Mummy. Come in.'

She was sitting up in bed with Donne's Sermons and a file of notes. Her tortoiseshell glasses perched becomingly on her nose's tip. Playing for time, Evelyn walked over and teased the curtains further from the window frame. Netia was back in her book, at least her eyes were lowered. She looked extraordinarily healthy for one who got so little fresh air. Blooming.

'Doc Fielding has gone, darling, and he says that everything's going to be fine.'

'Oh good,' said Venetia, looking up brightly, 'I've made you horribly late for your rehearsal. You must dash. Look, Ma, don't worry. All right? I can take care of myself. There's plenty of food downstairs and Mrs Whatsit can help me if I need anything from the shops.'

Evelyn bent and kissed her.

'Back soon,' she murmured, and left.

As she pulled out the bag of cashew nuts from under her file, Venetia smiled that her mother's embrace had been so unusually fervent. She heard the front door close. The cleaning woman's head came round her door with a denture-clad grin.

'All right, my love?'

Venetia smiled sincerely.

'All right.'

Evelyn stopped the Volvo at the crossroads and ran over to the call-box. She dialled the Keats Lane number, heard the answer-phone message, then replaced the receiver. Back in the car and speeding through the lanes, she dulled her shame by imagining Huw's frustration at the inevitable airport delays. So unlike him to rush off on a wild goose chase. But then, he hadn't been himself for several weeks. Those dreadful De Quincey headaches had grown worse and more frequent, and he had spent longer and longer in his study. He rarely came to bed, preferring to sleep at his desk, and he talked less. He even teased less. With the children away and so unable to corroborate her fears, she had talked to Jodie. God, that letter! Jodie made a habit of over-reacting. Evelyn hoped she could trust her not to talk.

From the radio came the announcement that in tomorrow's edition of *This Week's Composer* she would hear Sweelinck's earliest forays into the motet form. Ten o'clock. She hoped that Seth had made the right noises. A tractor swung out into the lane fifty yards ahead. She cursed and slowed down.

'And now an organ recital from King's College, Cambridge.'

She stared at the labrador that sat in the cabin with the driver and wondered at this talk of Venetia's neurosis. She would not pry. Every guide she had ever read on the subject had said how, more often than not, the disturbance was caused by the very presence of the mother. Mothers had a hard time of it. They were meant to have a hard time with sons too; strange that Seth should conform so little to plan. Dear, uncommon Seth. The labrador barked at a seagull that swooped over the hedge and into the neighbouring field. A Bach toccata. What had led her to assume that her daughter was racy; that she was not exactly loose, but far from Marian chastity? Clinically, she herself had ceased to be a virgin long before her marriage, but that was riding and bicycles at school. Netia had been reared in London so horses had been out of the question – far too expensive. A bicycle in Hampstead was plainly impractical. The tower appeared above the fields.

> Trenellion Tower cocked, rabbit-eared, above the corn,
> Sniffs apprehensive the encroaching foam.
> How sweet to worship in your warren!

Her mind sucked at the hoary nipple of immaculate conception and, though strong, the taste was good.

MONDAY two

Mo stood in the middle of the elegant room and watched the man from Forensic as he searched the desk for fingerprints, blood, hair, dead skin, anything. The m.o. was now predictable as clockwork. The flat had belonged to a Tarot reader and palmist, one who had lately received some degree of publicity. A lurid portrait of her hung spotlit in the hall. The victim in question had returned from a dinner party to find that someone had broken into her property through the skylight. She thought they had done no more than smash her crystal ball, until she smelt smoke and opened the kitchen door. Her latest work was burning in the sink. Apparently she had tried to put the flames out herself, and so had set fire to her dress. In a desperate attempt to save herself she had stumbled to the bathroom. Trying to turn on the shower, she had ignited the shower curtain and collapsed beneath the clinging sheet of frying plastic. A neighbour had been alerted by the smell as it slowly filtered through the luxurious hall. Suspecting an unattended pan fire, they had called the police. The burnt predictions remained in the kitchen sink, a soggy black pulp.

Accidental death, of course. Even a fool like McEnery could tell from his previous appearances that their man was meticulous. Had he wished to kill, his method would have been less messy, and he would certainly have stopped a flaming victim from racing so dangerously about the flat. There were two points that the Detective Inspector was left to ponder, however: the patently emotional touch of smashing the crystal ball, and the continuing lack of rational motive. Mo knew about weird burglars. They always made a mess and peed, or worse, on their victim's clothes and bedding. Tomcats leaving their mark. This man wasn't weird like that. His actions were unaggressive, by and large, and certainly lacked the hallmarks of a religious maniac like that bloke Gutteridge they'd just nicked at the pumping station. Each robbery was precise and, where uninterrupted, had been clean.

Mo walked out on to the landing and leant against the wall. Yet again she trailed her gaze along the scorched traces from kitchen to shower. Another man in a white coat was working at the top of the small pine staircase that led to the skylight and so to the roof garden. She stared at his brightly clocked socks and thought.

The skylight was a sliding one and had been left open by the intruder. Possibly he had heard someone downstairs and left in a hurry. Possibly he had dropped the ball by mistake and been afraid that the noise would alert suspicion. The staircase and stretch of carpet beneath it had been slightly damp. There'd only been one cloudburst all week and that was a short burst on Saturday at about ten p.m. He must have been here before dropping in on Fairy O'Leary's place. Depending on how deep the knife wound was, he might have gone into hiding.

Her mind spiralled off after motives again. She'd had a chat with Jack and he'd reminded her about that French dolly-bird in the fifties who'd gone loopy over a recurrent fortune-telling that said she was going to die young. She'd run amok in her neighbourhood one night, breaking into houses simply to smash clocks and watches. Extreme, obviously insane behaviour, but peculiarly logical in one who wants to bring a halt to time. This bloke had a thing about the future too, but his vendetta was an impersonal one; he seemed to be trying to enforce some kind of astrological silence. He didn't want people to know. Know what? That French bit had taken an overdose before they'd caught her, so it had all come true anyway.

Mo needed results badly, fast, if she was to save face with Timson and his toadies, but the more she thought about the matter in hand, the more futile her recent occupation had become.

She crossed to the kitchen. It was a bright, new affair of gadgets and glossy surfaces. She stared at her reflection in a cupboard door, stared balefully and let her eyes travel on. There was one cupboard with a perspex door. There were glasses of all shapes and sizes, little bowls for crisps, a large cut-glass jug and, incongruously, a metal hip-flask on the bottom shelf. She tossed a glance over her shoulder. The landing was empty. She pulled her snot-rag out from her cuff and, using it as an extempore glove, opened the door and lifted the flask out and down to her deep jacket pocket. It was heavy, definitely silver. She shut the door deftly and pushed the snot-rag back into her sleeve. She paused for a moment on the landing, looked first at one busy man and then at the other.

'OK, lads, I'm going back to the station now, if anybody needs me.'

'Cheers, Boss.'

She let herself out. Subversion was easier than one had thought.

MONDAY three

The orchestra was rehearsing Britten's *Saint Nicholas.* She heard a familiar tenor voice. Gregory Truscott, a rising opera star who had made time to pay one last visit. As she pulled open the oak door, Evelyn saw that conceited sculptor at work in the South aisle. He was painting a layer of preservative on an angel. He looked up as she stopped by a pillar and began to unpack her cello. He smiled and she mouthed a hello in reply. She made her way to her seat, flashed an apology at Peter and a glance at Seth. Her son was too intent to return it. Within seconds she too was rapt. The work posed no technical difficulties, and for the hours that remained until lunch, she entered willingly its iconic scenes of wondering faith. She remembered Venetia singing the part of a pickled boy at her school concert, and Seth playing the pleading introductory solo at one of his. In a beautiful church, with the sun emerging at last from the clouds, surrounded by people she admired, her ears full of favourite music, her thoughts daring occasionally to stray to her miraculous daughter, Evelyn found herself happier than she had been for months.

'Lovely. Now just once more through number three and you can all go for a well-earned lunch.'

Peter seemed on good form. Jemima hissed at Evelyn.

'Have you heard about the baby?'

'What baby?' asked Evelyn sharply.

'Peter's, I mean Helga's and Peter's. They're going to buy one.'

'What fun,' she said dully, but relieved.

'Gregory, if you wouldn't mind, number three once more?' Peter called the portly tenor back from the South aisle where he had been talking to the artist.

'My parents died,' sang Gregory.

'All too soon I left the tranquil beauty of their home
And knew the wider world of man.
Poor man! I found him solitary, racked
By doubt; born, bred, doomed to die
In everlasting fear of everlasting death . . .'

Seth glanced to his right but found Roly walking out, impervious, picking something off his fingernail. They were dismissed for lunch. Please would they all be back on time to set an example to the chorus who, heaven help them, were to join them this afternoon? Tonight they would please take home and study the parts for Roger's *Cantata* in preparation for tomorrow's preliminary endeavours.

Evelyn carefully laid her cello on its side by her chair.

'How did you get on with the doctor?' Seth asked, 'was it Robbie Fielding?'

'Yes.'

'How is he?'

'Very well. He says Neesh has got a stomach infection and that she had better stay in bed for a few days – nothing more.'

'Must have been a bad cashew. She's been wolfing the things recently. There's no need to look so worried.' At his smile she raised one as well, with a mute cry of thanks for the lacunae of a Public School Education.

'Let's go and have some lunch.'

'Yup,' he replied, discreetly scanning the place as he followed her rapid steps. She met Roly in the porch.

'Oh, Mrs Peake?'

'Yes?'

'Actually, I asked Seth if he'd give me a hand with some lifting in the break.'

As Seth caught up he could see that she was taken aback.

'Go ahead,' she answered, 'borrow him. But I want him back in one piece.'

Roly turned into the church and found him.

'Clever excuse,' Seth smiled.

'No. In fact I do need a hand. Could you help me pull this old girl outside?' Mortified, Seth took hold of the head while Roly held the feet of one of the old figures that had yet to be treated with preservative, and together they bore her, crumbling, into the churchyard.

'It's quite true, what they were saying yesterday,' he said.

'Who?'

'Oh. Just people before the first rehearsal began yesterday morning. They were saying how like yours the angel's hair was. It is.'

Roly laughed stiffly as they lowered the wood on to a tarpaulin.

'No,' he said. Then he looked up and met the feel of Seth's eyes and repeated, no laugh in his voice, 'No, Seth.'

'What?'

'You're too young. OK?'

Seth had no time to reply, as Mother had followed them out.

'So this is where you've been working.'

'Hello,' said Roly. A sixth-former on Parents' Day.

'I promise I won't tell a soul, otherwise you'll be bothered by women asking for busts of their children.' The two of them chuckled obsequiously. 'In fact, I have come to talk business, but I promise I don't want a bust of Venetia. I don't want one of this either, actually.' She placed a hand on Seth's shoulders as she spoke and he felt about twelve, forced back into shorts. He stood trapped and prickling, showing interest in the sea while his mother talked commissions. By an effort of will he managed not to look at MacGuire once for the rest of the interview. Evelyn was not long in finishing.

'Oh well, if you're going to be in London now, instead of Edinburgh, that makes you much more accessible. Come on, darling, we must go and get you something to eat.' She released Seth and he walked back into the cool of the nave.

On the doorstep, Evelyn turned for a moment and caught Roland MacGuire staring at her, or past her. She turned back quickly and went after her child. They walked in silence across the church and headed for cottage number two where lunch was laid out on trestle tables, and where chorus and orchestra would chat over bread and cheese about the morning's work. They joined the queue. Evelyn felt a barrier. Seth was sulking about something. Since Venetia was ill, he must be jealous. She would compensate with loving cheer.

'Seth?'

'Mmm?'

'Is Roland MacGuire a terribly sad person, or is that just me being romantic?'

'Just you being romantic. He's distinctly arrogant and secure. He's talented and he knows it. I think he's one of those people who will survive all their lives without anyone's help.'

'Oh dear.'

Seth wanted to cry, but talked about how perfect the Stilton looked. He followed the crowd into the orchard. Bronwen marched up to him, her plate laden.

'Bloody good grub,' she declared, 'Only bloody good thing about the festival so far. Ha! You're looking glum. Want to talk about it?' Seth opened his mouth to speak then just smiled wanly, waving a piece of baguette. 'Look,' she continued, 'I've got a schedule here and it's only semi-chorus and leaders wanted for tomorrow afternoon for Roger Whoodlum's monstrosity, which means neither you nor me. I'm going to walk along the coast to Pendarth Castle where I shall eat a bag of flapjacks and drink a bottle of scrumpy, and you're going to come too.'

'Oh thanks, Bronwen.'

The Madwoman of Saint Jacobs clicked her tongue and went to discuss Liszt's sex-life with Grigor. The breezy charity of a Matron. Seth forced down a piece of Stilton to find that it was really very fine, and went to join his mother in the shade of a pear tree.

TUESDAY one

The irritations of the morning had included a visit from a journalist from the *Standard* wanting to know about the 'Astro-Burglar', and why they'd hushed up the burning. Mo had been feeling sore about the entire affair and having some bastard trying to make a public joke out of it did little to ease her mood. The day had got off to a flying start when she woke to find that Andy had sicked up his kippers on the bathroom carpet, the computer at the bank had made a mistake over her statement – for the worse – and then she had come into work to face the sarcasm of first Timson and now this smug hack. Not content with insinuating that she couldn't catch Loobie Lou in broad daylight, he was going on to ask why she was one of the few policewomen of her rank being sent out in a patrol car, and to rake up the whole business of her fights with Timson and the rest. She was genuinely pleased to see McEnery when she rapped on the glass door.

'Boss, can I interrupt you for a second?'

'Be my guest.'

'Could this be action?' asked the reporter, and stood for The Perm.

'There's been another 999 about intruders. Hampstead have passed it on to us because they think it's another of our man's.'

'Where?'

'One of those roads running down behind the station.'

'Let's go.' Mo stood. 'They there already?'

'Yup.'

'No chance of my coming along?' asked the reporter.

Mo scowled.

'Yeah I guess you'd better. It'll stop you bringing all your friends. No phone calls, all right?'

'Thanks.' He laughed, and winked at McEnery who froze him. 'I'll follow you there.'

'Hi Gerry. All right?'

They met in the drive. Big place. Gerry'd been at training school with her.

'Hi Mo. Reverend, this is Detective Inspector Faithe.'

'How d'you do?'

'Morning. Are you the neighbour who telephoned?' They started towards the front steps.

'Yes. That's right, Officer. I say, I've never dealt with a lady Inspector before. My wife will be thrilled – very hot on that sort of thing, you know.'

In his rambling fashion the Reverend Jukes told her his story. Their neighbours had gone away on holiday and asked them to watch the house and feed the cats in their absence. Such a pleasant family – very talented. Anyway, it had all been plain sailing until the last couple of nights. His wife had woken him repeatedly with the promise that she had heard a car pull up in the garage, and that she had seen lights. This last night he too had seen and heard things. His suspicions aroused, he had walked down into the garden to take a look. Sure enough, someone was walking around upstairs. But on closer inspection, it had turned out to be the master of the house; at least it had borne a strong resemblance – hard to tell at such a distance. He had returned to comfort his wife with the suggestion that the man had returned early to get back to work. This morning, however, when she had walked over to pay her respects, she had seen the blood and the mess and been scared to death, poor thing. They had the work number and had tried that but the secretary had said no, he was quite definitely still away. The home number had produced only an answering contraption with the same reply. He was sorry, yes of course they should have got in touch earlier, but you know how it is. Mo knew how it was.

They certainly weren't badly off, that much was clear as soon as she was through the front door. Too big for comfort. Gemma and Robin twenty years on from Thornhill Square.

'The blood's in the kitchen, here,' said Gerry, leading the way. 'Bill's already taken some for processing.'

The French windows looked out into the garden. The trail of blood led through them to the kitchen table. There, a first aid box had been opened and the contents rudely scattered. The cut had been bad and the victim in something of a panic.

'It leads right out to the garage. Obviously came back in the car then ran in this way.'

'Right,' said Mo, 'what's been nicked this time?'

'Nothing as far as I can see but – well, I couldn't tell you this in front of the vicar but – looks as though this is his own place.'

'Ruddy Nora!' she mused. 'What else?'

'Come and look in the study.' Again Gerry led them across the hall. There wasn't much in there worth looking at until you looked over the desk. On one side, weighed down by a half-empty bottle of Scotch, lay all the papers and maps that had gone missing in the past few days. A diary lay open, a week-at-a-glance one, with a red circle drawn around Friday. As she glanced over it all, Mo blew out a breath between her teeth.

'Bill done this lot for prints?' she asked.

'Yeah.'

'Gerry, you're a bloody marvel. Thanks. I'll need to stay and look this lot over – may be able to tell where he's gone today. McEnery, you get back to the station and use that initiative. I don't reckon our little man's going to show up here again – not if he's got as much to do before Friday as I think, but this place had better be watched in case. Plain clothes job, of course.'

'Right, Boss.'

'Oh, and ask Our Father what kind of car it was and put out a search. Don't rouse his suspicions, if you can help it.'

'Yes, Boss.'

'I'll get one of Gerry's girls to drive me back.'

They left her sitting at the desk.

'Hard taskmaster, is she?' Gerry asked on the drive.

'Bloody granite-features!' snapped McEnery. 'Old Scarface!'

In the middle of the desk a book lay open. Mo covered her hand with a snot-rag and flipped to the front. *Principles of Hysteria* by Leon Berkowski. She frowned. Numerous pages had been turned down in one corner, and the text had been gone over thoroughly with a red pencil.

There were heavy underlinings and occasional comments in an illegible scrawl. She read the fly-leaf.

> In this, his latest work – one that can only prove seminal – Dr Berkowski, Founder of the Institute of Neural Research in Vienna, has turned his attention to the various manifestations and causes of the hysterical state. His thesis covers ground from the earliest recorded religious frenzies to the latest outbreaks of football hooliganism and pop idol-worship. In particular, he extends his previous examination of the powers of hypnosis to suggest that there is a mass-hypnotic foundation to all documented instances of the paranormal, not least the more celebrated biblical and legendary miracles and the widespread success of faith-healing. Berkowski draws on his first-hand knowledge of both Jewish history and the media to formulate startling conclusions concerning the potential of the human mind *en masse* to dictate the patterns of history.

Mo had read enough. Things were rapidly falling into place. She sifted through the piles of papers beneath the whisky bottle and found cuttings from the Yellow Pages and some specialist magazines. He had removed all the addresses and phone numbers listed under Fortune-telling, Magicians, and Publishing. Under the heading Titles on a memo pad was written '*Psychosomatic Apocalypse* – too pop?'

The telephone rang and the answering machine clicked into action. Mo carefully lifted the receiver and listened.

' . . . and do not expect to return before late next week. My wife and family are also away until that time. They can be contacted at Penfasser 53642. Should you wish to leave a message, please do so after the tone and you will be contacted as soon as possible.'

The tone sounded, there was a sigh and whoever it was rang off. A child laughed in a neighbouring garden. Mo pulled open the top drawer of the desk and looked through it. Nothing. Staples, paper and some photos. The dolly-bird was nice. Classy little bit. She picked out the man's photo and set it on the desk before her. Then she flicked through the directory. Jugs. Juhoor. Juicy. Jujitsu. Jukes. Jukes, Reverend Philip. She dialled the number and waited.

'Reverend Jukes? Hello. It's Detective Inspector Faithe here, yes, that's right. I was calling to ask you to give a description of the man you saw in your neighbour's house last night . . . No, just routine. Nothing's been taken. If you could just . . . ? Thanks . . . Tall? Ah, yes. Thanks a lot, Reverend. You've been a great help. My regards to your wife. Goodbye.' She replaced the receiver and sat tapping her fingertips on the photograph frame for a few seconds. Then she pulled out her notebook and glanced through the list of numbers. She dialled one.

'Hello. Faithe here. I've been looking over the burglary with Sergeant Bingham. Yeah, that's right. Oh, he's already told you. Well, if you can come and pick me up now, darling, that's great . . . yeah . . . hang on. Before you hang up on me, I want you to look up a number for me. Yeah? . . . OK. The number is Penfasser 53642. That's right . . . just the address. No. I'll wait, thanks.' Mo held the receiver under her chin and looked down at the photograph. Without the glasses he might have looked quite like Dad. Bit too thin, though. She tapped her pen on the glass, muttering at the impassive face, 'Gotcha, gotcha, gotcha!'

There was a flash.

'Gotcha!' laughed the man from the *Standard*. 'The First Lady of Crime goes into action and another one bites the dust.'

'Oh Christ! I'd forgotten I'd invited you.'

'I know. Sad isn't it? Still, I don't mind. I met your friend with the hair outside on the drive and she told me you were in here.'

'Now look,' Mo's tone was savage, 'you know you can't print anything about this place – not even the photo – until we've got something definite? I mean, we don't even know he's our man for sure, yet.'

''Sall right. Keep your hair on,' he leered, 'just wanted the exclusive, that's all. Tell you what.'

'What?'

'You keep me informed, and I promise – cub's honour – I won't tell another soul.'

'I'm not having you follow me around like bloody Lassie.'

'If you don't agree, you'll only get a whole pack of us.'

'Sod.'

'Wanta tell me how you got that impressive scar, then?'

'Oh . . . you've got the address?' She held her palm over the mouthpiece and looked up at her assailant. 'I'll deal with you in a minute. Yeah, I'm listening, it's just that I've got some wally with his Brownie up here. Fire away . . . La Korvy-what? How d'you spell that? . . . Stupid bloody name for a house!'

TUESDAY two

Venetia had woken on Tuesday morning to find her middle increased by another three inches. She had lain for a few minutes in the stupor of the freshly-stirred, gazing across the linen of her pillow at the pile of books on the chair by the wall, her mind an unruffled plane. Then, as her eyes picked their way, aimless, through the titles, and as her ears homed in on the sounds of the others preparing to leave, her bodily developments of the past forty-eight hours slid back into her mind and roused it inhumanly. She sat up and was disgusted. It felt as though an infant's naked buttocks were resting on her lap. She lifted the bedclothes, prepared for the worst and saw it. With a brave little sigh, she lay back so that her passenger would make its presence less felt. In the sunshine that poked through her half-opened curtains, the panicky schemes of the night gone by were ludicrous. She wondered what her father would do in such a predicament and at once found her lost resolve. If he lost a leg, if he grew a third one, if his colleagues confessed that they thought he was losing his mind, the one thing he would never stop doing was his work.

She rebuked herself for the dullness with which she had moped her way through the previous day. Since the affliction was so plainly psychosomatic, the worst thing she could do was to give it space for thought. So resolving, Neesh clambered out of bed, regained her balance and, pulling a dressing-gown around her, went on to the landing to salute the world. Seth had just disappeared towards the car, Evelyn was in the process of joining him. She looked up and smiled.

'Hello, darling. I tried not to wake you.'

'You didn't. I wanted to get up. I must ruddy well get on with some work. Any post?'

'No.'

'How long are you both out for?'

'All day. At least, I am. Seth doesn't rehearse this afternoon, but I think he's going for a walk with Bronwen.'

'Peace and quiet.'

'Yes. You make the most of it.' She had seldom heard her mother so bland, and was entertained to see how her eyes strayed instinctively down to where her daughter's waist had been.

'Bye-bye,' she said, and closed the bathroom door.

'Bye,' answered Evelyn, and left for the church.

Venetia refused to let her body think it was functioning abnormally. She took an invigorating shower, scrubbing the hateful mound as though it were Venus' greatest boon, even dusting it with loving talcum powder. She pushed her feet under the bed and performed a few sit-ups before coming down to a hearty breakfast. Without a pause to congratulate herself on the absence of morning sickness, she took a handful of books and a file and set up a study at the garden table. She read and took notes for the next few hours, pausing only to answer the telephone or to replenish her glass of pineapple juice. The sun was bright, her belly was full, and she only had eyes for Donne. She finished the sermons and spent the rest of the morning wrestling with the religious sonnets. Then she retired to the kitchen where she turned on Radio One very loud and, rocking her burdened hips as if they were a nubile twelve-year-old's, made herself a banana whip in the blender. Her favourite working lunch. She was just walking back to the garden with it when the telephone rang again. This time it was Daddy.

'Neesh?'

'Daddy! My God! Where are you? This must be costing you a bomb. Are you having a lovely busy time?'

'Well. Yes. Quite. How are you?'

'Very well. Thanks for your card. I found it in my room. What's wrong? You sound all odd.'

'Must be the distance. How's Seth?'

'Fine.'

'And your mother?'

'Fine. They're both fine. I . . .'

'Well, look, I'd better go. I was only ringing to say hello.'

'Hello,' she said, only he wasn't playing.

'And I'll see you again very soon. Bye-bye.'

'Bye.' A click and he was gone.

Venetia replaced the receiver and stared at the last inch of her drink as she swung it around the glass. She hated calls from abroad. The inbred mistrust of over-spending made any relaxed communication impossible. Most unlike him. Perhaps Leon's department had paid for the call. Maybe Daddy had chatted up a receptionist into giving him an outside line. It had been very clear – no interference at all. She recalled the pips at the beginning and realized that he must have paid for it after all. She drained the glass, catching the pieces of banana from the bottom on her tongue and relishing their taste after the pallor of the milk.

Then she dawdled back through the kitchen to wash up the glass, and turn off the radio. There were footsteps on the drive. She peeped around the curtain. Harry Barnes.

Her resolve fled. She ran back up to her room and shut the door. She dared not let him see her condition – imaginary or otherwise. She had sensed that he was an attractively squeamish man. The bell rang. She started to wait, then thought better of it. Leaning towards the open window she cooed out:

'Who is it?'

The morning had been spent with the orchestra getting to grips with the new composition by Roger Bevan. *Holy Innocents* was an oratorio of sorts. It combined texts from *Isaiah* and *Revelations* with sentences from eye-witness accounts of the bombing of Hiroshima. The work opened with a bass solo rendition of Saint Matthew's verses dealing with the putting of all male infants to the sword. The score was as taxing as the text was fierce, and matters were not helped by the fact that the orchestral parts had been pasted up from photocopied hand-written manuscript. A morning of frayed horse-hair and tempers. Roger had been persuaded to score the hardest passages for a semi-chorus and small ensemble of orchestral first-desk players, who would need fewer hours for rehearsal, but time would be short even to cover the 'simpler' movements.

Evelyn wore her 'Berio face' – a countenance of grim determination she assumed when tackling compositions whose effort in performance did not seem matched by their rewards. Her tastes expired after Britten and early Tippett. She had little sympathy with Seth's interests in late Bartok and Stockhausen. A very nervy three hours came to an end as Peter turned to Roger to ask yet again how exactly he meant this passage to sound. He dismissed the players, having decided that it would take a good hour to worm a coherent answer out of the man. Seth walked smiling over to Mother.

'Chin up,' he laughed.

'I hate you,' she said. 'Hope you both fall off a cliff.'

'Jealous?'

'Jealous is not the word.'

'If you take my violin home for me tonight, I promise to make supper for you before you come back.'

'Done, but leave it on that chair over there. Bye.'

'Bye. Don't frown too hard.' She laughed and he walked down the aisle.

The workmen had flown another angel to the rafters. Roly must have been at work at night. Seth wondered whether he had done so to avoid seeing him, then dismissed the idea as ridiculously self-centred. He waited outside the school room, sitting on the low stone wall. The choir were still practising. They seemed to be having less trouble than the orchestra, but then perhaps they had easier parts. His years in the north had not left Roger totally insane. Seth watched the other players walk, or drive away. Afternoon off: half-day excursions. Soon he heard voices behind him and saw that the choir too had finished. Doors opened and singers spilled out over the grass, some – the semi-chorus, Seth supposed – self-consciously showing an interest in the score they had just been rehearsing, and, pride of prides, singing short passages as demonstration of some point.

Pendarth Castle was their private name for a derelict

construction a few miles along the coast from Trenellion. Bronwen and he could never decide whether it had once served a military purpose, or whether it had always been intended as a home for animals on wintry nights. Standing barely six feet high and measuring about ten feet square, its interior, lit by a narrow slit-shaped window in one wall, was an unassuming mass of sheep pellets. The attraction of the place was the roof. One could command a fine view of the boiling sea beneath and the coastline to either side, while being sheltered from the winds by a raised edge roughly a foot high. It may have been because he had solemnly led Bronwen there on their first walk together that she led Seth there now.

The path to the Castle had remained miraculously within the domain of specialized local knowledge. For a right-of-way, though not marked on the map as a footpath, it attracted little attention. As the pair walked its length today, they met no one save the wind-swept sheep and the savage gulls. Bronwen rarely spoke when she was on the move, saving her energies for her eyes and feet. From time to time she would stop to uproot a plant or to snatch an interesting pebble, which she would toss into her carpet bag, or she would stop and stare awhile. There was no need to talk; she and the boy admired the same things. Seth found Bronwen a supportive but unobtrusive companion. He would walk in her wake, playing with his thoughts. Something in her enabled him to stand back from his world in calm contemplation. It may have been that her detachment from things 'normal' was so sturdy, her will so adamantine, that his more pliable spirit was drawn into her ways of seeing. As now they strode along the cliff-tops, the amazon and the acolyte, he felt her strength of purpose. The pauses were fewer than before. They passed by the blow-hole without the usual sit on the grass for a spout to erupt into the air above them. Bronwen barely greeted the sheep. They had to reach the castle roof and then they would talk.

After forty minutes they reached Pendarth Point, a narrow promontory that rose to a peak as it stood out from the pitted coastline. As one arrived at this stage in the path, the Castle was barely visible, masked by the rocks above it. Bronwen slung her bag over one shoulder and clambered before Seth over the boulders and patches of toughened grass. A path had been trodden out by the hooves of sheep. It was an indication of the coldness of nights that they continued to shelter in a place so perilous for them to reach. More than once, Seth had peered from the roof into the dank, black inlet to the left to see a shaggy corpse, bloating in corruption as it lay twisted on the rocks beneath. He had told Venetia the first time and she had warned him that he must always hold his breath when passing through a churchyard. Beneath the ground, she had said, all the corpses were twisting and swelling like that and every few minutes one of them burst. To inhale the filthy gas as it seeped from the turf would shorten his life by years. An unthinking uncle had expanded upon the theme to include breaking wind as a god-sent reminder of the tomb. The tease had long since been dispelled, but young Peake had never rid the water closet of this taint of mortality.

As he stepped across to the roof from the last rock, he found Bronwen flat on her back. A dead Viking putting out to sea with concubine corpses and faithful hound. She opened one eye.

'Took your time,' she said. 'Open the bag and tell me if that bloody scrumpy's stayed cold.' He bent down and felt in the bag. Among the pebbles, dried-out, forgotten herbs and feathers, he found cool glass. He lifted the bottle out and passed it to her.

'Perfect,' he said. She sat up, pulled out the cork with her teeth, and took a deep draught. He admired her unexpectedly youthful neck. She swung the bottle down again and wiped its mouth with the back of her hand.

'Just what the doctor ordered. Here.' She started to hold it out to him then stopped. 'I say, She doesn't mind you drinking this stuff, does She? I mean, after your grandfather and all that?'

'Oh no. She never seems to think that cider counts.'

'Dreadful for the stomach wall. Ha!' She winked, and held it out.

'How did you know about Grandpa?' he asked as he lifted the mouth to his lips.

'Oh, I think your father told me about him once,' she said and looked out to sea.

The scrumpy was so dry that it scarcely had a taste. It burned gently at the back of Seth's throat. He remembered that he had eaten no lunch. The drink was strong and the sun was hot. He would hold back.

Bronwen leant up against the little wall behind her. Slightly pink with the heat, she pushed her sleeves above her elbows and rubbed her forearms, enjoying the sun.

'Went for a swim across the cove and back this morning,' she said, 'bloody cold. Cigarette?'

'No thanks.'

'Good boy. Filthy habit. Have a flapjack instead.' She threw a plastic bag at him full of the things, rich with treacle. He fell on one with gusto.

'Isn't it better in the evening, after it's been warmed up a bit?'

'Suppose so, but it's not quite the same.'

'You mean it would be too soft?'

'Look, we're here to talk about you, not me.'

He laughed. 'We've got to talk about both of us, or it wouldn't be fair.'

'Cheeky, but OK. We'll start with you, though, because I'm older and more complicated. Chuck us that bottle like a duck.' He passed her the bottle and watched as she held her suspicious-looking cigarette in one hand and supported a swig with the other. Then she held it between her knees. 'No more until you tell me why you're looking so glum.'

'I thought I was radiating happiness.'

'Rubbish. I've been watching you and you're glum as a goat.'

Seth laughed softly and picked at a finger. Bronwen sucked hard on her cigarette and blew out the smoke in a sudden little jet.

'He's caught you hook, line, and sinker, that fancy bugger of yours, hasn't he?'

Seth was startled. Bron and he had never talked about such things. He played dumb.

'What?'

'Don't play the Mother of God with me. It won't wash. You can save that for him.'

Seth took another flapjack and teased a raisin from its flank.

'That's what's so odd. I can't play dumb with him. Right from the start he's treated me as an adult.'

'Well you are, or near as dammit. It's only Mother who treats you like a kid. Where does he live when he's not in a lighthouse?'

'He did live in Edinburgh, but he's sold the house and he's moving to London in the autumn.'

'Very handy.'

'Yuh,' he took a mouthful to give him courage, 'the trouble is . . .'

'What?'

'I don't think he's interested.'

'Balls.'

'No he's not, Bron. He thinks I'm just a little squirt. He's just playing with me. Typical Aquarian behaviour.'

'That figures.'

'What?'

'Leo and Aquarius: attraction of opposites.'

'Fire and water? I burn and he puts out.'

'You could make him boil if you tried.'

'I told you – he thinks I'm a squirt.'

'Even an Aquarian doesn't leave a party so openly to sit outside with someone if all he wants to do is call them a squirt. Don't be a goose. Here. You've earned some more of this.' He drank. The oats had made him thirsty. 'Steady on. I've got Her to answer to when you get home.' He lowered the bottle.

'The flapjack made me thirsty,' he explained.

'What makes you think he doesn't love you? Now be honest.'

'Well . . . I . . . It was all going so wonderfully at first. I just couldn't believe it. I mean, he really seemed to like me. He didn't just chat – right from the start he talked and made me talk. We even argued. Then we went and sat on the cliffs together and once he picked me up in his car. I think . . .' Seth thought back to the graveyard, the angel's hair. 'I think he's afraid. He's scared because I'm too young.'

'You're not too young. People used to get married at your age and God knows, that's a lot more responsibility than the lifestyle you're after.'

'It's the law, Bron. As from Friday I can get married, well, have sex with a girl. Two years after that I'm old enough to go and watch people doing it in a film and another three years after that the Government allows me to show my love for a man – provided that I don't do it in public or in a hotel.'

'But that's balls.'

'Nope. It's silly, maybe, but it's the law. If I went to bed with Roly I could get him sent to prison for child rape.'

'But you wouldn't, though, would you?'

'That's beside the point. He probably thinks that . . . we . . . I dunno. I think it's having a family as well. He's an orphan. Apart from the Trenellion bunch, who don't have a lot to do with him anyway, he doesn't have anyone breathing down his neck. I think he's scared that I'm surrounded by domestic spies. I mean, imagine if Mother found out and got the wrong idea because she was too frightened to ask me about it, and she went to the police. It'd be ghastly.'

There was a pause while Bronwen ground her cigarette into the stone. The herring gulls were wheeling overhead.

Seth threw a piece of flapjack on to the rocks and two of them pounced reptilian down on it.

'You do it with people at school. Doesn't that matter to her?'

'How do you know I do?'

'Seth, I've got eyes.'

'Well, school doesn't count. It's just character-building. Innocent fun and games for the growing boy.'

'And I suppose it's meant to help you with your Plato. Why on earth did she send you to that dreadful place?'

'It wasn't her, it was him, and I'm bloody glad he did.'

'Why?'

'Because I think it stopped me from getting screwed up.'

'You're not exactly normal, dear boy.'

'That's a debatable point.'

'Well, it hasn't given you much confidence in your power to please.'

'Yes it has. A bit.' He paused and smiled, shrugging his shoulders. 'It's just that I know my limitations.'

Bronwen frowned, as much to herself as on him. She bent forward and took a flapjack. Still thinking hard she bit off a piece.

'Well if . . .' Her mouth was too full and she pushed the food to one side, with her tongue. 'Well, frankly, if he can be put off you by the fact that some preposterous and unenforceable law makes you forbidden fruit, then I don't think he's worth pursuing. If he can be put off, that is. I don't think he can.'

'Bronwen?'

'What?'

'Yesterday. In the graveyard. He said I was too young.'

'Did he? Probably testing the water, then. He isn't going to take risks if he thinks you're only a bit infatuated – that *would* be stupid. Dammit, he's only known you for a few days; he doesn't even know if you're stable. For all he knows, it's just another schoolboy crush for you and he's terrified of you being unable to cope. He's moved too fast, on impulse, and now he's slowing up.'

'You mean he can't tell how I'd react?'

'Exactly so.'

'Well, what do I do?'

'Wait for him to make the next move. If he doesn't, which probably means he's being a coward and waiting for you to do the same, then go and see him. It's no use talking in gardens and churches and places where you can't relax. You'd have to walk along to the bloody lighthouse and, calmly and sanely, tell him that he drives you wild with desire.'

'But . . .'

'And if you don't have the courage to do that, then it probably *is* only another schoolboy crush and you'd do well to find someone at the RCM who you can't send to Dartmoor.'

Seth took another mouthful of scrumpy then lay back in the sun.

'Oh Bron, you are a help.'

'I know.'

'I never thought I'd have a conversation like this with you.'

'I'll bet you didn't. Ha!' Her laugh startled a resting gull.

'Doesn't it shock you a bit?'

'You sound disappointed. Why on earth should it?'

'Well it's not usual.'

She stared across and was jealous of his youth.

'It's usual for you and your friends. If something's usual for a few people then it's not very shocking any more, is it? The logic of insanity.'

'Do you think we're mad then?'

'Love is scarcely sane. It doesn't worry me. I'd be a lot more worried if you were in love with the youngest Pollock girl.'

'But you seem to have thought it all out before. Have you had this sort of chat with anyone else?'

'Just myself.'

It took a few moments for the full import of this to sink in. Seth raised himself on to an elbow and saw that, as she took a drag on a fresh cigarette, Bronwen's face was lined by mischievous smiles.

'No!' he gasped.

She blew out one of her little jets and stared at the horizon.

'I thought I'd told you to cut the innocent bit.' Suddenly her tone seemed less *gauche* than downright sophisticated.

'Actually,' he confessed, 'it had crossed my mind more than once.' He wanted to whoop and give her a hug, but she was too cool. Simmering, he managed to continue. 'She's got you hook, line and bloody sinker, hasn't she?' he said, then sensed he had made a terrible mistake. Her smile dropped.

'*She?*' queried Bron.

'But . . . oh.' Seth was covered in confusion.

'My dear child, you didn't think I was in love with your mother?'

'Well I . . .'

The chuckle in her voice did little to comfort.

'Bronwen the old dyke. I bet that's what she thinks, isn't it. Isn't it? Sort of absurdly self-centred conclusion she'd jump to.'

'But who?' Seth's mind raced.

'I'd have thought it was obvious.' She looked back out to sea. 'I know you're inclined to forget his existence, but you are blessed with a second parent.'

'You and Father,' he sighed.

'I shouldn't be telling you this. I promised him.'

'No. You've got to tell me now. Please. When?'

'Years ago. You were still a child.'

'When I first dragged you in at the garden door?'

There was a pause as she swallowed. 'Before that.'

'But how?' He faltered and sensed a welling feeling of betrayal. She had always been *his* special friend, his special, holiday friend. He found her first.

'Seth, I swear I had no idea you were his child.' He didn't dare look at her, but picked at some desiccated moss on the stone beside his arm, letting her continue. 'It was only a week, maybe two. He just wandered into the studio one day and started to talk. Wild talk. Something about being chased by a herd of bullocks in Puffin Cliff Field. I thought he was drunk at first. Seth, it was nothing – happened in a vacuum. He needed . . . I could have been anyone. Until you took me home that afternoon, I swear I had no idea he had a family.'

And then he saw that there were tears on her face. Desperate, he started to rise, but she forestalled his approach.

'No. No for God's sake don't touch me or I'll lose control. Just go on talking. Christ! Go on talking, *please*!'

Seth's mind went blank. He so wanted to say something but all he could do was stare at her, then at the ground, then at the cliff-face. If he could have disobeyed her and forced her into an embrace, the moment might have been shored up this side of pain – now he was powerless.

'Back in a sec,' he muttered, standing quickly. He climbed back across on to the boulders and staggered over to the field. The sheep had wandered close to the peninsula. They fled from around his sudden movement.

He kept visualizing her gaunt face capped by that crown of ginger and choking on its tears. He blushed at his reaction. Then the blush coagulated in his throat as he thought of the times his mother had joked about 'Bron the Man' and of how they had all joined in. Dear old Bronwen. Mad Bron with her Man's Bike. They had all joined in, save Father. He turned at the top of the field and saw that she had climbed down and was walking back to the path, outlandish among sheep. As he reached her side she held out her long arms and seized him in a mute hold that took all the breath from his lungs. Then the grasp relaxed and she pushed him gently ahead of her.

'Home, unnatural child, and cook some supper for that poor, unsuspecting mother of yours.'

'Hi there. It's Harry. Harry Barnes.'

'Oh. Hello.' She leant out of the window and smiled down at him. He had changed the cricket whites and blazer for a grey linen suit. 'Come round to the garden door. It's open.'

A distinct improvement. It was kinder to his air of receding youth. She looked closely in her mirror and ran a brush through her hair, wincing at the knots.

'Anyone at home?'

His voice from the sliding doors. She climbed back into bed with a couple of books she knew well enough for conversation and masked her little trespasser with her slightly raised knees and some bunched-up bedclothes.

'Hello. I'm up here. I'm afraid I've been sent to bed.'

'Oh. My word.' His voice was on the stairs. 'Perhaps I should . . .'

'Nonsense. I'm not infectious. Just bored.'

He came in. She saw at once that he had caught the sun. It made his milky eyes bluer and his hair a more interesting mouse.

'If I'd known that you were laid up in bed, I'd have brought some flowers for you to smell, or some gin to help you sleep it all away.'

'You can't buy flowers in Saint Jacobs, only fish. You haven't asked what's wrong with me?'

'Enlighten me.'

His teeth glistened. She mimicked Marilyn Monroe.

'Something unsavoury and intestinal,' she cooed.

'Enough said.'

'Quite.' She waved a graceful arm at the chair. 'Won't you sit down. Just shove those books on the floor. God, it's nice to see a human face! They've been rehearsing all day.'

He sat down and looked over the titles he had displaced.

'*Shakespeare and the Idea of the Play*. Now that *is* good.'

'Isn't it? A friend up at Oxford told me it was essential reading. He was taught by her, lucky thing.'

'Has no one been to see you?'

'Not a soul. Usually there's the charlady, but she isn't much of a conversationalist. Everyone's too busy making music. Even if they weren't, Mummy's very strange about illness and wouldn't tell anyone. She looks upon it as a sort of moral lapse – like doubt; one of those things that children go through which are best not discussed in public. She was ruthless about making sure we got through the worst as soon as possible. If a friend had measles, we'd be sent around to play in their sickroom for a whole afternoon in the hope that we'd get infected. She got terribly cross once, because she heard that I'd upset one little patient by insisting that Seth and I be allowed to kiss every one of her chicken pox scabs.'

'Monstrous!'

'Why are you so brown? I'd lain here fondly imagining that in all this glorious sun, I had at least one fellow sufferer, cloistered in the shade. I thought you'd have been slaving over a hot typewriter.'

'Heavens no. I find I can only write for about three or, at the most, four hours a day.'

'So you write all morning and visit the sick and fatherless all afternoon?'

'Usually. But sometimes there are variations. Right now I'm in one of the phases when I'm asleep all morning, bored all afternoon and only in the mood to write about seven-thirty p.m.'

'Well, what's so wrong with that? Sounds rather civilized.'

'Round about seven-thirty the Mob comes home from sawing on its catgut and we all have to sit around the farmhouse table for our convivial evening meal.'

'God, how awful!'

'What's more, it seems that most of these "Professionals" hadn't met one another before, and by the second night they were so busy making up for lost time that the place fairly reeked of licence.'

'Can't you lock yourself away in your room?'

'I try, but the noise comes through the walls.'

'At least you're spared the College horror of gory details over breakfast.'

'Thank the Lord.'

Barnes shuddered perceptibly.

'I remember there was a man who used to sound as if he was murdering this girl,' Venetia began. 'He'd start by the usual grunts and moans, and then the grunts got louder and louder. And all the time there was her pathetic wail, which I'm sure was quite fake – *that* kind of girl. Finally, he'd just be yelling with the effort as if he were belabouring her with a blunt instrument. I was quite frightened the first time I heard it. The word got around College and people started calling at unearthly hours on bogus missions, in the hope of catching the crucial moment. Benji, he's the friend who wants to write a thesis on you, by the way, Benji said it was a new concept in performance art and that I should learn to live with it as something savagely chic – a new dimension to interior design.'

Barnes laughed aloud.

'Why is it *so* ridiculous?' he asked.

'I suppose it's because lovers are so off their guard. It's

like catching someone dancing alone or talking to themselves in the mirror.'

'But don't you feel ridiculous when you do it yourself?'

'But of course.' She was caught off guard. 'That's why I try to do it as little as is humanly possible,' she lied. 'How about you?'

'Oh, it's worse for me. Well, I guess it's worse from one point of view and infinitely better from another.'

'Don't be so cagey. What do you mean?'

She wished Benji were a fly on the wall taking notes.

'Well.' He paused and recrossed his legs, leaning forward and looking fixedly at her knees. He picked his phrases deliberately. 'Clinically speaking, I suppose one would have to say that I was gay, and one of the charms of being gay is that the members of the fraternity tend to be either so unspeakably vulgar that one never meets them, or else so deliciously overwrought with confusions that in their company sex rarely finds a moment to rear its ugly head.'

'That explains it.'

'Explains what?'

'Well, not only why I liked your books, but why I felt sure when we were introduced the other night that I was bound to like you too.'

'Perhaps I shouldn't have told you.'

'Don't you like people to know?'

'Not much. It's so very limiting.'

'Then they won't. All the Professionals can think that you're making passionate love to me while they're out sawing catgut.'

They laughed.

'Seth's gay, isn't he?' he asked, with no air of enquiry. Venetia looked surprised. It seemed curiously irrelevant.

'Oh, no, I don't think so,' she replied at once, 'just polite and rather sensitive. Why do you ask?'

'Nothing really. Just a writer's magpie curiosity for character. Would you like to come to New York?'

'Who told you?'

'No one's told me anything.'

'I've been dying to go there ever since I was about twelve. I was planning on trying to get there after Finals next summer.'

'What would you do?'

'I don't know. Obviously, I'd want to get a job to pay my way, but it's meant to be almost impossible to get a work permit unless you show them written confirmation that someone will employ you once you get there.'

'I could employ you.'

Venetia's eyes grew as round as her midriff.

'Might I enquire, Sir, in what capacity?' she asked, Blanche Dubois.

'Can you type?'

'Not much, but I could learn by next June.'

'Well, I need someone to help me out, but someone with a brain and no American connections so that they could get on with the work on their own, and wouldn't keep sloping off to stay with said connections. You've got a brain, obviously, and you clearly don't have any friends in the States or you wouldn't be looking like Betty Boop.'

'Don't be mean,' she laughed.

'And I think I'm right in saying that we seem to get on OK.'

Their smiles met once more, clean and confident.

'What would I have to do besides give people the idea that I'm your good-thing-in-residence?'

'Well, I'd want you to take dictation, and you'd have to stop being rude, and help with research for novels and the lectures at Yale, and you'd have to be nice to my mother on a regular basis.'

'Oh, *God*!'

'No she's wonderful, honestly.'

'Well, of course *you'd* say that.' She felt it was time to take a little control. It was too good an opportunity to be lost in a mess of jokes. 'We've plenty of time to talk about it, at least to write. I've got a whole academic year to get BA'd, and you've got a whole one to think up a bloody good excuse for not employing me. No, but seriously.' She enjoyed stilling his smiles. He was a pushover. 'Seriously, I don't have any other plans. I want to find a job to use my brain, I *need* to find one, and I don't want to do another degree, even if I get a First. The chances of my finding an ideal or even a reasonable job over here at the moment are distinctly slender. I really can't see any reason why I couldn't come over.'

'So you're really interested?'

She assumed a US accent. 'You bet.'

'Well don't go having a change of heart and settling down in the Home Counties to have someone's babies.'

'No way!' There was a desperate edge to her chuckle. She blunted it by taking the initiative. 'Maybe you could find the time to come over to the Fens next term to give a lecture, then we could talk some more?'

He stood and walked over to the window, faking a yawn because he felt slightly ill at ease in this English girl's bedroom.

'Can your Mama see her church from here?' he asked, ignoring her suggestion. 'Oh no. Not quite. Ah, but I do see that kid brother of yours walking over the slope of the field with that old woman of the hills.'

'Seth and Bronwen?'

'Yes.'

'They've been on a walk along the cliffs.'

'Well. I must be off.'

'Stay and have some tea.'

'No thanks. It's my day to peel the potatoes. Try and get well for Thursday night.'

'Why?'

'So you can come and hear my talk on Trollope.'

'Oh yes. Sorry.'

'No. The talk doesn't matter, although it would teach you what you'd be putting up with for the next few years. No, I thought maybe we could go out afterwards. You can show me Penfasser by night.'

'Lovely. I'll try and get well.'

'Don't move. I can see myself out.'

'Bye.'

She grinned a farewell. He was rather good company. She nestled back into the pillows as he walked down the stairs. And far less acidic than Benji. She was astonished at the rapidity with which they seemed to have broken down all the usual barriers. She liked that Americanism in him. She heard him click the garden door to, and felt flattered to have become a chosen among women. She patted the hump, secure now in the belief that it could not last long. The door opened again downstairs. Her soul magnified itself.

'Hello,' called Seth, fatuously, 'I'm back.'

TUESDAY three

Mo chained her bike to a lamp-post and slung her helmet over one arm. Some kids were kicking an empty Coke can against a nearby wall. A tubby runt of a girl with carroty hair stopped and stared as Mo walked over and started up the stairs. Then she put on a Hilda Ogden accent and called out,

'Any more of them flaming bikers round these parts and I'm writing to Council, I'll give yer that straight!'

Mo climbed on through the peals of laughter. Kids gave her the creeps. She had slapped one once in a supermarket and the mother had screamed blue murder.

Suffolk House was one of the older blocks, probably from the late forties, before they started doing towers. It was red brick and long and six storeys high. The staircase ran up one side, giving on to a balcony corridor at each floor. You knew which was your floor by the colour of the doors. Green, yellow, blue, violet, red and brown. Mumsy's was a brown one: sixth floor. There was litter everywhere and a strong smell of piss. No lift, so Mo did most of her shopping for her. Mumsy said her friend had a lift and it was always breaking down and anyway, six floors were easier to climb than sixteen. A clatter of dance music and a couple of black kids with a ghetto-blaster ran out of the red balcony and passed Mo on the stairs. Off to beat the living daylights out of Carrot-Head. Mo grinned fleetingly.

She swung off the staircase on to the brown balcony and walked past the strings of gaily coloured washing to number twenty-nine. She rang the bell and waited. She rang it again. Still no one. She pushed open the letter-box and called out,

'Mumsy? Here! Mum?' The old love must be asleep. Mo pulled out her spare key and let herself in. There was a tiny hall, then a lounge, bedroom, bathroom and kitchen. Mo set down her helmet and walked into the lounge on the left.

'Hello, Mumsy.'

She had dozed off in her chair without even taking off her scarf and coat. A bag of shopping was at her feet. Mo touched her gently on the hand. In the window, Sandra let out a chirrup. Sandra the budgie. They'd been together now for so long that Mumsy wanted to get her stuffed. For the sake of the bird's dignity, Mo hoped that Mistress might go first.

Mumsy's eyes opened, blearily pink with strain. A broad smile dawned across her face.

'What? Oh, hello, lovie. Happy birthday for Saturday! Had I nodded off? How awful. Must be getting old. I must . . . oh gawd, look – I hadn't even taken off my coat!' She stood and gave her daughter a kiss. 'Hello, love,' she said.

'Hello, Mum. Ta ever so for the card.'

'Did you get it on time?'

'Yeah.'

'Oh good. I can never remember about Saturdays. Post goes queer at weekends. Did you get any nice presents?'

Mo thought of Hope.

'Yeah,' she said with a smile, 'one or two.'

'Well? What did you get?' asked her foster-mother, after a short wait.

'Come on. Let's make some tea and I'll tell you when we've sat down again.'

'No you don't. It's your special day. I'll make the tea and you sit here and put your feet up.' She pushed Mo into the settee and shuffled, humming, into the kitchen with her bags. Mo obliged, it was quicker.

'How's work?' called out Mumsy.

'OK.'

'Nothing exciting at the moment?'

'Not much. Just burglaries and that. I'm going to get my picture in the *Standard*, though.'

'Really?' There was genuine delight in the voice. 'When?'

'Later this week, maybe. Some stupid photographer of theirs following me about. Right pain.'

'But why are they photographing you?'

'I dunno. Got to photograph something, I suppose.'

'You're as bad as your father was. Too modest by half.'

Mo sat and stared at Sandra who sat and stared in her mirror. Mo tapped the cage so that the mirror swung slightly, and smiled to watch the bird move her ugly head to keep up with her image. Mumsy set down the cups and saucers, and a pink frosted cake. One candle in the middle.

'Now don't go teasing Sandra. You'll make her sick again.'

'How d'you mean "again"?'

'Well she took weeks to get over that Birdie-Chew thing you gave her,' said Mumsy, walking back to the kitchen. 'I think it was meant for mynahs or something. Didn't agree with her at all.'

The kettle started to whistle. Mumsy let it reach its highest pitch before she turned off the gas. Strict beliefs about the properties of tea and water.

Mo knew that she ought to suggest to her mother that she come to live with her in Hackney, but she could never bring herself to do it. It felt like giving up. They'd been much older than all her mates' parents at school. That was probably why they'd adopted in the first place; too old for kids of their own. They'd married late. It must have been for love because it certainly wasn't a shot-gun job. Dad had been a brikky, and trained the lads down at the gym at nights. Even at sixty his coffin had been enormous. Mumsy had always sworn he could tear a shirt-sleeve with his biceps, and Mo had boasted about this to kids at school. It made up for having only one skirt if your dad could tear a shirt-sleeve like that. Mumsy had worked nights as an usherette at the Empire, so it was always Dad who got Mo up in the mornings and saw she had enough breakfast. School was just down the road so he always walked her to the gates and then went on to his site. No boy trouble, of course, and she'd worked hard and never complained; the perfect kid. She looked at the sugar rosettes and decided that she hadn't got to know Mumsy properly until her teens.

'Tea's up,' said Mum, lighting the candle. 'Only one, I'm afraid, love, but then . . .'

'Yes, I know. I'm a blooming dinosaur.'

'That's not what I meant at all,' she went on, pouring the tea. 'It's just that, well, birthdays aren't so important once you've grown up.'

'It's a lovely cake, Mum. You are clever.'

'It's a pleasure to do,' she laughed. 'Well go on. Blow it

out.' Mo smiled up at her as she obeyed. Mumsy clapped then said cryptically, 'You stay here. I'll be back in a jiffy.'

Mo cut two slices of cake while she was gone. The cake-slice and stand only came out for birthdays. Mumsy'd gone to cake decorating classes once.

'Happy Birthday, dear Mo-oh. Happy Birthday to you!' Mum sang, returning with a large parcel. It stood about a foot high and was nearly twice as wide. 'Now,' she said, sitting down and taking a mouthful of cake, 'bet you can't guess.'

Mo's heart sank, but she kept up a smile as she undid the ribbon and pulled back the happy paper. Baring her teeth she lifted the cage on to her lap.

'Oh Mum!' she produced.

'Well, I know you're not very partial to budgies, even though I think they're much better pets, but then Bren across the way's got a hen canary as well as a boy one, and it laid a load of eggs and she let me have this fellow. Isn't he sweet? He's a boy, so he'll sing.'

The bird was enchanting; yellow, with a bright green cap of feathers on his head. He hopped from perch to perch then, as she put her head nearer the cage, he hung his head on one side and let out an inquisitive 'cheep'. Mo laughed.

'Oh Mum, he's a duck! He looks just like a little school kid with a cap on.'

'Now d'you *really* like him? I worried so much after I'd brought him back. You see I'd forgotten all about your Andy.'

'Oh heck, Andy.'

'Well, I gave it a bit of thought, and I realized how as you could hang him up in the kitchen. It's good and warm, and if he had a hook from the ceiling, Andy couldn't get up and frighten him. Bren says they like being where there's lots to see.'

'Like a bit of action, do you, lovie?' Mo asked. He chirruped back.

'There. He's talking to you. What'll you call him, love?'

'I'll have to think about it. How about Dennis – short for Dennis the Menace?'

'Oh yes. Suits him.'

'Better stay with you till I can come over in a car to pick him up, mind. He'd be blown to bits on my bike.'

'OK. Sandra'll be pleased of the company.'

'Delicious cake, Mum,' said Mo, grateful that Dennis wasn't a budgie.

'Not bad, is it? Hey, do you remember that time I made one for that nice friend of yours, Molly?'

'Maggie.'

'That's the one. And Dad said you'd said how as her parents never remembered her birthday and so why didn't we remember it for them, like as if she was one of our own?'

'I remember. You made her very happy.'

Mo remembered Maggie singing with glee as she danced round the flat in Earls Court afterwards in the shocking pink jersey dress Mumsy had knitted for her on her machine. Mo had bought her a car radio.

'Such a pity about her accident, and that,' said Mum, 'she was really nice. I remember Dad saying that he'd felt happier having you living with her for company than if you'd got married to Prince Charles.'

'Did he really say that?' laughed Mo, wanting Hope to hear.

'Something like. Here. Have some more cake. I can't eat it all myself.'

'No, honest. I had a big lunch.'

'Oh go on. Just a bit.'

'No. You'll make me fat.'

'I'd never. You've got a lovely figure. I've always said so.'

'Oh give over. I'm a barrel!'

'Stuff. You should have seen me at your age. Now that was a sight. Fat as Arbuckle I was and your dad wasn't slim. Your Nan used to say she worried how the bed could cope with the two of us at once.' Mum laughed. Then, more serious, she said, 'You know I wish you'd settle down, though. Find yourself a good upstanding man to take care of you. I don't want you getting lonely after I'm gone.'

'Mum, please. We've been through this before. I'm not lonely. I've got friends.'

'Yeah, well, friends aren't always enough. And you know it.'

'Well, they're enough for me. Now don't worry. You're the one I worry about. How's that leg? Have you been down the clinic again, like I said?'

'Well,' the old woman paused, then looked pleading. 'Well, no. You know I don't like it down there. It's so noisy and you have to sit for hours.' She rubbed the greying bandage under her knee. 'Besides, he'd only put me on some pills and they cost money.'

'I've told you, the Health Service will pay as you're an OAP.'

'Well I don't like the doctor.'

'What's wrong with him?'

'Well he's . . . he's one of them Asian ones.'

'Oh for God's sake, Mum . . .'

Once again the fond heckling of the one gave way to the tender bullying of the other. The mother was meekly led, but the daughter knew her sway would pass with the visit. In her cage, Sandra had discovered how to swing her mirror without the ugly lady.

TUESDAY four

Evelyn sat on a bench eating Dolcelatte and watching the sun go down, while the strains of his Bach solos floated from an open window. He had seemed oddly subdued over supper. Perhaps the sea air. He should have stayed at home to work on the Bevan obscenity; she had noticed his trouble with counting this morning. The sun sank almost out of sight and the garden grew too cool for comfort. Pulling her cardigan around her shoulders, she stacked the debris on to a tray, then remembered her daughter.

Venetia was sitting up with a mound of pillows behind her, reading *Barchester Towers*. Her supper tray lay on the carpet. Evelyn picked it up then sat on the edge of the bed.

'How's my girl?'

She looked up.

'Perfectly healthy and very cross.' Evelyn smiled sympathetically to let her talk. 'I know you're wondering what the Hell's the matter with me,' the girl went on. 'Well, I didn't think I was the hysterical type either. It certainly isn't wish-fulfilment.' She gently punched her abdomen. 'I didn't want a ruddy baby. I never have.'

She looked up at her mother and puckered her lower lip in mock misery. Evelyn gave her a hug then leant back and looked at her, a hand on one of her shoulders.

'Perhaps if we can both learn to relax it'll go away. Your body's trying to tell you something.' Venetia made a scornful snort. 'Well I'm only trying to help.' Evelyn, wounded, withdrew her hand.

'I know. I'm sorry.'

'I have to admit . . .' she faltered.

'What?'

'I was quite surprised at what Robbie told me yesterday. I mean about your still being . . . being a virgin.'

'Are you glad?'

Evelyn paused. 'Bloody hell! Yes. Yes I am. I'm proud of you! I know that sounds dreadful and old-fashioned of me.'

'My God! And here was I all this time, thinking that you'd be worried about me not having a sex-life.' Venetia laughed, true relief on her face. For a second, Evelyn looked concerned.

'Everything is all *right*, though, isn't it?'

'I'm not a lezzy, if that's what you're getting at.' Now Evelyn was relieved in turn. 'It's just that I've never understood this overwhelming urge to go out and get laid,' Venetia continued. 'Is it so very great?'

'It's not bad. But don't feel you have to rush.'

A pause of evasive smiles.

'How was your day?'

'Medium to long-wave vile. I'm not awfully good at new things. I think I must be getting old.'

'But you've never been "good" at them.'

'Well then, I've always had a mature outlook. How about you?'

'Lots and lots of work, *and*,' she put on a New England accent, 'Harry Barnes came to see me.'

'Really? Did he know . . . er?'

'No he didn't know that I'd a hysterical bun in my

oven – and neither does Seth yet, so he might as well not. No, I managed to hide the little stranger under lots of books and bedding, and by staying firmly where I lay.'

'How was he? I haven't talked to him yet, not properly.'

'Oh, very well. We talked about Trollope and Cambridge and things. He wants me to show him Penfasser by night. I said I'd see how I felt later in the week.'

'That's nice. Is it nice?'

'I think so. He's not horribly American, but at the same time he's pleasantly un-Etonian. I think he might be about to offer me a job.'

'A job? What kind of job?'

'As a researcher. He needs one for his books and lectures and he doesn't have much faith in US universities to produce what he wants.'

'Flattering.'

'Yes. Isn't it.'

Evelyn stood. 'Don't read too late.'

'Mother, I'm not really ill.'

'I know. But let me worry.'

'All right. If you're very good. Night-night.'

'Sleep tight.'

Evelyn walked down to the kitchen where she yawned profusely. Seth was still practising. She slid the tray on to the worksurface beside the other one. Lady Log could do them in the morning.

WEDNESDAY one

This was Jamie's first job. So as to live a little before starting at Exeter, he had come from his Gloucestershire home to stay with friends in their parents' spare London flat. The book department had claimed him because he'd done English A-Level. His school suit was too small now, and rather hot, but he preferred it to the polyester jackets of the uniform; it stopped girls from thinking he worked there properly.

He and Michelle sat back on their stools and watched the shop floor. Michelle had worked there since leaving school at sixteen. She thought Jamie was a laugh.

'Where d'you go in the break, then?' she asked. 'Didn't see you in the staff room.'

'I went out.'

'Where?'

'I went to the library.'

'You're loopy.' She clicked her tongue. 'What d'you want to go there for?'

'They've sent me a huge list of books I've got to read before starting at . . . er . . . college.'

'Christ, how boring!' she laughed. 'Whereabouts d'you go to college, then?'

'Exeter.'

'Where's that? In Dorset or something?'

'Devon.'

'Is it a poly, then?'

'No. University, actually.'

' "Actually",' she imitated his accent to perfection. 'Posh git. Only hoorays say actually.'

'Don't be cruel. I don't imitate you.'

'Go on then. Do an imitation of me.'

'It wouldn't be fair.'

'You're sweet. Oh. Can I help you, Madam?'

'You can but try. I'm looking for a collection of Radio Four religious talks. I think it's a BBC publication. They talked about it the other day. I think it's in paperback, too.'

'Oh. Well. I'm not sure. Jamie, do you know?'

'*Parson's Pleasure*, Madam?'

'Ah yes. That's it. Well done.' She smiled, seeing at once that Jamie didn't work there properly.

'You'll find it over there by the stairs on the BBC rack. There's a paperback version of it, but it may have sold out. If it has, we should be able to get you a copy by Saturday as they deliver before then.'

'Oh. Lovely. Thank you so much. I'll go and take a look.' She smiled again and was gone.

'How come you know so much, then?' asked Michelle.

'I don't. I just read that pamphlet thing Mrs Jones gets from Head Office each week. It says what all the new books in stock are. No one ever seems to ask for anything but new books – it's that kind of shop.'

'Jammy dodger. Here, have you heard about the fire?'

'No.'

'Course. You wouldn't of as you weren't at lunch. Old Dog Jones made an announcement. There was a fire up at the old warehouse in Finchley. Night-porter died.'

'Really? Was that the one they mentioned on Capital this morning?'

'Yeah. I heard that too. But they just said a book warehouse, not ours or anything. Anyway, Jones said it was suspected arson because there were only certain bits burnt – like he'd poured paraffin over just the bits he wanted to get rid of and not the rest.'

'What went, besides the night-porter, that is?'

'Well, lots of magazines – you know, not the good ones, just the useless things they print themselves. Not glossies, things like *Prognosticate* and *Monthly Almanac*. I think it's really spooky.'

'What?'

'He only went for things to do with fortune-tellings and that. Weird stuff. Old bags' stuff.'

'Sounds a bit far-fetched.'

'No, but it's true. It's that loony that's been doing all the burglaries on the Gyppos and Greeks and people. Didn't you read about it?'

'No, I don't think I did.'

'Second victim that's burned to death, thanks to his machinations. What's the time?'

'Three-thirty. Why?'

'Thank God! Time for a cup of tea and a couple of fags. Can you hang around till Jones comes to relieve me?'

'Sure.'

'Thanks, Toff. Be seeing you.'

Three customers later, Mrs Jones arrived at the counter. Since his arrival she had ignored the fact that Jamie obviously knew more about literature than she had gleaned in thirty years of service. She settled down in Michelle's place and started to tidy the biros and credit card forms there.

'Michelle gone to tea?' she observed with a question mark.

'Yes. What's all this about a fire at the warehouse?'

'Oh. Of course, you weren't at lunch, were you?'

'No.'

'Well it's that madman, the Astro-Burglar, or whatever they call him. He broke in and set fire to all the books and magazines he didn't like. The sprinklers got to it, of course, but not before hundreds of pounds of damage was done.'

'How awful.'

'Criminal. Absolutely criminal. That poor night-porter. Mr Pratt was saying in his office – I was up there just now, taking in the order dockets – he was saying it's a wonder the fire didn't spread. A lot of people live round there. What a way to go! And you know what else?'

'What?'

'I had O'Leary on the phone this morning.'

'Who?'

'You know. O'Leary. The O'Leary Column in the *Express* and things like that. He's on *Breakfast Time* sometimes, as well. No?' She was concerned at Jamie's ignorance of popular culture. 'He's a well-known astrologer, does things on the Royals, too. Well, he was on the phone to Head Office to complain about the security at the warehouse.'

'What had it to do with him?'

'He'd written a big feature on Doomsday Cookery for *Prognosticate* – you know, our fortunes magazine?'

'I know.' The boy nodded. Not wholly stupid.

'Head Office got muddled up, or something. It was dreadful. Didn't catch his name, thought he was trying to order some books and put him through to me!'

'How embarrassing!' Jamie crushed a yawn and glanced at his watch.

'And the poor man!' She assumed an intimacy with the famous. 'You know it's the *second* time he's been got at by that maniac, the horoscope one? No wonder he's feeling fractious.' Suddenly she was all masked surveillance. 'Here. Look at that one there.'

'Where?'

'Over there, by the swivel stand. He's the sort you have to watch. Big coat like that at this time of year, buttons open – they're the sort to keep an eye on.'

'Do you think he's a shop-lifter?'

'Never give them the benefit of the doubt – that's the way to lose valuable stock. Yes, sir. Would you like them wrapped?'

'Lovely.'

While Old Dog Jones busied herself with giving satisfaction, Jamie watched the suspect. He was tall and thin. He needed a shave. Were it not for his shoes, he'd have looked like a tramp. He was staring about him. No self-respecting crook would look so suspicious; he was simply unwell or confused. Knightsbridge women were forever being caught with stolen goods in their pockets; always something futile, though, like a packet of marge, as proof that one only did it for the thrill. Rich woman's bingo.

He sat up as an old man approached the counter, and stiffened with surprise to see that the suspect was coming over too, suddenly intent. Beaten to the post, the old man waited behind. The man in good shoes was almost breathless. He had a slight limp.

'You still have some copies of the *Almanac*, I see.'

'Yes, sir. That's all that's left for this month. The other stock was burnt in the fire at Finchley.'

The pocket-sized magazines lay in a display box beside the till.

'I'll take the lot, then.'

'All of them?' Jamie checked his tone; even batty customers were always right. 'I'll put them in a bag for you. Let's see. Two, four, six, eight, ten, twelve, fourteen, sixteen, eighteen, twenty, at twenty pence each; that's four pounds exactly, please, sir.'

'Thank you.'

Jamie took the notes and rang up the amount on the till. The old man pushed forward.

'You aren't taking the whole lot, are you?' he mewed.

'Why not?' Batty did not look round.

'But . . .'

'There you are, sir.'

Jamie sensed that there was to be a scene and handed over the bagful in the hope that he could thus play no part. Batty took the little magazines and started limping for the stairs. The old man was quite worked up, even angry. He followed closely and eventually dared to try a restraining hand on his fellow believer's arm.

'But that's monstrous! You only need one and there aren't any left now.' A few customers' heads turned as the thin voice rose. Jones lifted her perm.

'What the . . . ?' She checked herself.

'Just get out of the way. I need them all.'

'But you heard the lad say that there weren't any left. I really must beg you . . .'

'Damn you! Leave me alone!' Batty pushed the old man aside and ran halting to the stairs. The force of the push was ill-judged. The old man tottered backwards into the swivel stand and brought it crashing to the floor. A woman gasped out loud, and another caught him by the shoulders to prevent him falling also.

'I'll go.' Jamie took the initiative and left Jones behind. As he reached the top of the stairs, there was a piercing scream from below. He ran forward just in time to see Batty rolling down the last few steps to crack his head against the podium of a huge marble pillar. There was a momentary hush then a surge of noise as customers bore down on him. Jamie wavered helplessly at the top of the stairs. He watched as someone called out,

'No. He's alive. But look!' She had pulled back the coat to feel his heart, and now lifted up, triumphant, handfuls of books that he had stuffed into his poacher's pocket. As the crowd swelled, two policemen cut through it, called in off the street. They searched his pockets while the store medics unfolded a stretcher.

At Jamie's elbow the old man peered down to the tableau.

'I say. It was you at the till just now?'

'That's right.'

'Well do you think it would be possible for me to buy back one of his copies of the *Almanac* by some kind of credit exchange system?'

His smile bordered on the winsome.

WEDNESDAY two

Bronwen's talk had done little good for Seth's morale. The next move would never be made and so he stood in the lunch queue and made noises about what a scream it had been when Henry had kept missing that *da capo*. Jemima sailed up, good deeds waving.

'Godson?'

'Hello?'

'How's that Brahms sonata?'

'OK. Why?'

'Only OK?'

'Marvellous,' Mother chipped in.

'Why?' repeated Seth.

'I've just been attacking Peter in the nicest possible way about sycophancy to professionals and neglect of the younger generation. I won. I'm inviting myself to dinner tonight. You can play me the Brahms, and if it's more than just OK, you're going to play it half-way through my recital tomorrow.'

'Oh but J . . .' he began to protest.

'Look. If you can't accept a favour gracefully, I'll get Sophie Pollock to come and recite some Rupert Brooke.' He laughed. 'Good,' she said, 'thought you'd see the light. Are those really strawberries?' So saying, she joined the queue, some way from the back.

Seth's mind was a blank except for Brahms. He turned

with a broad grin to Mother as they walked towards the garden.

'Well, that's put the colour back into your cheeks,' she said. 'No, I promise, cross my heart, that I had nothing to do with it.'

'How dreadful. I didn't even say thank you. I was too excited.'

'She hasn't heard it yet, you know. She may decide it's just OK.'

'Beast!' he retorted. 'Seriously do you think it's up to scratch?'

'Don't ask me. I'm only a teacher, and not even yours at that. *I* think it's marvellous, but then you're my son.'

An hour later, he was sitting, tuning up, when Bronwen entered the nave, head and shoulders above her companions. She walked slowly so as to be left behind and, catching Seth's attention, jerked her head impassively to show that they had to talk. He glanced across and saw that Mother was discussing some matter with a cellist to her rear, then rose and went to his violin case on the pretext of rubbing some more rosin on his bow. Bronwen stood briefly beside and murmured:

'He's coming to see you tonight. He's coming late, so for God's sake put a light in your window and don't fall asleep.' He could ask nothing since she carried on towards the rostra. The rehearsal passed quickly. Peter was concentrating his criticism on the chorus, unaware that his leader was far away, being discovered tastefully arranged in a gloomy chamber of a lighthouse. On the way home, Seth sat readily in the back of the Volvo to be allowed to dream a little longer, while Jemima asked for Evelyn's advice on various matters without waiting to hear it. When they arrived at *La Corveaurie*, Evelyn went to get hot and bothered in the kitchen, while Seth and J said a brief hello to his sister – who had barely arranged herself in time – and withdrew to the music room. J sat at the old Steinway, playing what she could of the accompaniment, but stopping from time to time to concentrate on Seth. She was pleased, even excited. The Bach solos had given her some idea, but she had entertained little inkling of just how much progress he had made. Over the moussaka and cheerful red plonk, she said as much.

'Now, now,' Mother restrained her. 'Don't go swelling his head. He still has a great deal to learn, don't you, Peake?'

'Yes, Mamma.'

'How soon do you start at the College?' his godmother asked him.

'September.'

'Do you know, I first fell in love at that place? He was a deep and utter dish. He was at RCM with me and his sis was at RADA and they shared a wee flat off Baker Street, up in the attics. So romantic. He was a trumpeter and he played in secret with a jazz band. Frightfully sexy!'

'Why in secret?'

'He'd have lost all his credibility if people had known. He led a sort of double life; vaguely scholastic director of a mediaeval ensemble by day, hot syncopator and macho man by night.'

'How could you bear to keep him a secret?' asked Seth. 'Didn't you want to tell all your friends?'

'Not on your nelly!' Jemima looked quite shocked. 'I

was leading a double life too. In those days nice gels didn't do it. At least, they didn't talk about it. I think we were supposed to sit primly on the shelf, thinking of other, purer things until some beastly man came along and took us horribly by surprise – all within the sanctions of holy wedlock, of course.'

'What about you, then, Ma?'

'I thought you were supposed to be in charge of his spiritual welfare,' Evelyn growled.

'Only in the event of your being gathered, thank the Lord. Seth, don't go asking your mother questions like that. I've always nursed a rankling suspicion that she was one of the *really* good gels.'

'More salad, J?'

'I was reading the other day,' said Seth, 'that Deirdre Comstock's novels sell even better in the Latin countries than they do over here and in the States.'

'That abominable creature with the white coiffure and all the rocks and poodles?'

'Yes. Apparently, her ideals of the sexes – chaste, withdrawing women, and slightly, but not too rakish men – appeal to their sense of how things should be.'

'Stupid Roman Candles!' Jemima ladled scorn, 'I think that woman's disgusting. And she makes a fortune out of it, to boot. Catholic, of course.'

'I suppose,' said her schoolfriend, 'that some of them really believe in the justice of those absurd ages of consent. I mean, imagine not being allowed to get married before you're twenty-one!'

'Is that still the rule in Italy?' queried Jemima, 'I thought it was only in China now.'

'No, I think so,' Evelyn said, 'so by the time the man gets the poor thing, he's only got two images of woman in his mind – the saint who has been waiting for him all this time, and the tart he's been visiting in the interim.'

'Oh, Bath Olivers – delicious!' said Jemima, tucking in.

'When do you think girls ought to be allowed to have sex then?' asked Seth. Evelyn frowned at her plate for a moment.

'I think,' she lied, 'ideally, they should be allowed to as soon as they want to – providing they have passed some kind of contraceptive knowledge test.'

'What about the parents?'

'They aren't having the sex.'

'Yes,' said J, 'but they might beat the poor little things up when they got home. Lovely Brie, darling!'

'Well, if the little girl knows that they won't like it, I suppose she should be careful that they don't know. I mean, there's no point in being pious about it. What they don't know can't harm them. As long as she knows how to avoid getting preggers.'

'Well what about the poor little fags?' Jemima asked suddenly, in no particular direction, and making her god-son's heart lurch in its progress.

'The what?' asked Evelyn.

'Fag, darling, faggot. It's New York slang for a gay man.'

'Oh, I wish they wouldn't use that word!' Mother went on. 'It used to be one of my favourites.'

'But you *can't* say homosexual,' wailed Jemima, 'it sounds too like something people bring home from one of those warehouses in the back of the car, and put together them-selves. "The Home-O-Sexule – a new concept in living."'

Seth snorted. Evelyn continued.

'Well, I don't know. I thought we'd made it all terribly easy for them. Hasn't the law made it legal now?'

'Yes, but my dear, only the *laws* have changed, not the attitudes, and only after they're twenty-one! Personally I think it's inhuman.'

'Perhaps,' dared Seth, 'they thought that leaving sex until they were that age might put as many as possible off the idea, like enforcing celibacy on to young Italians to interest them in the Church.'

'As far as I can see,' said his godmother, 'it can only screw the little darlings up. I mean, not only do they go so mad with frustration that they spend hours in gyms and discothèques working off their excess energy, but they have to spend the crucial years of their emotional development feeling that they're a pack of crinimals. I mean criminals. Strong plonk this, Eve. Sainsbury's?'

'No. M & S, actually.'

'Seth, just think,' said J, 'the day after tomorrow you'll be free to marry Sophie Pollock!'

'Not without my permission, which I refuse, in advance, to grant him.'

'Oh Mamma, mayn't I? Please?' joked Seth. Then he thought of Bronwen and felt a little sad. Evelyn stood.

'Yes,' she mused aloud, 'it is cruel, very cruel, but the law's the law I suppose. Who's for coff?'

The topic was dropped.

When Mother looked into his room before going to bed, Seth was sitting at the table by the window writing letters. She pulled the curtains for him and kissed him on the head.

'Don't stay up late. Tomorrow's an important day, young man,' she said.

'I won't. I must just write to some friends from school.' She turned to go. 'Ma?'

'Yes?'

'Who's a lovely girl!'

'Who's a *wunderkind*!'

'G'night.'

'Sleep tight.' And she was gone.

He waited for the shutting of her door then drew back the curtains again and, having scrumpled up the bogus letter, pushed the light right up against the glass. Then he waited. And waited. The room started to feel cold because he had been sitting still for so long. He gazed at his reflection in the window-pane, made clearer by the brightness of the light, trying to pout his lips and suck in at the same time to form a miraculous cheekbone where puppy fat still lay. He tapped out the Brahms with his left fingers in the pool of light on the table top. He tried blowing bubbles with his spit. He hoped he smelt nice. He cut his nails. He cleaned out his ears with a cotton wool bud. He sat and twined the hair of his fringe while he started to reread *Rebecca*. And then he fell asleep.

His first thought when he woke was that someone had knocked at the door. In a moment of terror at the idea of Roly standing, horribly visible, on the landing, he ran over to open it. No one. Another pebble struck the window. He opened it and peered down. His slightly, but not too rakish man was standing in the road. Behind him the silver charger, circa 1930, stood waiting in the moonlight.

The night was mild and clear, and the roof of the

MG was folded back. Roly sped away as soon as Seth sat down.

'I thought you'd never come.'

'I nearly didn't; I'd fallen asleep.'

'So I gathered. Where shall we drive, Sir?'

'Show me your lighthouse.'

'I was hoping you'd say that, nowhere else is open.'

Seth laughed. All he could think was how much he loved Bronwen and how heartily Jemima would approve.

'Do you want some music?'

'Yes, please . . . or is it anti-social?'

'We've passed the last house now – only cows and sheep, and they won't mind.'

'What's the choice?'

'Let's see. Well there's *You, the Night and the Music* on the radio, or a cassette of some Wagner.'

'Not *Tristan*?'

'How did you guess?'

Roly clicked the cassette into place in the new-looking machine, and there was Brangaene singing from her turret top as the lovers abandoned themselves to untrammelled ardour in the bower beneath. Seth groaned with pleasure and lay back on his seat, the wind in his hair. By the violet light of the dashboard, he could see a wide smile on the driver's face.

'Don't tell me it's your favourite bit?' Roly asked over the roars of music and engine.

'Well . . .'

'Not very subtle, but you've room for growth.'

'Arrogant monster! Where've you been for the past few days?'

'Where've you been all my life?'

'Oh,' said Seth nonchalantly, 'sleeping, ageing, things like that.'

'Wretch!'

'All right, all right, I admit I've been waiting for a moment like this all my life.'

'Have you really?'

'Well, I can't help it if you're one of my clichés, can I?'

'For the past two days I've been doing my damnedest not to clap eyes on you. I've even been working at night to avoid rehearsals.'

'But why?'

'You know very well why, Jail-bait. Don't fish for compliments, it's Harrovian.'

'I wasn't.'

'Then Bronwen came stalking around to the lighthouse last night, tiddled as a coot – said she'd brought the flask along with her in case it turned nippy on the cliff-tops. Before she settled down for a coma on my sofa, she gave me a long lecture on *Carpe Diem*.'

'On what?'

'Living life for the here and now in case it suddenly comes to an end. She said that Modern Youth had too much respect for authority and that the essence of genius, whether artistic, philosophical or mechanical, was a total lack of faith in anything beyond the bounds of one's own impulses. Then she passed out. Oh yes. And we talked about you a bit. That's why I'm here.'

Brangaene shrieked and Mark's hunting party arrived.

'Oh, I hate this bit,' said Seth sharply, 'it all goes wrong and I hate it. Can I turn it off?' He pressed a button and the tape clicked out again. The radio came on in its stead with some black woman crooning *Stormy Weather.*

'That's much better,' he said, and lay back once more. They turned off into a field and bumped along a track.

'Look,' said Roly.

Seth looked and saw the lighthouse. The moonshine was bright after the narrow lane. Seth saw how the track ran down to some railings at the cliff-edge. Beyond that, out on the rocks, stood his lover's tower. Roly parked the car. As he got out, Seth saw that the field stood on the tip of a peninsula. Penfasser's street lights shone far off to the left. Darkened Saint Jacobs was tucked away somewhere in between.

'Why haven't I seen this before?' he asked.

'Mainly because it was so badly placed, but also the footpath stops a long way back. Bronwen was both foolish and trespassing. The last mile and a bit is all Trenellion land and there are rock-falls every year. Not safe for walking at night.'

'I know the path by the church, but only in the other direction, towards Pendarth Point. No, you go first so I can see where to walk.' Seth followed Roly down the steps that led across the rocks to the lighthouse. 'Why isn't it working?'

'No need any more. There's no heavy shipping around here now, only the local fishermen, and they know their way. Anything further out to sea uses the buoys and bells. In bad weather the light-boat goes out, in any case. I think this was a companion folly to the mine.'

'Rather like shoving a lamp-post in your front garden.' But Roly was too busy unlocking the door.

'Mustn't stay long,' he said. 'You've got to get back to catch some sleep before your big day.'

'News travels fast,' said Seth as his hopes foundered.

'Yes. Peter Grenfell came to dinner at Trenellion tonight – that's where I've just come from. He mentioned that there was to be "a slight change" in the first night programme.'

'Will you come?'

'Will you be good?'

'You can tell me afterwards.'

There was a space at the bottom of the tower's staircase filled by a mass of fruit boxes, coats, oilskins and seaside paraphernalia. There was a strong smell of paraffin.

'This is the hall,' said Roly, as they started up the stairs. 'It gets washed out by the sea about fifteen times each winter. I've got to whitewash it for them before I go.'

'I'd love to stay here in mid-January.'

'You're mad.'

'No. I love thunder and rain, as long as I'm safely indoors. Does anyone stay here then?'

'No. Jane and Lachlan usually leave it empty. They move all the rubbish from the hall upstairs, out of the wet, and lock and nail up the door. It gets quite a beating from the surf – even though it's on the inland side of the tower.'

'Oh, but it'd be marvellous! You could lie in bed and pretend to be out on the Atlantic, only without the danger of throwing up.'

'Mad. Quite mad.'

They turned another bend in the stairs and came upon a surprisingly large room. For all the snugness of sofa, bed, cooker and a few books and maps, there was still a pleasing sense of incongruity.

'Sorry about the mess. Even bachelors gay can get a bit squalid.' Roly tugged a handful of bedclothes into place.

'No, no,' Seth muttered aimlessly. 'God, what a view!'

'Good, isn't it? Lachlan knocked that window out. There used to be a dreadful porthole affair which was too claustrophobic. Of course, they have to put a shutter over it in winter. The surf reaches right up.'

'Could it smash glass this thick?' Seth admired the moonlight on the waves.

'Not on its own, maybe, but there are pieces of driftwood and pebbles it can hurl up. Also I suppose the salt would rot the frame eventually.'

'I want to come down here one winter. Bronwen says that she has to board up all her windows too. Apparently even slates get pulled down. She says it's like the Blitz.'

Seth could hear himself prattling. He wished he could find the conviction to fall silent. While Roly carried a few things over to the sink and tidied up in a vague fashion, he sat on the sofa. There were clothes discarded all over it. An old, thick cardigan was draped by his shoulder. He sat back and took a luxurious sniff while his host's back was turned.

'Sorry, it's bloody cold in here. It's being on the sea and having only the one window – it never really warms up. I'll put the stove on.' He turned and made towards the paraffin heater by the sofa.

'No, honestly, I'm fine,' Seth fibbed.

Roly reached out and touched his hands as they lay in his lap. The movement was brisk, like a doctor's, so that Seth had no time to react.

'Liar,' he said. 'You're freezing.' He crouched, opening the little door, and lit the wick.

'That's what the smell was when we came in,' Seth said. 'I love it. We used to have one of those in the bathroom at home in winter.'

'Getting up for school when it was still dark?'

'Yes, that's right.' Seth smiled at the shared recollection.

'Bung some music on. It's behind you. Do you want some brandy? All I've got, I'm afraid.'

'Please.' Seth leant over the arm of the sofa and looked through the records. 'Are these all yours?'

'Yuh. Don't sound so surprised.'

'No, I'm sorry. It's just that I hadn't . . .'

' . . . thought of me as the musical type? I'm not, really. At least, I have to have music around, but I'm hopeless at talking about it to people.'

'The instinctive artist?' Seth said, putting on a Saint-Saëns piano concerto.

'That's right. Brand me. Muscular inarticulacy stumbling into genius.' Seth laughed, then stopped as the wrong music began. It was on the other side. The powerful speakers, the only things in the room that stood free of the pervasive clutter, declared the jazzy surprise of the Ravel G Major concerto.

'Oh, sorry. Wrong side,' said Seth.

'I was going to say, it's not exactly nocturnal. No, don't take it off.' Seth was reaching for the tone-arm. 'Just jump to the slow movement.'

'Now who's being cliché-ridden?' he laughed.

'But it's good. It works. Here.' He passed Seth some brandy in what looked like a cleaned-out mustard jar. Duralex. A school glass. 'I suppose you want to see the studio.'

'Yes please. But only if you don't mind.'

'I'm not *that* pretentious. A bit of stone's just a bit of stone. No, let's go up there anyway – it's more comfortable.'

Seth knew of nothing more comfortable than sitting surrounded by the dirty laundry of the one you love, but he stood up and took a sip of brandy. It brought tears to his eyes. He had only had the stuff on Christmas pudding. Roly picked up the stove by its handle and headed towards the staircase, pausing only to flick a button on the stereo system. At once the music sprang up the stairs ahead of them. Suitably impressed, Seth followed.

Instead of a narrow walkway around a battery of revolving lights he was surprised by a circular room almost as large as the one they had left. The entire light mechanism had been removed. A floor had been laid, and was covered in rugs; the Indian kind, decorated with bold stripes of colour. The ceiling was a metal dome, supported on wooden beams and on a wall of glass and metal that ran all the way round. There were two elderly armchairs of the formless, engulfing kind. Roly hurried ahead and hid something beneath one of them as he entered.

'It's incredible!' Seth exclaimed, walking around by the windows. 'How on earth did they get the lights out?'

'Apparently it was a terrible job. They virtually had to rebuild the top section. It was all over some architectural mag.' He flopped into a chair, and watched in amusement as Seth stopped by the trestle table of works and works-in-progress.

The pieces were small – none more than a foot high. Carved in smooth, white stone, flecked with tiny fossils and shells, each carried reflections of the human form while maintaining an overall design that was wholly abstract.

'Roly, they're beautiful. Could I pick one up . . . if I'm very careful?'

'Go ahead. They're meant to be held.'

Seth took one gently in his hands. It was like a tiny curtain fashioned in stone, at least, it had gentle undulations in its form like the folds in a hanging cloth. At one point, though, the folds were disturbed by what seemed to be a part of a human face pressing from the other side. Seth felt the surface. He turned the piece in his hands to see the other side, but where he'd expected to see the back of the head that was pressing through, he found only the reverse of the folds on the front. He smiled, tricked by a conjuror.

'What?' asked Roly.

'It's like a ghost.'

'Top marks.' Roly sounded pleasantly surprised. 'It's a ghost piece. Most of them are. It was Bronwen's idea. She drove over with me to Portland for the day to collect the rocks – she wanted to go fossil-hunting below the cliffs – and on the way home she told me that fossil stones are special because they have a memory. I thought about it when I started playing around with the stuff to see what it could do. On the first day it kept misbehaving, splitting open because of the shells and ammonites. Then I remembered seeing photographs of the excavations at Pompeii and Herculaneum – you know? – where they found whole bodies trapped in dust and turned into living sculptures. I thought I'd . . . well,' he snorted bashfully, 'thought I'd try to raise the memories of each stone.'

'Don't laugh at yourself,' Seth said, as he set the piece

down again and let his gaze trail, lingering, over the others. 'It's a strong idea.' He turned, and parodied Roly's grudging aesthetic. 'It works . . .' He walked over to the other chair and sat with a painless sigh.

'Suppose so,' said Roly, taking another sip of brandy and wishing it wasn't so hard to make the next move.

Seth listened to the Ravel. The assumed naivety of the slow movement would be drawing to a close soon. He had to make a move before the finale broke in and reminded Roly to drive him home. He took a gulp of brandy, wincing until the burn had soaked down to his chest, then he stood with his eyes down and went to sit at Roly's feet.

'You're better placed for the speakers. Can't have a lopsided finale.'

Thankful for the muttered half-truth, Roly made room for Seth's shoulders between his knees. Safe from the gaze and smile, Seth could relax. He leant his head against the leg on his left, delighting at once in the warmth of the spirit, the spirit of the music and the music of battered, slightly dusty jeans. When Roly ran a hand through his hair, he leant his head back and smiled up from the young man's thighs.

'Hello,' he said.

'Hi.'

Bending forward, Roly kissed him lightly on the top of his forehead, where the down merged into the line of his curls. He had meant to check himself, to lift his head back afterwards, but Seth quickly raised an arm, putting his fingers softly but firmly on Roly's neck. Roly brought his lips down once more, this time between the boy's eyebrows. Seth smelt the brandy on his breath. He put down his empty glass and twisted around into a kneeling position, taking Roly's head between his hands, and pulled the other's mouth against his own. They kissed, hesitant at first, then more fiercely, as Seth tightened his grip behind his lover's neck and slowly compelled him out of his seat.

The music was now rushing along, hopelessly frisky beside such concentrated solemnity. For the first time in his life, Seth was kissing without keeping an ear open for an approaching junior, or wondering where the next breath was going to come from. The concerto crashed to an end and was replaced by the sound of the sea and the rhythmic bumping of stylus against record label. Heedless, the embrace continued. Seth had now slid away from the chair and was lying on the rugs, holding Roly tightly to him, his eyes forced shut by the keenness of sensation. He moaned to himself as the sculptor traced a line of kisses across his jaw to an earlobe.

Then Roly's glass toppled from its perch on an arm of the chair and smashed on a small patch of bare boards beside his head. His hand rushed to Seth's face to shield it from any splinters of glass. He laughed as he sat up. Seth smiled up at him as he picked pieces of glass from his guest's splashed hair.

'The world intrudes,' he said quietly.

Roly stood and tossed the broken glass into a bin by the trestle table. Seth sat up against the chair and stared at the ring of flame inside the stove.

'Oh shit!' said Roly.

'What?'

'Look.' He held out his watch. 'It's two-thirty. You've got to be up at sparrow's fart.'

'At what?' laughed Seth.

'Very early. I'd better drive you back. I won't be responsible for your giving a sub-par performance.'

'I guess not.'

'But I want to see you. How about tomorrow night? I'll come to the concert and we can talk afterwards.'

He turned off the stove and they started downstairs. A brisk walk from temptation.

'I'm playing just before the interval. We can talk halfway through.' Seth stood in the doorway and watched as Roly switched off the record player and grabbed his jacket.

'Didn't you have a coat?'

'No. Just this.' Seth tugged at his jersey.

'Pull this on.' Seth took the cardigan and pulled it on. It was huge and well-worn. He hummed his approval.

'That better?' asked Roly, grinning.

'Smells good.'

And they stood in the doorway for a final kiss before walking down to the rocks and up to the waiting car.

Evelyn had lain in bed and tried vainly to read. Her concentration strayed to the comments at dinner, and to Jemima's jibe at her priggishness. She disliked it when contemporaries mentioned love and marriage because she could tell they were sitting there looking at her and wondering what it must be like to go through life having been to bed with no one but one's husband. Marriage was one thing, but love . . . as she brooded, uncomfortable and sad, Berlioz's *Memoirs* sank neglected to her lap and the spectre of Camilla Blair rose before her once more.

Camilla had been sombre sixteen. Her back was straight

as a silver birch, her arms were graceful and long, and her hair was dark and glossy as a concert grand. Together they had been sent riding because they were too tall safely to join in lacrosse. Together they had sworn vows of fidelity till death, lain in the woods reading Browning and Catullus, knelt at the altar for Confirmation, and together they had learnt the pungency of secret passion. They swore to withhold the vessels of their spirit from male desecration with due savagery but their dreams never encompassed anything beyond the bounds of the school. When they left, Camilla trotted off to the Sudan to do VSO. There had been a farewell tea in Fortnum's and a few excited letters, then a hurtful silence. At last, after months of waiting, there had been a strained note from Commander Blair in some village near Lowestoft, explaining in bleak English that Camilla had died in a fever hospital, that the funeral had been a quiet family affair but that, as a close friend of his late daughter, would Miss Davenham care to attend a memorial service the following Saturday. Miss Davenham had never summoned the courage to go. Of course, she knew now that she was not, well, that sort of woman; she had given the matter considerable thought and had come to the conclusion that Camilla was an exception to a rule.

As she tried once again to read Berlioz's account of his dealings with the Ministry of the Interior, she thought of Huw in some clinical Viennese library, and was perturbed, as she had been countless times before, by the gnawing suggestion that the only person for whom she had ever felt passion uncoloured by duty lay tossed across a rose-bed in a Suffolk churchyard.

A landing floorboard creaked and Venetia came in. In

her hurry she had come without a dressing-gown and her once long t-shirt clung absurdly to the bloated contour of her abdomen. Evelyn was shocked – the girl was even larger than she had imagined. Venetia looked excited.

'Mummy?'

'Are you all right, darling?'

'It's Seth.'

'What's wrong with him?' At once the book was thrust aside.

'Well I was woken up by this noise. And I lay there for a second and then realized that someone was throwing stones at the house. I waddled over to the window and saw that boy – the blond who was at the party, the one who talked to Seth for ages. He was throwing pebbles up at Seth's window and the next thing I heard was Seth "tiptoeing" out to join him. They've driven off in his sports car.'

'Well, I never!' Evelyn laughed.

'Aren't you a bit nervous? I mean, it's well past midnight.'

'No, darling, it's OK. They've just gone for a night drive along the coast, I expect. It was probably all pre-arranged and frightfully exciting, and we weren't supposed to know. Don't let him know you found out.'

'But . . .'

'Honestly, he's perfectly safe. Roland's rather nice, actually, a sculptor. Terribly talented. I expect he's partly doing it to humour Seth; give him an adventure. You know what boys are.'

Until Venetia saw Seth being driven off by that pompously good-looking young man, she had never seriously entertained the possibility that he might be queer. One never did imagine it in one's own family; rather like burglaries, or babies with spina biff. Of course she knew plenty of the creatures. Being friends with queers was one of the things that made her coterie so trendy. (Benji was one of her closest friends.) Still, one never liked to think of them *doing* anything; they simply *were*. The whole attraction was that they wanted to do nothing to her, and tended to do nothing to anyone else. At least, they kept it quiet. Men like Barnes came with all the advantages of a boyfriend and none of the squalor. She despised the titles 'fag-hag' and 'fruit-fly' since they suggested that the advantages were less mutual than they seemed, placing one in the same category as the Useful Maiden Aunt. She might not stay a maiden, but it now seemed less likely that she would ever become an aunt. Perhaps Seth was worth cultivating after all. Then she remembered that he had disappeared into the night with another man, and not simply been discovered, like Benji, in one of her ball gowns. Once one of her pet faggots hoisted the lurid fact of S.E.X. before her unwilling notice, he fell from grace, no longer sensitive but rather common. Aligning standards of chastity with those of breeding could salve a catalogue of social grazes. Breathless with the discovery therefore, she had hurried to the maternal bedside, only to find herself cast in the unenviable role of sport-spoiling sneak. Mummy was being even more Victorian than usual. Venetia tried to penetrate the moral bombazine.

'You'd never have let me drive off into the middle of the night with dishy men when I was his age,' she thrust.

'Yes, but . . . in my former ignorance, I'd have suspected you of wanting to run off with them for more than just the sea-view by starlight.'

'Well how do you know that that's all there is to this little jaunt?'

'What? Oh Venetia, *really*! It's just a jolly jape.'

Her daughter gave up the attempt and wandered off to bed.

Evelyn set Berlioz back on the bedside table, turned out the light and worried like hell. At last, after wrestling with her conscience, and Camilla, she decided not to bring the matter up unless forced to do so by her son or by the production of, ye gods forfend, concrete evidence.

She fell into a fitful sleep and then was jolted awake by a terrible sound. She turned on the light and saw that it was exactly two o'clock. What had started as a scream and now broken into an hysterical laugh, was coming from Venetia's room. She threw back the covers and ran out on to the landing. She shivered. Standing there in the dark with that girl's helpless laughter was unnerving. Her mind lurching back to the years of nightmare-comforting in Hampstead, she pushed open her daughter's door.

She was struck immediately by a strong scent of roses. It was almost overpowering; like walking into an overheated florist's shop.

'Darling, what's . . . ?' she began as she turned on the light, then was stunned into silence. Venetia lay on her bed. The bedclothes were pushed aside. She was quite naked; the t-shirt had been tossed to the floor. Her face was streaming with tears, her eyes tight with mirth. Her hands were clasped to her belly which, in the seconds following Evelyn's entry, finished the last inches of what appeared to have been a lengthy deflation. There was no blood, apparently no pain, only the laughter and that sweet, unaccountable scent of roses.

Overcome, Evelyn quickly flicked off the light, closed the door and leant for a while against the landing wall. She gazed out into the darkness beyond the banisters until her heart's pounding stopped. Then, with the poised humility of one who has just received a reprieve from a new career as the latter day Saint Anne, she withdrew to her chamber and fell weeping to her knees.

THURSDAY one

McEnery looked up from her desk as Mo walked into the station.

'Hello, Boss,' she said, 'sorry to drag you from your sickbed.'

'That's OK,' said Mo, 'just a belly bug. Either that or my mum's baking. Had me up half the night. It's worn off now. How's our friend?'

'He came round late last night. Medical have given him ten stitches across the scalp. No fracture, which is pretty amazing. They didn't need to keep him in another night, although there seems to be some mild amnesia. They brought him in here after lunch. He's in number five.'

'What kind of amnesia?'

'Can't remember name, address or family.'

'Convenient for them.'

'Doctor Stuart said it was possibly some kind of compensation – that he might be protecting himself from the shock.'

'Has Timson or anyone been in questioning him?'

'No one. He's been asleep, but he rallied about an hour ago, when I took him some tea, so I thought it best to ring you and let you talk to him first.'

'Good girl. I'll go in now.'

'It's a bit embarrassing, really.'

'What is?'

'Well. I dunno. The way it's all turned out, with chance playing into our hands.'

'Never mind.' Mo's manner had hardened. 'We've got him – that's the main thing.'

McEnery raised an eyebrow and passed her the keys from a board that hung beneath the desk.

'Oh, yes,' she said, 'a letter came for you this morning.' She proffered the envelope. Mo took it, then walked aside and opened it. She recognized the rough handwriting at once.

> From:– The Squat, Pollock House, 123, Jackson Road, London NW1 (Behind Marylebone shunting yard). Forgive hasty departure and nasty message. *This* little pig says she's sorry. Come and say it's all right, tonight (Thursday) at tennish. Your loving Sister.
>
> 'Happy Birthday – late,' the back said.

Feeling a rush of blood to her face, Mo folded the note as quickly as she had opened it and, thrusting it into her pocket, walked downstairs to the basement. She let herself into the corridor of the detention area and leant against the cold bricks for a few seconds to check her breathing. The surroundings soon killed her smile for her.

The detention area had recently been refurbished and was clean and impersonal as a hospital. The cells upset her. Something sinister about the way each had the essentials – bed, light, toilet and basin – and yet all adapted for the 'safety' of both prisoner and keeper. The toilet had no seat, its tank was inside the wall and the flush was automatic. The radiator was boxed away beneath the built-in bed and automatic. The table and chair were fixed to the floor. The light was built into the ceiling and operated from outside. The first time Mo had seen inside a new cell, she'd thought immediately of a story she'd read as a kid where a boy climbed through his washbasin mirror and found a world similar to his own in general respects, yet eerily different in detail.

Mo stopped outside the fifth door, pressed a button and spoke into a grille in the wall when a green light shone.

'Barry? Yeah, I'm going into number five now. If I'm not out in ten minutes, come and find me, there's a love.' She unlocked the door and went in.

He lay on the bed staring up at the low ceiling. They'd given him a shave in Medical, on the scalp as well as the face, so they could put in the stitches. As Mo sat down in the chair, he turned his head and stared at her.

'Hello,' she said, 'I'm Detective Inspector Faithe. How's the head?'

'How can I tell when there isn't a mirror?'

The voice was educated, as she'd expected. It was also dead and tired.

'How does it feel?'

'How would you expect?'

'Point taken. I'm feeling rotten too, so I won't keep you long. Just a few questions. What can you tell me about Marina Stazinopolos, Papas Mercouri, Katya Garcia, Seamus O'Leary and Millicent Du Cann?'

He swung himself around into a sitting position and stared back at her.

'Apart from the fact that they're all Catholic, they're a bunch of fakes. Rather, they are; Du Cann was – being dead.'

'How d'you mean "fakes"?'

'They make a fortune telling fortunes and telling fortunes is one of the oldest con-tricks in the history of mankind.'

'You don't believe in it?'

'Correct.'

'Sensible fella. Then why did you break into each of these persons' flats and steal or destroy items connected with their work?'

'Not because I believed.'

'So you admit you committed each burglary?'

'It would be a lie to deny it.'

'You'd be prepared to admit to each charge of burglary in court?'

'Of course.'

'What do you know about the warehouses in Sandridge Road, Finchley?'

'I committed an act of arson in one a couple of nights ago, as I recall, which resulted in an accidental death.'

'Why haven't you asked for a lawyer yet?'

'Because my case is plainly indefensible.'

'Did you break into each property because you had some kind of a grudge against these people? Did you disapprove of them as "fakes"?'

'I disapproved of them, but my actions bore no taint of personal malice or moral judgement.' He winced minutely and passed a hand across the stripe of shaven, tapestried scalp.

'Can you take this, or shall I came back later?'

'No. Just a twinge. I won't bore you with details of my work. Suffice it to say that I am, I was, an academic in a field situated somewhere between theology and history. In the course of researching my next book – research that started, let me see, some five or six months ago – I made an alarming discovery. Doubtless this'll seem unlikely to you. It did to me at the time . . .' He stopped suddenly.

'Go on.'

'There's no point in my telling you all this. I've admitted guilt. Further details would be irrelevant.'

'Detection's over now. This is on private time. You've got me interested.'

'That wasn't detection, it was a bloody catechism.'

'You what?'

'Never mind.' He smiled for a second and sighed. As he continued, tears began to brim in his eyes and run down his cheeks. He didn't seem to notice. Mo had seen many a grown man cry in this room. It seemed to be a result of relaxing. 'I was following up some ideas a colleague of mine had had concerning the powers of mass-hypnosis.'

'Yeah. I saw the book on your desk.'

'You've been to my house already?'

'Yes.'

'How amusing.'

'Went there on Thursday morning.'

'You saw my notes?'

'Yeah.' She opened her notebook and found the word. 'What does "psychosomatic" mean, then?'

'Induced by the power of mind. I was delving into the history of the apocalypse concept, and various men's views of how the world would end. Then I got side-tracked, at least, it seemed like a side-track at the time, into the realms of prediction by astrology, the Tarot and so forth. It had struck me that, given the idea that something must happen, and given the will – possibly subconscious – for it to take place, the human mind could order its own destiny to a remarkable extent. My colleague had already applied this theory to political genius and the way in which a will to dominate can rise so effortlessly to domination.'

'Yeah?'

'I simply applied this concept on a racial scale to prophecy, and deduced that, theoretically, the human race could will itself to an end simply by a preoccupation with the Apocalypse, with a sense of ending. The horror started when I visited a cross-section of the "profession" or read their books. By a disgusting coincidence, patterns of upheaval, an immense change, such as could be taken to refer to the end of the world were lined up right the way across the board as it were. The palmists don't have much to do with the Jehovah's Witnesses, who in turn don't have much traffic with the Tarot readers or the astrologers, but in visiting such people and in doing some supportive "prediction" of my own by their techniques, I saw . . .' He broke off, startled by the realization that he was weeping. 'Oh dear,' he said, in the same dead voice that he had used all along, and wiped his face and eyes with a handkerchief. When he looked up from doing this his face was quite calm.

Mo's first impulse was to laugh. There had been such a promising build-up, starting with the discovery of that fat Greek baggage strapped to her chair, that the final motive rang out stupidly in the blankness of the cell. There was something in his dignity that killed the impulse however, and she found herself gazing back in sincere, nervous curiosity, and asking,

'When's it going to happen, then?'

'Tonight. In a few hours. Now I am very tired. Do you think I might . . . ?' He lay back on the bed and returned to his staring at the ceiling. There was a knock at the door.

'Boss?'

'It's OK, Barry. Nearly through, thanks.' She slid a hand into her pocket and felt Hope's letter. 'That's why you don't care, isn't it?' she went on. She thought of the huge house in that row of huge houses in NW3, and of the dolly-bird's photo. He stared at the ceiling.

'That's right,' he said.

Mo stood and walked over to the bed. When he snatched her hand she didn't flinch. He was helpless. She could break his arm if he tried anything. He snatched her hand and pulled her palm against his cheek. His face was twisted with sobs. His stringy body shook. The hand that wasn't holding hers clenched and writhed at his side. She sat on the bench beside him, watching his tortured features, letting him press her hand. His face was all bone. He was racked with one last spasm. A faint, wet sighing issued from the back of his throat. The silent wail past, she laid a hand, gentle, on his shoulder.

'Here,' she asked, 'is there anything you want?'

He controlled himself with a deep intake of breath. 'Can I trust you?' he managed.

'I'm all you've got. They don't listen in.'

'There were several things of mine in my coat and trouser pockets. When I arrived here, that girl with the dreadful hair locked them up somewhere just outside the door. I was pretending to be asleep; I heard everything.'

'Well?' asked Mo, with a ghost of a smile.

'There's a letter from my wife with some pills in it. Could you bring it to me?'

Mo stared for a while at the empty man who stared at the ceiling, and breathed, 'Yeah. You've earned it.'

She drew her hand from his grasp, and stood. She let herself into the corridor. She glanced along its length. No one to be seen. She unlocked the small cupboard set into the wall beside the cell door. It said 'FIVE' on it. The coat dangled from a hook and the contents of its pockets were set out on a shelf. Mo made a quick mental note of what was there, then snatched the envelope and locked the door. He didn't move as she set them on the bed beside his head, but he thanked her and said that he didn't feel like any supper.

'That's all right, my lovely. 'Course you don't. We won't disturb you till the morning.' She left quietly and locked him in. Outside she pressed the button and spoke into the grille.

'Barry? Mo. I've finished in there now. While I remember, he's feeling pretty terrible and he doesn't want anything else tonight so you can tell Bella to leave him off her tea list, OK?'

She walked back to the office, sat at her desk, and quickly typed out a list of the personal belongings, save the letter and pills. Then she took it next door. McEnery was sipping a cup of tea.

'Tea. Yes, please.'

'OK, Boss,' said McEnery.

'Bad girl, by the way.'

'What have I done now?'

'Forgot to make a check-list didn't we?' She waved the piece of paper. 'Most unlike you.'

'Oh Christ! I'm sorry.'

'That's all right. Lucky I thought to check. I've done one here, but file it away will you, and put a copy of it back inside his locker when you've a second?'

THURSDAY two

On what appeared to be the first day of a heatwave, the vestry was mercifully cool. Seth's suit jacket hung from the back of his chair; he had no intention of putting it on until the last possible moment. He suffered from the heat, and knew that, once surrounded by over-dressed, sun-shocked bodies, he would melt. His violin lay on a chair beside him, tuned to perfection. Twice over. He sat forward, his elbows resting on his knees to keep his armpits exposed to the remaining minutes of cool air. His nose and cheeks prickled, for he had fallen asleep in a deckchair that afternoon. The day had passed by at a rush, but now, as he sat listening to Jemima's performance, all was still. To the other side of the door a churchful of impassive bodies and serene, motorway faces stared at her: soon they would be staring at him. He stirred himself to check once more that his fly was secure and his nostrils void.

As they prepared to go their separate ways in the churchyard, Mother to talk to friends, he to tune up, she had thrust a small packet into his palm, with a 'Happy Sixteenth in advance, because you're a brave boy,' and then left him to his nerves. A watch. Oddly enough, his first. Restrained, with no innovations beyond a window where the date appeared, the present circled his wrist.

The last movement of the Beethoven sonata (Jemima's adaptation) came to an end and the vestry caught the applause. Seth stood at once. He had momentarily lost concentration. He whipped on his jacket, lifted instrument and bow, then stood a few feet from the nail-studded door. He was poised and calm now, but for safety's sake, as the old latch lifted and the oak mass started to swing towards him, he muttered between his teeth.

'Yes please, God. But not for me.'

Venetia had helped Harry with his day's chores at the farmhouse, and drunk hibiscus tea with him in his room. Then the two of them had escaped the communal meal – an early one on account of the recital – driving over to Saint Jacobs. Seeing that the Volvo was still parked outside *La Corveaurie*, she had made him turn into a field by the crossroads and there they had waited, plunged in helpless giggles by their conspiracy, as mother and son drove past them to Trenellion a few minutes later. During the short wait, she had praised his lecture in detail and he had reiterated an invitation to his motherland; both were now effervescent as a consequence.

'Now,' she declared as they walked into the deserted house, 'if we're going to have a real *Soirée des Prolétariats* we have to start it by getting in the mood. So, off with crappy Radio Three and on with something boppy.' She twiddled knobs on the stereo system and found her way through the haze of interference to a disco goddess singing, with panache and scant evidence of regret, of her failure in love. Smiling, and feeling younger in the company of this heady blossom, Barnes lounged on the sofa.

'Wooh!' went the blossom, tapping her feet, 'and now,' she smacked her slender hands together, 'we've got to have a beer and a packet of crisps!' She skipped to the kitchen, where she clicked the radio on as well, and sang along to the song as she fished some crisps out from behind the bread bin and found some beer in the fridge.

'If only I'd realized that this was our last time, I'd have hugged you 'n' kissed you until you was all mine,' sang the Goddess. Venetia joined Harry at the sofa where he was dipping into a catalogue of a recent exhibition of Victorian pornography at the Hayward.

'Uh-uh,' she said, snatching the publication away and tossing it to the floor, 'books is *streng verboten.* All you can have is beer from the can, my gorgeous body and,' she scrutinized the packets, 'Prawn Cocktail or Bar-B-Q flavour crisps.' Harry moaned delightedly and raised his can.

'To next summer,' he toasted.

'Up yours 'n' all,' she replied, and they drank.

She took a handful of crisps and stuffed them into his mouth.

'Aren't they filthy?' she cried, 'Mummy made such a fuss about being seen with the things in the supermarket queue – macrobiotics and indestructible bags and all that – so I pacified her by saying that I was trying to give our visitor a genuine cultural experience.' He giggled and puffed crumbs on to the sofa. Venetia fell back and wailed. At last he recovered and asked, with a faint note of sarcasm in his honey and sun-cream voice,

'Say, won't your kid brother be a bit sore at you missing his concert? I'd have thought it's a bit special to be playing in the first one of the festival.'

'Yes, I suppose it is. I guess so,' she mocked his accent because he liked it, 'but Seth prefers it if I don't go to his recitals. He says that it's too painful knowing how bored I am. Besides, he's playing something I've heard before. If he ever gets "sore", I could get "sore" back at him for not reading my essays and for only coming to plays that feature good-looking sensitive types. Oh God! It's *this*. I love this song! Dooboo ba da da Dee doobee doo bawa,' she sang along, clicking her fingers for a while, then took some more beer. 'It's really great. I think it's meant to be based on some old Zulu chant about freedom, or something. No . . . while I remember. You reminded me.'

'You *are* excited, aren't you?'

'Of course. I'm spending a night on the town all alone with a famous novelist. It's about Seth. You were quite right.'

'Really?'

'Well, I think so. At least, he was picked up well after midnight last night by that rather dishy hunk who's been making angels for the church.'

'No! Not the blond with the broad back and the biteable chin?'

'Don't tell me you fancy that *prick*?'

'Well, no. I was admiring him as a purely aesthetic object.'

'Have some more crisps.'

'Thanks.'

She rocked to and fro with her legs up on the sofa and felt the conversation lapse. The euphoria threatened to burn out too soon. She stared at the smiling face on the cover of *Tatler* and complained,

'God! I could really do with some coke right now.'

'Surely you're forgetting that we're honorary members

of the Prole Front for the evening. I don't think Happy Dust is quite their scene.'

'True. Very true.' Her concentration had faltered quite. He smiled and opened the breast pocket of his shirt.

'But,' he said, smiling as her interest rekindled, 'but I do have these,' he said, passing one over, 'and *these* I think they could afford.'

'Grass?' she laughed with disbelief in her eyes.

'Home-grown, hand-rolled, and very Prole.'

'Wooh! Tacky, man. Got a light, babe? Thanks. Oh, this is *so* seventies!' And she was happy again. She took a few drags, glad that he didn't notice her failure to inhale, then jumped into action.

'My God, we can't sit around here getting mellow, we've got a night to organize. Now where's the local paper? A film, then a fish'n'chiperama, then a bop.' She found the paper and squatted on the floor, scanning the entertainments column. In seconds she was shrieking with pleasure.

'Yes! *Emmanuelle and the Sisters of No Mercy*, followed by *Sex in a Women's Penal Colony*.'

'Wonderful.'

'OK? Won't make you park a custard or anything?'

'I managed the crisps, I can manage anything.'

'Great. Then we can go to the Happy Dolphin. Actually the fish is really good and fresh there. Then I thought the Tintagel Palais. It's full of fags on Thursdays.'

'How do you know?'

'I spent a happy afternoon with Josh once, flipping through a dreadful gay guide he'd found.'

'Which is he?'

'Just another of your rivals for my affection. Now look,

we've got to get our skates on or we'll miss the local adverts and they're the best bit. I would suggest taking the bus a) so you could drink and b) so as to savour the true mindless tart experience of catching the last one home, but I think we're too late. You'll just have to drive really fast to make up for the want of authenticity.' So saying, the Virgin and her Fairy set off for a good night out.

After the final chord, Seth froze for a moment, then dropped his arms to his sides and was engulfed in clapping. His mouth twitched involuntarily into a smile and he gave a little bow. There was a cheer from the back of the church where some late-comers had been forced to stand. He turned to Grigor to bow again with him, but his accompanist had moved obstinately behind the piano, and stood smiling. As Seth tried to wave him over, he merely smiled more broadly and began to join in the clapping. Defeated, Seth gave one more shallow bow, and started for the vestry. Then he remembered his music and stumbled back to pick it up and tuck it beneath his arm. There was a friendly burst of laughter amid the applause. As he closed the vestry door and leant against the chill stone of the wall to recover, he heard the rumble of displaced seats and a burst of pent up conversation. Mother and Jemima would be round soon. Still slightly dazed, he strapped his violin into its case and stood gazing across the churchyard as he loosened his bow.

'Bravo!' They had come straight from the church, to avoid the crowds. J clapped.

'Well done, darling!' Mother rushed forward and held his head in her hands, taking him in. Jemima laughed.

'The great wet blanket. D'you know, she got through two of her hankies and my one, to boot, during that?' Seth laughed. Mother's eyes were still pink.

'You great ninny,' he said, 'I made so many boobs. Grigor coped wonderfully.'

'Probably didn't notice. He rarely does, it's part of his job.'

'And well done, Godmother Beale,' Seth went on. 'You've no idea how hard it was going on after your Beethoven.'

'Oh, bilge. You're a very clever boy and we're both proud of you, ain't we, Mum? Now I could do with a good stiff gin.'

'Get you in the mood for Bartok?' asked Seth.

'Hole in one. As performers and family, we should be able to jump a few queues. Come on.'

The sun was half-way below the horizon and had suffused the few clouds with a deep pink.

'Lovely,' pronounced Evelyn, as they scaled the wooden steps placed over the wall for the evening, and rounded the church.

A drinks tent had been erected outside the porch. The grass around it buzzed with a well-behaved audience rewarding its virtue. Most of the crowd were in evening dress. First timers and a few one-off visitors stood awkwardly out from the mass, declared by their leisurely holiday appearance and the interest they were taking in the church and surrounding coastline. A few practised Friends of the Festival were wolfing picnics around their cars or against walls. Guilty Glyndebourne. Grigor emerged from the back of the tent beaming, with a trayful of Martinis.

'Bless your cotton bedsocks, darling!' said Jemima, as he presented the cocktails.

'Grigor, that was marvellous. Thank you,' said Seth. He still felt touched and embarrassed at the man's refusal to share the limelight.

'Oh, I don't know . . .' he grinned. 'You were not so bad yourself.' Then he laughed aloud at his wit.

The four of them had no need to circulate. The people they wanted to see came to them. Seth tripped up increasingly in his attempts to swing the praise on to Grigor and Jemima. He glowed as he saw heads turning in the crowd outside the tent, and as strangers smiled shyly at him on their way back to their seats. J and Grigor hurried back to the vestry, Martinis in hand, leaving mother and son together by the cliff-top walk.

'Did I come up to scratch?'

'I'll say. Jane was sitting by me and she was a perfect brute, trying to embarrass me in front of the others by making loud references to my being your mother. By the time you came on I was almost as nervous as you.'

'How did you know I was nervous?'

'Your shirt collar had jumped up on one side and you hadn't noticed.'

'Oh my God!' Seth gasped as his hand flew up and turned the flap down. 'It must have been when I put my jacket on in the vestry. Did it look very obvious?'

'Yes. Well, rather. But it made you look sweet and vulnerable. Look. Everyone's going back in. Drink up.'

'I'll put your glass back for you and join you in there.'

'OK. But don't be late in.' She handed him her glass and strode over to join the stragglers by the porch. Seth drained his glass and, chewing Mother's olive, walked back into the tent. As he handed over the glasses to the waiter behind the tables, there was a voice behind him.

'Now it's my turn to be admiring.'

'Roly. Were you in there?' Seth darted a helpless eye over his evening dress.

'It was brilliant.'

'Where were you sitting? I never dare look.'

'Up in the gallery so I could sniff in peace.'

'You don't mean I managed to pierce that stony heart?'

'Well Brahms did, but he had a little help.'

Seth started towards the porch. Everyone else had gone in.

'You aren't going back in, are you?'

'Yes. I think I ought to hear the rest of Jemima's stuff. It's thanks to her that I got the spot at all.'

'Well I know, but you'll have to stand at the back.'

'Why?'

'It's packed out. If your mother kept a place, someone will have taken it by now. And there's absolutely no room left upstairs.'

'Oh God! Ma said she'd see me in there.'

'Don't worry.'

'She'll be furious. Things like that are so important to her.'

'It's not your fault. Just write her a note and put it under her wiper or something.'

Seth hesitated. He felt he should pay Jemima the courtesy of hearing her out, yet he wanted to see Roly more. It would be slightly anticlimactic to sit out in the audience after standing before it.

'All right. I don't really want to go back in anyway. Have you got some paper?'

'Yup. Have a bit of diary.'

The living quarters had been transformed. The bed was neatly made and hidden beneath a counterpane and cushions. Dirty clothes had vanished, as had the pile of washing up. Records were back in their sleeves, books on their shelves, and a bunch of yellow roses stood in a milk bottle on the table.

'Well!' teased Seth, setting down his violin. 'And what happened in here?'

'It was getting a little too sordid even for me. I nicked the roses from Jane's garden. She's got plenty to spare.'

They stood side by side for a few seconds. Seth wanted them to roll around on the sofa but they didn't. Instead, Roly asked if he was hungry.

'I'm ravenous.'

'Watercress soup, chops, spuds and ice-cream do you?'

'You can't . . .'

'I'm not a starving artist. Not yet. I'm still their guest, even if I'm not especially welcome under their roof.'

'Then – yes, please.'

'I'd do something more inspired, but I'm not very adventurous yet.'

'It sounds lovely.'

'Better than taramasalata and quiche?'

'Leave poor NW3 alone.'

'Pax.'

Seth made himself comfortable on the sofa, and admired Roly's back. The cook called out from the sink,

'Not over there. Chuck a record on then come and sit on the bed, where I can keep an eye on you.' He ground a blenderful of watercress while Seth looked through the records.

'I hope Ma won't be too cross about my shirking the second half.'

'I saw her face in the interval; you're infallible for the next fortnight.'

Seth found the Chopin *Préludes* and put them on. He sat on the edge of the bed and took off his shoes because they pinched, then curled up against a mound of cushions in the corner by the window.

'That's better,' Roly said.

Seth found his smile too much, and turned his face to the waves. The sun had vanished and the night was clear.

'Know anything about stars?'

'No. Why?'

'I wondered if I could see Leo up there. It's the right time of month. The trouble is I can only make out constellations when someone draws a sort of dot-to-dot on top of them.'

'Do you believe in horoscopes?'

'I'm not sure. I'm very bad at disbelieving anything. I certainly read them, and if they're good I get excited. I suppose that means I believe.'

'Well, Aquarians are meant to hold the keys to the New Society. I haven't found mine yet.'

'What about that table-load upstairs?'

'It's not exactly permeated with social relevance.'

'How would you define "social relevance"?'

'You are feeling confident tonight, aren't you?'

'Of course. I've shown you I can do something.'

'Indeed you have.'

'You haven't answered my question.'

'Leave me alone. I'm trying to cook.'

'Round one to Peake. Anyway, who says that art has to contain some reference to society? I thought art was a social event in itself, like tea-drinking.'

Roly just grinned, threw his dinner jacket on the sofa and continued arranging chops in the grill pan.

'Aquarius is a very gay sign,' said Seth.

'And what do you mean by that?'

'Well, it's detached yet gregarious, obsessed with individuality, yet eager to be popular. Most Aquarians are idealistic, too.'

'Who says idealism goes with being a fag?'

'It's fairly hard to be a fag without nursing some hope that the social structure will change. Any outcast who wants to be accepted is an idealist.'

'Are you an outcast?'

'Until I tell people I'm crazy about you, I'm not properly gay, I suppose – just an unknown quantity. Once I do tell them, then I run a fairly high risk of being treated differently. I know my mother won't throw me out on to the streets, because she's Protestant and can take me up as a cross to bear. I'll be another cause for her collection, and you don't get that kind of pity from people when you're considered socially dead-centre.'

'And I'm shoved out on a lighthouse.'

'Quite. But being Aquarian you don't care, in fact it makes you pleasantly different. And when you move to London you'll enjoy becoming part of a lighthouse community. Joe Bloggs'll think you're all sad outcasts, but your idealism will transform your circle into a high-minded élite.'

'I know someone who's been reading one of those trashy star sign profiles . . .'

'Well,' confessed Seth, 'I did dip. But it's all true, isn't it?'

'Hang on.' There was a pause while Roly turned over the chops and smeared some more butter on to them. 'Christ! They're almost done,' he said. 'Have your soup.' He lifted two bowlfuls out of the fridge and put some sour cream into them. Seth joined him at the table as he poured out some Chianti. It was warm from standing near the stove.

'Looks marvellous.'

'You haven't tasted it yet.'

Seth tasted it. 'It is. Clever boy.'

'Thanks, kiddo.'

'So you don't think we're the new super-race?'

'It's a romantic thought, but I don't see why we should be. Quite apart from the fact that we can't reproduce, we've been around so long.'

'Well, so have the ants, but they've never had a nuclear holocaust to clear away the opposition; we've never had a Gay Movement to consolidate our forces and beliefs.'

'We're not a religious army!'

Seth smiled across the roses. 'Round two to MacGuire,' he said. 'How did you get branded the black sheep?'

'It was so stupid of me. I'd just finished my first term at art school – just like you, talking about my sexuality *ad nauseam* as it was the first chance I'd had . . .'

'Well, I'm only young.'

'And *how*! Anyway, first term over and I was madly in love for the first time, all starry-eyed, and I brought him to stay at Trenellion with no explanation.'

'Was it so obvious, then?'

'We touched rather a lot, and then Jane was out walking one evening when bloody Hera tracked us down in the long grass.'

'How dreadful!'

'You had to look at the funny side. She just wouldn't stop barking. Jane was standing several yards away from her. When she still wouldn't shut up or heel, she got worried in case she'd sniffed out a body or something, so she ran over, green wellies and all. Her poor face was indescribable.'

'Poor . . . er.'

'Jimmy. Yes. I think it was worse for him. They'd been treating him as an alien from the start anyway, ever since he announced to Lachlan that he'd been reared in a bed-sit in the Gorbals. We left the next day under a cloud.'

'Is this the first time you've been back?'

'Yes. You have to hand it to them, they were very kind. They didn't kick us out. We left because Jimmy was feeling so embarrassed. Then, after Nanny died, they sent a sweet letter making no mention of the ugly incident, but saying that the lighthouse was at my disposal whenever I felt like getting away. Lachlan wrote again a few weeks later with the idea of restoring the angels. He'd just heard through some grapevine that I wasn't a total dilettante, and reckoned he might as well get them done for love by an up-and-coming, than for a fortune by a "name".'

'So carrying on the family tradition of patronage.'

'Exactly. Do your parents really have no idea yet?'

'I don't think so. Why should they? I've been away at school for almost half my life, and I'm only sixteen. Well, nearly.'

'Straight boys are dating by sixteen. Some even have jobs.'

'Do they really? I wouldn't know.'

'No. I don't suppose you would. You know about the bill, though?'

'What bill?'

'Where've you been all the past year?'

'Under lock and ruddy key. What bill?'

'There's one about homosexual ages of consent trying to squeeze through the Lords today. If only I had a radio we could find the result.'

'You mean, lowering it to the same age as the straights?'

Roly took away the soup bowls and brought over the chops.

'They could hardly raise it any higher. Yes. The Europeans have put us all to shame at last, and sanity may be about to blossom forth. In one quarter, at least, but it's a start.'

'It hasn't got a chance, though. Mmm, this smells good.'

'It hasn't got a chance now, but there hasn't been enough preparation. The shoot-em-all-at-birth lobby have to be educated first, and one of the best ways of doing that is to show that someone who went to the same schools, has two parents, two arms, a wife, children, and a title, who isn't even *gay*, has the humanity to support the bill.'

As the meal carried on they spoke of schools, families, dreams, food, aspiration – anything that arose from the topic before. By the time a third record had been chosen and the washing-up was piled up once more, Seth had lost his self-consciousness and could say whatever came into his head. He didn't feel especially drunk.

'Coffee?'

'Please. Actually, no thanks. I rather like feeling well-fed and woozy. That was delicious. Thank you. What's the time?'

'You're the one with a watch.'

'Oh hell! I completely forgot.'

'What?'

'Mummy gave me this tonight just before I went to get tuned up, and I forgot to thank her in the interval. *And* it's three minutes to twelve.'

'Quick, then! Upstairs so I can give you your present.'

'You haven't . . . ?'

'Upstairs. Hurry. I'll follow you.' They started up the winding staircase to the studio. 'Bronwen told me – that's how I knew.'

'Oh.'

Roly had flicked the appropriate switch and the Schubert quartet preceded them.

'Now sit down, close your eyes and open your hands.' Seth did as he was told. He smiled broadly in expectation. There was a squeak as Roly pushed forward the other armchair to retrieve whatever it was. Then something heavy and wrapped in cotton was lowered into his upturned palms.

'Careful not to drop it.'

'Can I open my eyes?'

'Yes.'

Seth found he was holding something wrapped in a pillowcase. Roly sat on the dhurrie in front of him, faintly embarrassed. Seth smiled down at his frown.

'Go on. Open the thing. Your birthday's any second. Sorry I didn't wrap it properly, but the papers were hideous.'

'I'm too excited. What is it?'

'Go on, you nit.'

Seth pulled off the dressing-gown cord that was tied around the bundle then, slowly, he slipped his hand inside the pillowcase. It met cold stone.

'Oh Roly, you haven't!' he gasped as he pulled out the sculpture.

It was about a foot high, and just small enough to be held. It was a figure, possibly an angel, with one arm held protectively across the top of its forehead and the other clutching a book or a tablet of rock to its chest. By the same technique that had suggested distorted cloth in the other pieces, Roly had made it seem as if the figure were flying upwards through a thin sheet. Arms, hair, torso and features were conveyed through the folds.

Seth ran his fingers across the surfaces, feeling the whorls made by the chisel in the clean, almost soapy stone.

'Well?' asked Roly, at last.

'You know it's beautiful, damn you. Thank you and thank you.' He smiled briefly then looked at the figure once more and said more solemnly, 'And I promise it'll stay in my room and I won't let her shove it in her garden or have it in the drawing room. And when you start having exhibitions, I'll send it to the galleries, carefully packaged with a small card, "From the intimate collection of . . ."'

He twisted round and laid it behind him in the chair, then turned back to the creator and reached for him. 'Thank you.'

The kiss was sudden, the harder and greedier for having been broken off the night before. Seth slipped down into Roly's arms, feeling his suit jacket crumple up beneath him. He stretched back his head on the rug and sighed as his lover fed off his ears, his jaw, his neck and began to nose his way beneath the loosened fabric of his shirt. Allowing his hands to stray across Roly's hair and the back of his neck, listening to the music, he began to sense that he was almost incapacitated by alcohol. Lying down so fast had made him hopelessly dizzy. As Roly sought his mouth again, he clung to him tightly in an effort to rouse himself with the pressure, but his blood only sang the more.

'Here,' Roly said, gently raising him and slipping his jacket from off his shoulders. Seth felt suddenly cooler. His back had become sweaty and the sharp feeling of the air playing across it stirred him for an instant. He defied the wine and tugged Roly back on to him. The unexpected passion amused Roly and as they kissed again he rolled over, wheeling Seth around and above him. Seth ached to relax, to lose himself in the appropriate manner, but now a new sensation began to stir from his depths and his lust ebbed before it. With each fresh touching of lips or laying on of hands came an intensifying of the knowledge that he was about to be violently sick.

'Oh no!' he groaned and began to sit up. 'Is there a window, I . . . ?' He rose unsteadily to his knees and rocked towards the door that led out on to the platform outside. Roly was there before him and swung open the door with seconds to spare. He held Seth by the shoulders as, beneath a starry sky and brushed by a rising sea breeze, the boy vomited generously over the railings into the foam. Seth clutched the bars when the attack seemed to have stopped and tried to say that he was sorry, but was checked by another spasm.

'Sssh. Poor boy. It's all right. Come on. You'll feel much better when it's all out.' Roly made kind noises and held a supportive hand across Seth's forehead. After a couple of minutes all was silent again. Seth swayed where he leant, gulping, dribbling, shivering, and staring miserably ahead, then was meekly led indoors.

'I'm sorry, Roly . . .' he managed at last.

'Don't be stupid. Look, come down to the kitchen and wash your mouth out.'

'I always forget how vile it feels. I haven't been sick for years. Actually, I think I must have had too much to drink.'

'Don't try to talk in case it starts it up again. Poor old boy.' They walked back to the kitchen. Roly handed him a glass of cold water, then offered him a toothbrush and paste when he had rinsed out his mouth. Seth hesitated.

'You don't mind?'

'Don't be a twit. Use it.'

'Thanks.' Seth brushed his teeth and felt a little stronger. Roly draped his suit jacket across his shoulders.

'We'd better get you back home to bed,' he said.

'Oh but this is awful,' wailed Seth, and blew his nose. Roly took him by the arms and said,

'Listen. We've got all the time in the world. You're here for another week and after that I'm moving to London.'

'But I wanted it to be tonight.'

'Right now you've got a mother and an impending hangover to face.'

Seth tried to laugh but only mustered an aimless grin. Roly handed him the old cardigan.

'Pull this around you for the way back. Pull on your shoes and I'll get your present.' So saying, he turned to climb back up the stairs.

'Does my breath smell so very foul?' Stopping, Roly turned with a surprised grin.

'No, but I thought . . .' He was silenced by the look on Seth's face.

'Could you . . . could we have the light out?' asked Seth, letting the cardigan fall to the floor. Roly turned out the light and came across to the bed.

There was still a glow from upstairs. The window had been opened to let out the smell of cooking, letting in the rhythm and scents of the sea. Seth was aware for the first time of the habitual heaviness of his lover's breathing; also, when they kissed standing up, of the difference in their heights. They tumbled quickly on to the bed, then had to get up again because of the difficulty of removing trousers while lying side by side on a narrow single bed. Roly's body was more muscular than Seth had expected, his skin less smooth. He had formed few definite preconceptions, but had expected, dreaded perhaps, something more spiritual. He was pleasantly reassured.

Seth kept quiet on the journey home. As they drew up outside *La Corveaurie* he saw that all the lights were out and, glancing at his new watch, found that it was very late.

'Should I come in and apologize?' asked Roly.

'No. I think they've all gone to bed. I'll face them in the morning.' He tapped the angel in his lap. 'This'll pacify her, anyway.' Seth bent across and kissed him lightly. He paused with his hand on the door handle.

'Tonight.'

'What?'

'When you said I should go home earlier . . . you weren't just using my being sick as an excuse?'

'What do you mean?' There was an encouraging chuckle in his voice.

'Well . . . well I thought perhaps you were nervous because I'm under age – only just sixteen.'

'Did you honestly think that?'

Seth thought a moment then smiled, hugging the angel to his chest.

'No. Not really.'

'Now go to bed.'

'Bye. Thanks for supper.'

'Go to bed.' Seth got out and shut the door. 'Seth?'

'Yuh?'

'Well played, birthday boy.'

'Idiot!'

Seth walked, smiling to himself, up to the front door and heard the car pull away. He let himself in and climbed the stairs. As he turned on his bedroom light he saw at once that his mother was asleep on his bed, in her dressing-gown and slippers. The sudden light woke her quickly. Her anger was foggy only for a moment.

'What? Oh. Seth.' She sat up. 'Would you mind telling me where you've been exactly?'

'Sorry. Didn't you find the note on the car?'

'Of course I found the bloody note.'

'Oh.'

'J was very hurt. She didn't say anything but then, she never would.'

'I'll telephone her in the morning.'

'Oh will you? That *will* be nice. Have you been to the lighthouse again?'

'Yes.'

'What's happened to your suit? It looks as if it'd been rolled up.'

'I had dinner with Roly MacGuire.'

'Tête-à-tête?'

'Yes.'

'I saw you go off last night.'

'I thought perhaps . . .'

'Wasn't it rather irresponsible, the night before a concert?'

'Yes. I suppose it was.'

'Lucky for you you played so well.'

'Thanks. He gave me this.' Seth held out the sculpture for her to see.

'It's beautiful,' she said, less harshly. 'He's very talented. Can I see?'

He passed it to her and sat at her feet on the bed. She held it, running her fingertips over the ridges as he had done, and weighing it in her palms. Then she placed it on the bedside table and looked down at her hands as they returned to her lap.

'Was supper all you had tonight?'

'What do you mean?'

'What I say.'

He spoke at once. 'No. I had sex. We made love.'

Evelyn flinched minutely, her eyes firmly down.

'Is he the first man you've, er . . . ?'

'I'm not a virgin, but he's the first man . . . the first man I think I could love.'

'Does it worry you?'

'Why should it?' He reached out and held the back of her hands as they lay. 'I'm more worried about you. Does it worry *you*?'

'I don't know. I'm not shocked. Perhaps I've always known and not spelt it out to myself. You know it's against the law?'

'You didn't know until Jemima spelt it out to you last night.'

'Well, I know now, and you've just broken the law.'

'It's not a law I choose to respect. Besides, who would hand us over to the police? We're not going to walk around hand in hand.'

At last she looked up.

'When I found you'd gone off again tonight, I was so worried.' He saw at once that all the anger was gone. He hugged her to him.

'But why?'

'For God's sake, because you're my baby, that's why. I'd worry if Neesh rushed off like that with someone, too.'

Seth rocked her gently and said, 'Well there's no need to worry any more.'

'You have grown up in a hurry. I thought it would be at least another summer.' Her tone was wistful. 'He's awfully nice.'

'I'm glad you like him.'

'Can he come to stay?'

'Now you're not going to take us on like some cause.' They laughed, still hugging. Seth looked across her at the angel and smiled privately.

'Thank you for my lovely watch,' he lied. 'Made my evening.'

THURSDAY three

She'd left her bike at home and come on a double-decker. She'd sat on top to have a smoke. It was a warm night and sitting up there, with the narrow window wound down, the warm city draught in her face, the mounting tension had grown intense. Saturday night had been unexpected and strange, and the drink had fogged her feelings, but tonight was sharp, and announced. Despite the high number of the address, there were hardly any other buildings in the street. The old office block stood incongruously among fenced-off sites. It was hard to tell whether the area had been badly bombed and left undeveloped, or whether the demolition was new. The long stretches of corrugated iron were daubed with names and slogans. 'I may be Jewish, but I still like sticking Pigs.' She stood at the foot of the building in the light of a street lamp and gazed up. No lights, but perhaps squats had no supply. She had never been sent to one before, never had the bad luck to be called out to help on an eviction. A piece of paper was pinned to the door. 'Come in before the big, bad wolf gets you. I'm at the top.'

She pushed on the door and it swung open with a creak. She peered around her awhile to accustom her eyes to the darkness, then started up the broad staircase. There was a dim smell of dust, but no damp. She hoped the stairs were safe. From above came the swelling blare of a sax. *Stranger on the Shore.* She glanced up inside the stairwell but could see no light. At the top of the stairs a heavy curtain hung from the ceiling as a rudimentary door. She pushed through this and found another 'door' made of two sheets of translucent plastic. A candle burned in a bottle on the other side and lit the words 'Hope's Place' slashed across the barricade in dark paint. As she came between the sheets the sax was clearer still. She could see very little by the candlelight. She picked up the bottle and held it higher. It showed her a ladder leant against a skylight opening. The sax came from on the roof. Afraid of fire, she snuffed the light, and climbed.

By the wash of the stars and the amber glow off surrounding streets, she could see more clearly than in the murk below. She turned around and found a barbecue glowing and spitting on the gravel. Behind it, sitting on a mattress against the chimney stack, was Hope, playing her sax. There were two old fruit boxes pulled together as a rough kind of table, and plates and mugs and a bottle of wine. Hope carried on playing the familiar song. Unable to contain her smiles, Mo came forward and crouched on the other side of the embers, watching her. Hope went through the refrain once more, raising her eyebrows in greeting, then crooned to an end.

'Brilliant,' said Mo.

'Hi. I'm sorry I called you a piglet.'

'Don't worry, it suits me. I'm sorry I didn't tell you.'

'Well, it was quite a surprise. I could have done *anything.*'

'I'm only a piglet on duty. I'd probably have joined in.'

Hope laughed. She held out her hand and the other came

around to join her. They kissed tenderly, muttering apologies between mouthfuls, then falling about in helpless mirth at some remark of Hope's about cowboys and Indians.

'This is amazing.'

'What?'

'You, this roof, the view, the sax, the food. Everything.'

'The food. Shit!' Hope jumped up to poke around in the barbecue.

'Is it all right?'

'Yeah. Done to a turn, Superintendent.'

'I'm only an Inspector.'

'OK, Porker. You'll get your promotion soon enough.'

'What is it?'

'Guess.'

'Is it . . . it isn't pork?'

'Straight up. A fresh joint of copper.' Mo started to laugh. 'That's why I had to nick a bluey.'

Mo's mouth watered at the charcoal-flecked smell as Hope lifted the pieces of meat on to the plates. Baked potatoes were raked out from the embers and salad tossed from a Co-op bag. Hope produced a bottle of sauce, Mo poured out some wine, and they started to eat.

'You're marvellous,' said Mo.

'Shut your gob, Wonderwoman, and eat.'

'I got you a present.'

'What for? You're the one with the birthday.'

'How did you know?'

'That cow with the hair asked if it was a birthday card. I told her to mind her own.'

Mo laughed. 'Good on you,' she said, 'she's a right slag.

Here.' She tossed a package to Hope, who caught it with a whoop.

'What's in it?'

'Open it.'

She tore off the paper and gasped at the silver trophy.

'Blimey! Where d'you get it? It's beautiful.'

'You'll never guess.'

'Where? What? It must've cost the earth.' Hope giggled at Mo's grinning silence. 'Go on. Tell us.'

'Well,' said Mo, with affected cool, 'I was in this dead bird's fancy pad, checking out a burglary case, and she had loads of the stuff to spare . . .'

'You never! Shit! That's the best present I've ever had; a silver hip-flask nicked by a genuine copper!' she whooped and, laughing, kissed the metal. 'Oh Mo, you're fantastic. I take it all back, you know, I take back everything I thought and nearly said.' She laughed again and went on, 'You know it's just like what you said about Trace, my friend who turned piglet and that, about . . . what was it?'

'Subverting from the inside?'

'Yeah. That's what you've been and done, in a way, isn't it?'

'I suppose so.' Mo glowed.

'Brilliant!'

'That reminds me. I've got to get up at dawn tomorrow and go on a trip to the seaside.'

'Why? Business or pleasure?'

'Bit of both, my lovely. A bit of both.'

BIRTHDAY

The first thing Seth saw was Roly's statue. It summoned a clutter of images, and with them, the recollection that he was now sixteen. He could have lain in as it was a free morning, but he wanted to open his presents, and meet his new, enlightened mother. He dressed, and walked to the bathroom. He washed his face and, as he was patting it dry, heard the door bell, and his mother talking to someone. He listened and caught a woman's voice moving with Mother's across the sitting room and into the music room beneath him. Too deep and slow for Jemima. He returned to his bedroom to find his shoes and put on his watch. It was late, nearly twelve. Shocked that he could have slept so long undisturbed on a birthday, he hurried downstairs.

Venetia was lounging on the sofa with a cup of coffee and a biscuit tin.

'I see you've finally stirred after the excesses of last night,' she murmured. 'Happy Birthday.'

'Thanks. Why didn't anyone wake me?'

'We thought you might need a lie-in. You obviously did. Was it good?'

'Not bad,' he said, and found he didn't blush. 'How was yours?'

'As a matter of fact, Harry and I spent a civilized evening together and he's insisted I go to New York and work for him after next summer term.'

'But that's brilliant!'

'Isn't it.'

He dropped into a chair. 'Aren't you excited?' he pursued.

'Well yes, of course I am,' she sighed, 'but I've got exams to think about first.'

'Oh yes. Finals.'

'Aren't you going to open your cards?' He stared at the pile of cards and presents on the table.

'I will in a moment when Ma comes out. Who's she talking to?'

'It's a policewoman. With a scar.'

'But she didn't send for one, did she?'

'How the hell should I know? I was in the kitchen and just saw her letting her in at the front door and walking into the music room. I doubt it, actually. She respects that what you do with that grubby body of yours is your own affair.'

With a slight frown, Seth stood and walked through to the kitchen to make some breakfast. With the informed confidence of the post-liberation male, he assumed that her period had started again with a vengeance. He happened to be right. He turned on the kettle to make some coffee and poured himself a bowl of muesli. Trying to conjure up some birthday spirit, he gave himself some black cherry yoghurt on top of it. He switched on the radio and ate his cereal, perched on a stool rather than face the unappealing atmosphere by the sofa.

'The headlines again. A public enquiry has been demanded by the Home Secretary into the narrow escape at the

Havermere Nuclear Plant in the Peak District, where, through the apparent negligence of the night staff, a radioactive core was allowed to overheat to far beyond regulation level. The danger was only spotted within minutes of an explosion, say the specialists.

'At the end of last night's session in the House of Lords, the startling debate on the Age of Consent Bill ended in favour of a reform to the existing laws governing homosexuals of both sexes. Following a lead from the European governments, the debated private members' bill suggests that sixteen, not twenty-one, is the fair age of homosexual consent. In addition, the bill suggests an unprecedented law be brought to bear upon female homosexuals, or lesbians, preventing sex before sixteen. At present there is no law governing lesbianism. A considerable number of complaints at the bill have been raised, not least from the extreme Right who say that society could never be the same again in the event of the present laws being changed, I quote, "for the decadent worse".

'And finally, we have just had word that Dame Audrey Fox, the novelist unanimously crowned the Queen of crime fiction, died peacefully in her Sussex home last night after a week-long illness. She was eighty-four.'

As the full import of the second announcement sank in, Seth rinsed out his bowl at the tap and began to feel more of a birthday boy. He looked around and saw that Venetia had returned to the garden. She was fighting with a deck-chair. He heard Mother's voice from the opening music room door.

'Are you quite sure you won't stay for a cup of coffee, or

something, Officer?' She walked to the front door with the policewoman.

'No thanks, all the same, Mrs Peake. I just wanted to be the one to tell you myself. I've got to be hurrying back now.' Seth walked to the doorway to look. 'Morning,' said Mo, with a smile. He nodded in reply, then went to cut some bread.

'Oh well, thank you for being so considerate,' said Mother.

'My pleasure.'

Mother shut the door and walked smartly over to the kitchen. Seth looked up from the toaster. She was talking brightly and fast.

'Happy Birthday, darling!' she sang, and planted a warm kiss on his forehead.

'What did she want?'

'Oh, wasn't she funny? She was a real Cockney. She'd come all the way from London to tell me. And did you see that scar? Quite awe-inspiring!' She laughed unexpectedly, 'Oh my God! You didn't think I'd called the Fuzz to set them on your new sculptor friend? Really Seth, how could you forget my keenness to patronize the Arts?'

As she heard herself babbling on the brink, the newly-widowed mother of two was surprised that she could not begin to tell them.

A PLACE CALLED WINTER
Patrick Gale

Harry Cane has followed tradition at every step, until an illicit affair forces him to abandon the golden suburbs of Edwardian England and travel to the town of Winter in the newly colonised Canadian prairies. There, isolated in a beautiful but harsh landscape, Harry embarks on an extraordinary journey, not only of physical hardship, but also of acute self-discovery.

'Gale's confident, supple prose expresses the labour and hardship that toughen Harry's body as they calm his mind . . . Harry Cane is one of many, the disappeared who were not wanted by their families or their societies and whose stories were long shrouded with shame. This fascinating novel is their elegy' *Guardian*

'Gale's novels are imbued with clear-eyed psychological truths navigating the emotional landscape of characters it is impossible not to care about deeply. Sensitive and compelling' *Irish Times*

'A mesmerising storyteller; this novel is written with intelligence and warmth' *The Times*

TINDER
PRESS

ISBN 978 1 4722 0531 5

A PERFECTLY GOOD MAN
Patrick Gale

'A writer with heart, soul, and a dark and naughty wit, one whose company you relish and trust' *Observer*

On a clear, crisp summer's day in Cornwall, a young man carefully prepares to take his own life, and asks family friend, John Barnaby, to pray with him. Barnaby – priest, husband and father – has always tried to do good, though life hasn't always been rosy. Lenny's request poses problems, not just for Barnaby, but for his wife and family, and the wider community, as the secrets of the past push themselves forcefully into the present for all to see.

'This being Gale there's a compelling tale to be told . . . a convincing, moving account of man's struggle with faith, marriage and morality' *Sunday Times*

'A thoughtful and moving novel about love, morality and faith. Marvellous' *Mail on Sunday*

'A heartfelt, cleverly constructed read' *Independent on Sunday*

TINDER PRESS

ISBN 978 1 4722 5542 6

ROUGH MUSIC
Patrick Gale

'Sparkling with emotional intelligence. A gripping portrait of a marriage and quiet, devastating fall-out of family life' *Independent*

Julian is a contented if naïve only child, and a holiday on the coast of North Cornwall should be perfect, especially when distant American cousins join the party. But their arrival brings upheaval and unexpected turmoil.

It is only as a seemingly well-adjusted adult that Julian is able to reflect on the realities of his parents' marriage, and to recognise that the happy, cheerful boyhood he thought was his is infused with secrets, loss and the memory of betrayals that have shaped his life.

'A subtle, highly evocative tale of memory and desire' *Mail on Sunday*

'Like the sea he describes so well, Patrick Gale's clear, unforced prose sucks one in effortlessly' Elizabeth Buchan, *Daily Mail*

'A painfully acute but never reproachful examination of a past that will not vanish' *Daily Telegraph*

ISBN 978 1 4722 5540 2